Larceny

Triple Crown Collection

Larceny

Triple Crown Collection

Jason Poole

www.urbanbooks.net

Urban Books, LLC
97 N18th Street
Wyandanch, NY 11798

This title is published by Urban Books, LLC under a licensing agreement with Triple Crown Publications, LLC.

ISBN 13: 978-1-62286-949-7
ISBN 10: 1-62286-949-4

First Trade Paperback Printing July 2015
Printed in the United States of America

10 9 8 7 6 5 4 3 2 1

Distributed by Kensington Publishing Corp.
Submit orders to:
Customer Service
400 Hahn Road
Westminster, MD 21157-4627
Phone: 1-800-733-3000
Fax: 1-800-659-2436

ACKNOWLEDGMENTS

For my son.
Everything I do, I do it for you. Live by the jewels that have been handed down to you, and I assure you that there will never be any room for error .

Love always,
The one who has given you life, Dad

Also I would like to thank Vickie Stringer, Triple Crown Publications and Kathleen Jackson for all of their help and assistance.

DEDICATION

This book is deeply dedicated to my most truest and
dearest comrades,
James H. Fowler, Ishmael Ford-Bey, and
Ruben "Rat-Man" Bell, R.I.P.

Forever I shall remain loyal, even in my death.

J. Rock

Special dedication to
My brother, Eric "Fat-Cat" Poole, and my cousin,
Michael "Six Pack" Modlin, R.I.P.

CHAPTER 1

"When We Met"

SONYA

It was a cool day in May of 1994 when we first met. As I entered the building most famous in Washington, D.C. for its political scandals and often seen on every news channel after 5:00 p.m., I felt good.

For some reason, today seemed so good. I woke up this morning feeling more beautiful than ever. As I looked at myself in the mirror of my one-bedroom condo on Connecticut Avenue in Northwest D.C., I must say that I was proud of the reflection I saw. I could tell that the low-carb diet that I'd been on for the past month was doing my abs supreme justice. My stomach was almost flatter than Janet Jackson's and my ass was more shapely and fatter than a Las Vegas stripper. Thanks to my mama, I had inherited one of her greatest assets. Also, I could see that the Palmer's Coca Butter that I used kept my golden brown skin as flawless as Halle Berry's. If I was to compare myself to someone famous, I'd say it would be Toni Braxton, but I am slightly thicker in all the right places.

In most men eyes, I'm considered a perfect ten—a straight dime piece is what they call it—and to my surprise, not just men but women too, especially the ones who desperately want to sleep with me. I'm always getting indirect invitations from bisexual women, and to tell the truth, these women are gorgeous also. Although it may seem interesting letting another woman lick my pussy, I still decline. I'm not into that, and I don't think I ever will be. I'm strictly dickly.

I opened my bedroom windows this morning to get a feel of the summer's cool breeze. The weather was nice. It was in the high 70s. As I opened my walk-in closet full of upscale business suits, casual tops and bottoms of the latest designer fashions, I thought it would be perfect to wear my new cream-colored Dolce & Gabbana short halter-top dress. I pulled out a pair of medium-heel ankle-laced sandals by Joan & David to show off my freshly pedicured toes. Since I felt so good, I planned to wear my hair back and let its tail fall down to crease of my spine, sort of how the famous singer Sade wore hers—and no, I do not have a big forehead.

I stepped into the shower and turned on the radio to the station that played all the coolest jams. I turned the volume up as they played Tanya Blunt's new song, "Through The Rain." Tanya was also from Washington, D.C. and it was so good to see people from D.C. getting a chance to show their true talents.

When I got out of the shower, I hadn't realized that time had flown past so quickly. I had gotten in the shower at 9:30 a.m., and it was now 10:15. Damn, that shower felt so good. I guess I had gotten caught up and lost track of time, sorta like lovemaking, huh? Anyway, I let the cool breeze from my bedroom window dry my golden brown skin off, and then I lotioned my body with my Victoria's Secret Amber Romance body lotion and put on my clothes, pulled my hair back, and looked in the mirror one last time. Oh, did I mention I'm also bowlegged?

Here I am, Ms. Sonya Chanell Dunkin, an assistant producer at B.E.T. Studios, with a lavish condo in the upper northwest and the proud owner of a new emerald green convertible BMW 325, and for the record, I'm single, sexy, and free.

I didn't have enough time to grab a bite to eat because my appointment was scheduled for 11:15 a.m., so instead, I grabbed a granola bar, got in my BMW, and headed for 500 Indiana Avenue Northwest, Washington, D.C.'s Superior Court.

It was this day that I met the man of my dreams, the most gracious and perfect gentleman I've ever met in my life. This was the day I met the man I plan to spend the rest of my life with. As I entered the elevator and the door was about to close, it opened back up again and there he was. There were two other women on the elevator, one who seemed as though she was a nervous wreck. I assumed she was an untrained court clerk getting the run around from her boss. The other one was an elderly woman with a pretty smile who wore the worst perfume I'd ever smelled in my life. And there he was, just about six feet tall, caramel complexion, jet black wavy hair, which he wore semi low with the grain. He had a precise shape-up, as though his barber had outlined it with a razor, and he wore a light, perfectly trimmed goatee.

It was as if I had X-ray vision because when I pierced my eyes through his clothing, it was obvious this man was in extremely good shape. He had a body similar to the actor Shamar Moore. His face was very handsome. It reminded me of Denzel Washington when he played Malcolm X. As I glanced up and down at him, shoes first, I saw that he wore about a size 9 and he had on a pair of black calfskin slip-ons by Salvatore Ferragamo with the silver buckle, a pair of thin black slacks by Ferragamo with a matching black belt. His slacks weren't tight nor too baggy; they fit him just right. When he stood still, the cuff of his slacks lay over the top of his shoes, and when he walked, the cuff would pop up, exposing the buckle of his shoes, which matched his belt. He had made sure that his outfit was perfect. He also wore a thin black long-sleeve mock neck shirt, which enhanced his Movado watch.

On the other wrist he had a plain white gold bracelet designed like a bicycle chain. He also carried a small notebook case, and his walk was a gracious, cool, superior walk, as if to say "Nothing or nobody can fuck with me!" It wasn't a thugged-out, "I'm trying too much to look hard" walk. It was more of a glide with a sense of security, boldness, and assurance.

The elevator reached the third floor and the doors opened. As I was getting off the elevator, I couldn't resist the sensational smell of his cologne. I imagined it might have been "Curve" by Liz Claiborne or "Blue Jean" by Gianni Versace. Before the doors closed, he leaped out of the elevator and followed me as I continued to walk down the hall.

"Excuse me, Miss. May I please have a moment of your time?" he asked.

Although I knew he was talking to me, I still played it off. I looked up and down the hall and answered, "Are you talking to me?"

"Yes, I am. Hello, and how are you?" he said, his voice sounding smoother than he looked. "My name is Jovan Price, and I normally don't go out of my way much, but for you I had to make an exception. It is obvious by my actions that I'm extremely attracted to you. Is there any kinda way that you and I can get to know one another better?"

Normally, I would have told the average brotha that I was either involved or engaged, but with him I respected his approach, so I said, "Well, Mr. Price . . ."

"Jovan. Please call me Jovan. Mr. Price is my father," he said, smiling.

"Okay then, Jovan. My name is Sonya, and it wouldn't be any harm in us getting to know each other a little better, but right now I'm running late. I have an appointment in about sixty seconds. I shouldn't be that long; maybe fifteen to twenty minutes."

"So, Ms. Sonya, is it good to say that you'll have lunch with me?"

In my mind, I was saying, "Hell yes, with your fine ass!" But, as always, I was too ladylike to be acting like my hood rat cousin, Trina, so I said, "Yes, I will have lunch with you."

"Good, then you can meet me on the first floor about twelve o'clock, which is a half hour from now."

"Okay, I'll be there."

"I'll be waiting, Sonya."

It was now twelve o'clock, the busiest time in downtown Washington, D.C. As I stepped off the elevator anticipating my lunch date with Mr. Jovan, I maneuvered my way through the crowd of lawyers, district attorneys, criminals awaiting trial, and busy protesters who often frequented this building. I looked all around for a minute, and I still couldn't find him, until all of a sudden I heard that full, smooth voice, followed by that familiar sensational cologne scent.

"Excuse me, Miss Beautiful, are you looking for someone?" Jovan asked.

There he was, standing behind me. I didn't realize he was that close at first, and any other time, when someone crept up on me like that I would have been on some type of guard, but with him for some reason, I felt a sense of security.

"Oh, there you are. So what's up?" I asked.

"Where should we go for lunch? Do you like seafood? I was thinking we could go down to Phillips Seafood restaurant on the waterfront," Jovan said.

"Yeah, I could go for some shrimp and a salad," I said.

"Good then, are you driving?"

"Yes. I'm parked in the garage over on C Street."

"Well, I'm parked about two blocks down from you."

"We can take my car and I can bring you back to your car after we finish lunch," I said.

"Oh, no, you don't have to do that. I'm not due back in court. The hearing is over with. How about we meet each other in front of the restaurant?" he said.

"Cool," I said.

As I pulled my BMW out of the parking garage, I started to contemplate what I was doing. Should I go to lunch or just head on home as though I never met this man? I started thinking as I retraced every step from the moment we met in the court building. He seemed okay: very sexy, polite, good manners, and fine as hell. I would say the perfect gentleman, but when he told me he wasn't due back in court and that the hearing was over, my antennas immediately shot straight up.

Now, I grew up in Trinidad northeast, one of the most treacherous neighborhoods in D.C., and there wasn't too much you could get past me. Most of the game niggas ran on other bitches out there was so weak you could see right through it. I'd seen niggas talk a virgin into fucking on the first night, so whatever game a nigga was shooting at me was getting batted down off the break. So, I did what most people in my position would do: I took a chance because for one, he could be some type of criminal, which I doubted, or he could have had some type of lawsuit hearing, or he may have been some kind of lawyer. Who knew. I'd never know until I went to lunch and found out more about this man Jovan Price.

As I pulled up in front of Phillips Seafood restaurant, I could see that Jovan had gotten there first and was standing in the walkway of the restaurant waiting for me. There were four other cars parked at the restaurant: a black corvette, a blue MVP mini van, a 500SL white Mercedes-Benz, and a gray two-door Acura Legend. Since Jovan had gotten here so fast, I guessed that the black Corvette was his, or maybe the Mercedes. Most guys I knew from D.C. wouldn't be pushing a 500SL and wearing a Movado watch. They'd be rockin' a Rolex.

When I got out of my car, Jovan was a complete gentleman. He opened my door, grabbed my hand, and helped me out. He even added in a little humor.

"Ms. Sonya, so glad to see you. For a minute I thought you had a change of plans." When he smiled, I just looked up at him and imagined kissing him on those pretty, full lips.

"No, I didn't have a change of plans. I guess your car is just a lot faster than mine," I said, giving him the opportunity to tell me which one of those lovely cars was his; but he just smiled and positioned me in the direction of the restaurant.

CHAPTER 2

"The Paralegal".

Jovan

Around nine o'clock in the morning, I got a call from my employer at his law office. There must have been some type of problem, because usually he would be in court around that time, trying to get one of his clients out of jail, or at least trying to fuck any district attorney who wanted to prosecute one of his clients. Here I was, Jovan Conrad Price, getting harassed by my boss at 9:00 in the morning, especially on my day off.

I worked for Mark Rohon, an attorney with the biggest criminal law firm in Washington, D.C., Rohon and Robinson. He was the leading attorney at his office, and he was very well known for his many highly publicized cases. His legal skill attracted the biggest drug dealers in the city.

If anyone who was getting some type of papers in D.C., or at least on trial for some murders, wanted to get off and win the case, then Mark Rohon was their man. Believe me, his services did not come cheap. It's been said that Mark worked so hard getting his clients out of jail that the government wanted to investigate him to see if there was some kinda way that he was involved with their criminal conduct. Like any other smart attorney, Mark always had a way of getting out of any scheme.

I'd only been working for Mark for about five months, and the more I worked for him, the more I saw how crooked lawyers were. But for me, a nigga from the streets of Southeast, I respected his game, and besides, this mu'fucka was getting paid out the ass. Niggas came by his office every day, dropping off shoe boxes full of money, and out of all this money, this fucker only paid me a punk-ass thousand dollars a week. Now, I was no lawyer, but most of the cases that were put in Mark's motions came from my labor.

I took a paralegal course for two years and received my graduate diploma about six months ago. I knew Mark from paying him on previous cases for some good friends of mine. We connected well and became cool, and he always told me if there was anything he could do to help me legally, he would; so when I received my diploma in paralegal studies, I went straight to Mark.

At first he seemed a little hesitant about hiring me, but once I explained to him my position and the need for money to continue my education, he graciously obliged. I was more than happy to get the job, but for real, I was still fucked up financially. I not only needed money for school, but I also had a lavish spending habit. I liked the finer things in life. I was used to having money.

All my life I'd been getting that money, loot, dough, cash, cheese, or whatever else you may call it. I had always had a lust for that paper. I craved it like a junkie craves a fix.

It used to cross my mind to get back into hustling, but I always knew that it took too much risk, time, and hard effort to achieve the type of bank I really wanted, and besides, there was too much competition in D.C. at the time.

The summer of '94 was a booming year. Everybody was getting it, doin' they thang. I often thought about kidnapping and robbing a few of these niggas out there getting that money; especially those punks who ain't suppose to have it. Nowadays, everybody was hustling, slinging them thangs. Niggas who ain't put in any work or come up hard from rock bottom was getting money, pushing 600SL's, Lexus Coupes, LS400's and 850I BMW's.

When the notorious Big Silk was on the scene, none of these niggas was flaunting their bank like that, let alone coming off their fucking porches, but as soon as they heard that this killer had gotten three life sentences, all of a sudden niggas started poppin' up with shit. Don't get me wrong; there were some real gangstas out there getting money when Big Silk was on the scene, but them punks who he peeped as variable niggas who wasn't fit to play in this game definitely got what was coming to them. They were being robbed at will.

Now that I was changing my life, it was hard for me to get used to not having a lot. Oftentimes I felt depressed, unfocused, and just plain ole broke as hell. I knew I had to put a plan together, the perfect plan that I'd been working on for the last two years. I called it the Political Move, and all I needed to make my plan work was a nice bankroll and a down-ass bitch.

I considered a few females that I was dealing with at the time, like Barvette. She was one of the top-flight broads in the city. Barvette looked good, and she had a business head on her shoulders, but the only thing about her that I couldn't get with was that she fucked around with too many major niggas. She wasn't looked at as some freak-ass hood rat. She was more like a female player who knew how to play her cards right. She was the type of female you could take anywhere and she'd adjust to the situation.

At one time we were considered almost an item. We had the most fun together. Although I still saw her every now and then, I still couldn't put her down with my move. It had been rumored that she was now dating an NBA star who played for the Washington Wizards. When I found that out, I just knew there was no way to fit her into my plans.

There was also Keda, who I called my gangster bitch. She had the total package: a pretty face, pretty eyes, nice body, nice job, education, good pussy, bomb-ass head, and was down for whatever. There was one area Keda lacked: she had two little boys from a previous relationship—not to mention they were bad as hell—and kids were not a part of this move.

Lastly, there was Peppa. Pep was cool. She fit all the criteria but only one thing: she was too much of a hood rat and loved the party life. Pep was the type of female who would walk into a business meeting with a Donna Karan Spandex suit and tennis shoes on. I definitely couldn't use Pep.

What I needed was a straight-up educated but down-for-whatever, no-children female. Face it; I needed a real live straight-up bitch like in Bonnie and Clyde.

Ring, ring, ring. As I got up off the floor from doing my daily routine crunches to answer the phone, before I could even say "Who is it?" I heard a panicky voice.

"Hello? Jovan? Jovan! Are you there?"

"Yeah, I'm here. Who's this?"

"It's me, Mark."

"Damn, Mark, I'm supposed to be off today, remember?"

"Yeah, yeah, I know, but right now I need you. It's urgent."

Damn, usually I was the one telling a lawyer I needed him. "Okay, what's up?" I asked.

"Well, I need you to come down to the office and categorize a few cases for me and help format this motion for this evidentiary hearing we got coming up. I'll be calling you from court, giving you certain cases in between the hearings, and you can fax them to me," Mark said.

"Damn, Mark, why'd you wait so late to file this motion?" I asked.

"Because the court didn't give the proper notice of service that one of my clients was just granted this evidentiary hearing on appeal."

"So you mean to tell me this is an appellate case?"

"Yeah," he said, "and I've got these fuckers by the balls."

I laughed. "That's good then. Who's the client you're representing?"

"His name is Bilal. Bilal Davis."

Sonya

As Jovan and I entered the restaurant, we were greeted by a young, shapely white waitress.

"Hello, and how are you? Welcome to Phillips waterfront restaurant. Today's menu includes our lavish seafood buffet of grilled tuna, baked salmon, lobster bisque, filet trout, and the soup of the day is shark fin chowder. The patio will be open until three o'clock, and we have a smoking and non-smoking section inside," the waitress said.

I wondered if Jovan smoked, because that would be a complete turn-off. I looked at his lips to see if I could see any traces of purple that most smokers have. My cousin has the darkest lips ever from smoking, and every time we go out, it's a must that she cover them up with bright red lipstick. Since I wasn't able to detect any signs of smoking on Jovan, like the smell of his clothes, yellow-stained teeth, purple lips, and a need for a fresh pack of Newports, I assumed that he didn't smoke.

Jovan interrupted the young waitress as she continued to tell us about damn near everything the restaurant had.

"Excuse me. We would like to be seated outside on the patio if you don't mind," he said.

The young waitress looked at Jovan as if to say "Why in the hell did you cut me off like that?" I liked that in Jovan: a sense of aggressiveness.

When we were seated, I thought I'd add a little humor to the situation. "Thanks. For a minute I thought she was gonna tell us how the place was built and give us a grand tour," I said.

We both laughed, and then Jovan said, "You better be quiet, 'cause here she comes with the menus."

"Shhh. I thought she already told us the whole damn menu." We both laughed again.

I liked that about Jovan: he carried himself very well. I could see that we were starting to connect and feel a little more comfortable with each other.

Jovan

Bilal Davis. All I could do was think back and reminisce about the last time I saw Bilal. It was the winter of 1985, and I had just turned 15 years old. He was from Northeast D.C., over there on Sixth and K, across the street from Wilson Elementary School, an area which would later be known as the Gold Mine that helped D.C.'s biggest drug dealer, Ray Edmonson, rise to multimillion-dollar status.

My grandmother lived a few blocks over on Ninth and G, right across the street from Golden Elementary and Sherwood Recreational playground. This is where all the major players and future NBA stars played basketball—people like Sherman Douglas, who played for the Boston Celtics, Curt and Charles Smith, Lawrence Morton, and

Michael Gram. On weekends, some of the players from the Georgetown Hoyas would play against local drug dealers in exchange for certain gifts.

My favorite was to see Big Fat dunk on any and everybody that got in his way. Sometimes my big cousin Poochie and Uncle Bobby would go over to play, and I'd watch them, along with almost every pretty female from around the way. The playground was always packed with pretty females, but as usual, they were all too old for me, and besides, pussy wasn't the first thing on my agenda back then.

It was a cold day in November of '85, and I was at my grandmother's house, bored as hell. No one else was there but grandma and me. My father was a smooth nigga, and he wasn't around that much. He was mostly outta town on some type of business—at least that's what I thought. As I got older, I came to find out that he was on the run for some bank robberies he did back in the late '70s. This is why, when he came by grandma's to see me, he wouldn't stay long, but he'd give me a few dollars, throw a couple of jabs at me to make sure I knew how to fight, drop me a few jewels, and step off.

The one jewel that stayed with me the most was when he'd say, "Trust no one, master your condition, and keep all suckers in the bounds of moderation." Of course, I wouldn't understand any of this shit until later on in life when it became reality.

Sonya

Jovan ordered baked salmon filet with sun-dried tomatoes and a side order of creamed spinach, along with a glass of freshly squeezed grapefruit juice. I could see from his order that Jovan was very alert toward his health, which was something that we both had in common. I wondered if he drank occasionally, like myself. That would be a plus.

When it was my turn to order, I got a seafood salad with blue cheese dressing and a side order of steamed shrimp, along with a glass of lemon ice tea.

"Got a big appetite, huh?" Jovan asked me.

"Yeah, I was in a rush this morning and wasn't able to eat a thing."

A slight grin came on his face. "So that's why you took my invitation to lunch. You wasn't even thinking about getting to know me better, huh?"

Before I answered, I blushed a little. "Look, Mr. Smarty Pants, if I didn't want to get to know you, I would have made the first right on Pennsylvania Avenue, headed home, fixed myself my own seafood salad, and watched the daytime soaps. And for the record, I must find you somewhat interesting, because I don't miss my soaps for nobody."

"Well, excuse me."

We both laughed while looking each other in the eyes. I wondered if he was thinking what I was thinking, did he feel like I felt, and did he want what I wanted.

"Well, Sonya, where are you from?"

"I grew up in the northeast over in Trinidad, all the way up until I got in the ninth grade, and then we moved uptown to Webster Street Northwest."

"Is that where you went to school?"

"Yeah, I went to Roosevelt High, and I stayed there until I graduated. I had a rough time in school mostly because my mother stayed in the hospital a lot. She had cancer and died when I was in my last year of school."

"Damn, boo, I'm so sorry to hear that."

"It's cool. I've learned to deal with it. I can't let that hold me back from achieving higher things in life. In fact, I use it as motivation," I told Jovan.

"That's good. Do you have any brothers and sisters?"

"My brother is—hold up. I just met you. I shouldn't be telling you all my personal business like this."

"Sonya, your business only becomes personal when you hold it in; and when you hold it in too long, sometimes it may hinder you from getting what you really want in life."

At that moment, whatever he said sounded good, and I thought about it for a second, especially when he said it may hinder me from getting what I really wanted in life. Right at that moment what I really wanted was to get to know Jovan better, so I continued with his little interview and anticipated the wait for my turn to ask the questions.

"Okay, I have a younger brother. His name is Anthony, but we call him Li'l Tony. He's locked up down in Lorton, Virginia, behind the wall. He's been in prison since he was sixteen and he's twenty-four now. He got thirty years to life for killing a guy who tried to rape me."

While I was telling Jovan about Li'l Tony, my eyes started to get watery, even though it had been a long time since that day when Li'l Tony heard me screaming in the alley on Sixteenth Street. He came to my rescue, only to see that the man he thought was his father was holding my throat and choking the life outta me while pulling down my pants and trying to take my virginity.

Jovan

Bilal stopped over at my grandmother's house to see if I was coming outside. He had his little brother, Jamal, with him. Jamal was eight years old, and Bilal had nicknamed him Mal-Mal. He was the only true love

Bilal had. Everything Bilal did, he did it for Mal-Mal. Their father was killed in a bank robbery shootout with the feds, which left Ms. Cookie, their mother, a nervous wreck. She didn't know how to take care of her two boys because she had always been dependent on Bilal's pops. To make matters worse, they were both dependent on heroin, so when he was killed, that left Ms. Cookie, the worst addict that northeast D.C. ever had, to take care of her two boys alone.

Ms. Cookie never had any food in the house, so Bilal was the one who had to take care of Mal-Mal. He would go to the Safeway Grocery Market on Seventh and H Street Northeast and steal whatever kind of food they could eat without cooking because they didn't even have gas on in the house.

When Bilal and I used to go down to McBride's Department Store to steal, we would see Ms. Cookie on the corner of Eighth and H Street, nodding and scratching. Once when he went up to tell her about Mal-Mal being sick, she lifted her head up real fast as if she was concerned and then said, "Baby, you got ten dollars so I can get my fix?"

Bilal began to hate Ms. Cookie. He used to say, "Jovan, one day I'm gonna be rich and I'm gonna take Mal-Mal to Disneyland, Sea World, and all them other places parents take their children. I'ma get a real big house for Mal-Mal and me, and that bitch Cookie better not ask me for shit!"

Although we both knew that Bilal was dreaming and it would never happen, I still had to add to it to keep his mind off of Ms. Cookie.

"What about me?" I asked. "Whatcha gonna do for your boy?"

"Oh, I'ma get you a white Nissan Maxima, about fifty pair of New Balances, and a fat gold rope like Run DMC.," he told me. "Yeah, nigga, it just gonna be Mal-Mal, you, and me."

Sonya

Jovan held my hand tight while I sat in silence for a moment, and then he said, "Sonya, if you don't want to continue, we could move onto another subject. I understand how it is, believe me, and when it comes my turn to talk, you will hear things similar to your story."

For some reason, I kept feeling a sense of security with Jovan, as though his words were sincere and his heart was pure. He was the perfect gentleman. It was all too good to be true. I couldn't wait until it was my turn to ask him questions.

"Okay now, Sonya, is it all right if I ask how old you are?"

I gave a slight smile and said, "How old do you think I am?"

"Well, you definitely don't look old. In fact, for a minute I was kinda skeptical about asking you to lunch because you look so young," Jovan said.

I laughed. "Yeah, right."

"No, but seriously, you are a very gorgeous woman and also in tremendous shape. I wouldn't care if you were sixty years old. I'd still ask you to lunch."

I laughed again. "Now you're pushing your luck."

"Well, you know all I can do is try."

"Don't worry. You're doing a good job; and, baby, for the record, I'm twenty-seven and my birthday is April third."

Oh, no. Did I call him baby? I hope he doesn't take that as a sign of weakness. I barely know this man and I'm calling him baby already. What in the hell has come over me?

"So you just turned twenty-seven?" he asked me.

"Yeah, but sometimes I feel like I'm eighty-seven."

"Damn, sweetheart, you going through that much drama?" We both laughed.

No, he didn't just call me sweetheart. This little lunch date is going well.

"No, I ain't going through that much drama, but I do have a very difficult job," I said.

"Oh, so you do work."

"Yes, I do. Why'd you say that?"

"Oh, because earlier you said something about watching the soaps."

"No, baby." *Oops, there I go again.* "I watch the soaps whenever I'm off, and sometimes when I'm at work, I tape them so I can watch them when I come home from work."

"Oh, okay."

"I've been doing that for years."

"So, what type of work do you do?"

"I work at BET Studios. I'm the assistant to the producer."

"Damn, so you call the shots, huh?"

"No, not really. What I do is run around like a mad woman for the man who calls the shots. Remember I'm an assistant."

Again we both laughed. Damn, it felt good to be in a man's presence—a fine-ass man at that. Little did Jovan know that if he kept up the good work, then maybe this little lunch date would turn into a dinner date.

Jovan

When Bilal and Mal-Mal came into my grandma's house, you could tell that Mal-Mal hadn't eaten. He was quiet and he looked cold. I went upstairs, got him one of my old sweatshirts and a coat I had back when I was young. Grandma always kept those types of things. She didn't believe in throwing nothing away. I then fixed us some Oodles of Noodles and Steak-umms that Grandma kept in her freezer for me to cook when she was gone. I made Mal-Mal and Bilal two sandwiches apiece and a bowl of Oodles of Noodles. Mal-Mal ate all of his food but Bilal didn't. He wrapped his sandwiches up just in case he wasn't able to find Mal-Mal anything to eat later. Bilal was taking on a big responsibility, because no matter what was going on, he always made sure Mal-Mal was all right.

While Bilal and I went downstairs to play video games, Mal-Mal stayed upstairs and ate cookies and watched cartoons. I was killing Bilal on Ms. Pac-Man. We played a couple more games and then we started to talk.

"Hey, let's go down to Hechinger Mall and steal some cologne and leather belts," Bilal said.

"What the fuck are we gonna do with cologne and belts?"

Bilal laughed and said, "We gonna sell 'em, stupid!"

"To who?" I asked him.

"To the fucking hustlers on Ninth and I, and the ones on Orleans Place. They love that type of shit."

"How you know?"

Bilal dropped his head to his chest before he said, "'Cause my mother's a fuckin' junkie and she do it all the time. That's how I know."

So we all walked down to Hechinger Mall and went into the Safeway Foods first. We stole enough food to feed Mal-Mal for about a week. So far our shoplifting spree was going good. No police were in sight, and no one would ever suspect two teenagers with an eight-year-old would be stealing like it's going outta style.

When we went into the Cavalier Men's Shop, we used Mal-Mal's innocent looks to get what we wanted. The salesperson was a fat, pudgy lady who looked like she was in her thirties. She was the only salesperson on the floor at the time. Bilal must have done this before, because he knew right where the belts and cologne were.

"Go 'head, Mal-Mal. Do your thang," Bilal told him.

Mal-Mal went over to the lady to distract her and said, "Excuse me, pretty lady."

"Why, hello, young handsome fella. How can I help you?" the saleslady asked Mal-Mal.

"My daddy's birthday is tomorrow. Can you help me pick out a hat?" Mal-Mal said.

"Why, I sure can, little man. Come on over here with me."

The fat lady took Mal-Mal over to the hat rack, while Bilal and I opened our coats. Each of us wrapped five Pierre Cardin leather belts around our bodies. Then we stuffed our inside and outside coat pockets with bottles of Ralph Lauren, Geoffrey Beene, Stetson, and English Leather colognes.

When it was time for us to leave, Bilal went over to Mal-Mal and said, "Hey, you brought Daddy a hat last year. Why don't you get him something else?"

"Okay, I'll be back. Hey, pretty lady, when I come back, can you help me pick out a pair of gloves?" Mal-Mal said with his innocent look and whiney voice.

"Why, I sure can, little man. You just promise to come on back, you hear."

Damn, Mal-Mal did that shit too perfect, but I already knew where he got it from. Ms. Cookie used to make him do that whenever she was "ill" and trying to get her fix.

Sonya

"So, where do you live?" Jovan asked.

"Why, aren't we getting a little too personal?" I said, giving him a sexy smile.

"Oh, I'm sorry. I'm just starting to fee'
able with you, and I could sit here and tal.
long," Jovan said as he leaned back in his sea.
my body language.

"Well, since you don't look like some kinda sta..
or anything, I guess it wouldn't hurt to tell you where i
stay. I live on Connecticut Avenue in a condo called The
Saratoga."

"Nice place, ain't it?" Jovan said.

"You've been there?" I asked him.

"Yeah, a few years ago. A friend of mine had a nice
condo there. Do they still have those marble bathrooms?"

"Yeah, they do."

"That spot reminds me of a hotel in Vegas."

"Yeah? Which one?"

"The MGM Grand."

"I've never been there."

"You've never been to Vegas?" he said.

"No, silly, I mean I've never been to the MGM Grand.
I went to Vegas a couple of years ago." I hoped Jovan
didn't ask me who I went to Vegas with. That would be
the start of many lies, so to keep from lying, I shifted the
conversation in another direction.

"So, since I sat here and told you all my business, now
it's my turn to ask the questions," I said.

"Hold up," he answered. "I've got one more question."

Jovan

With our shoplifting spree over, it was now time to drop
Mal-Mal off and go try to sell our goods to the hustlers on
Ninth and I and Orleans Place. On our way back, Bilal
had a look of unhappiness on his face. I wondered what
was wrong. We had just stolen about a hundred dollars
worth of shit, so why the fuck was he mad?

"Hey, what's wrong, nigga?" I said to him.

"Whatcha mean what's wrong?"

"Man, you look like you just lost your best friend."

"Naw, nigga, I got something on my mind, and for future reference, I ain't never gonna lose my best friend. My best friend is right here, and he ain't going nowhere. Ain't that right, Mal-Mal?" Bilal said, looking at his brother.

Mal-Mal looked up at his older brother, all smiles, and said, "Yeah, Lal, we best friends for life. I can't wait 'til we get rich, get our big house, go to the movies, the park, play games, and eat candy all day."

"Naw, little nigga, you ain't gonna be eating no candy all day, but we is getting our house and all that other stuff." Bilal grabbed a hold of Mal-Mal's head and said, "I love you, Mal-Mal."

"I love you too, Lal."

As I looked at them expressing their deepest love to each other, I began to think about my big brother, and the pain grew deep in my heart. All I could do was block it out and hold it in until the day I would be able to release it.

Bilal was only fifteen years old, but he took life very seriously. He knew that he had to do something to be able to raise Mal-Mal like he wanted to. He looked at me deep in my eyes, and from the way he was looking at me, I knew that whatever was about to come outta his mouth was to be taken seriously. Bilal was a grown man trapped in a little boy's body.

"Hey, Jovan?" Bilal said.

"What's up Lal?"

"Look, man, you know it ain't nobody but Mal-Mal and me. You know he's my life and my only love, right?"

"Yeah, Lal, I already know that."

"Can you promise me something?"

"Yeah, what's up?"

"Promise me that if anything was to ever happen to me, you'll look out for Mal-Mal."

At that moment, I didn't know that my promise would mean taking on such a big responsibility so soon, but we were friends, and all I could do was be loyal to our friendship.

"Yeah, nigga, you know Mal-Mal's my little man," I said. "Sho'nuff I'll look out for him."

"Thanks. You my only true friend," Bilal said with all sincerity.

As we continued to walk down H Street, we saw Ms. Cookie coming in our direction. She looked clean. She wasn't scratching or nodding, but she was getting very skinny.

"Hey, Mommy!" Mal-Mal yelled with a big smile on his face.

"Mal-Mal, my baby," Ms. Cookie said. She grabbed her youngest son and hugged him as if she hadn't seen him in years. Mal-Mal was happy to see his mother. It wasn't often that he saw her in a healthy state of mind.

"Hey, Mal-Mal, you wanna go over to Aunt Gloria's house with me?" Cookie asked him.

Bilal interrupted with the most serious look I'd ever seen. "Naw, he a'ight. He ain't trying to go nowhere."

Ms. Cookie immediately snapped, "Look here, Bilal. This is my son, I carried him for nine months to bring him into this world, so I can take him wherever the fuck I want to!"

"Lal, I wanna go with Mommy over to Aunt Gloria's house," Mal-Mal whined.

Lal didn't want Mal-Mal to go, but he could see that Mal-Mal missed their mother, so he said, "Okay, Mal-Mal, you can go; but Cookie, let me tell him something first."

"Go ahead, but make it quick," Cookie said while coldly looking at her firstborn as if he were her archenemy.

Bilal took Mal-Mal's hand and whispered in his ear, "Look, Mal-Mal, when you go over Aunt Gloria's house, be good."

"Okay, Lal."

"And if Cookie tries to leave you over there, don't cry, 'cause I'll come and get you tomorrow, okay?"

"Okay, Lal."

"I love you, li'l nigga."

"I love you too, Lal."

"You my soldier?"

"Yeah, for life."

Then he hugged and kissed his little brother and said good-bye as if it would be the last time he'd ever see him.

"I wish your ass would stop acting like you his father. You ain't his daddy," Cookie said to Bilal.

"Well, when you start acting like a mother, then I'll start acting like his big brother; but until then, I'm his father and his big brother," Bilal said, giving his mother a hard stare.

Before Ms. Cookie could cuss Bilal out, I interrupted and said, "C'mon, Bilal. We got something to do. See you later, Ms. Cookie."

"Bye, Bilal. Bye, Jovan."

Sonya

"Okay, what's your last question?" I said curiously.

Before Jovan opened his mouth, I could see that the expression on his face became very serious. His eyes had a mixture of boldness and bashfulness. He sat back in his chair, crossed his left leg over his right, put his left hand under his chin, and asked the question that would change the whole tone of our lunch date.

"Well, I know this is a little too early, and if I'm in any way outta place, I expect you to let me know. Also, if you feel the slight bit of discomfort, I would like to apologize beforehand."

After hearing him apologize, I became anxious and curious as to what he wanted to know. "Okay, Jovan, go ahead shoot your shot."

"My question is, do you have a man?"

At that moment, I was unbalanced, and I knew that my future friendship with Jovan would depend on my answer. Although I hadn't been seeing anyone, I did have a very serious relationship two years ago. Even though it was over, I knew that I was still in love with this man. But shit, that was over two years ago, and life must go on. Besides, I was tired of playing with my pussy all the time. I needed some good dick. I needed someone to hold and cuddle me, someone to make passionate love to me while fucking my brains out at the same time. Even though my vibrator did the trick at times, in reality, I still needed the flesh. Bad as I wanted to tell Jovan this, I couldn't. He'd just have to stick around to find out for himself.

"Well, this is kinda awkward for me to tell you this, but I'm gonna give it to you in the raw," I said. "No, I don't have a man, although it would be nice to have one. I haven't had a man in over two years, and to be honest with you, my body hasn't been touched by a man in over two years."

Jovan raised his eyebrows, and I wondered what he was thinking. Then I remembered that I said I hadn't been touched by a man in two years, so I retracted and said, "And no, I'm not gay. I don't go that way."

"I didn't say that," Jovan said, smiling.

"I know, but in case you were thinking that, I just had to put that out there."

Jovan

Bilal and I were headed over to Ninth and I and Orleans Place when all of a sudden something came to my mind. First of all, this was Bilal's neighborhood, and I didn't know any of the hustlers out there. Although my pops and my uncle Howdy had a vicious reputation for being stick-up boys, I was still a little skeptical about going around there.

"Hey, hold up!" I yelled to Bilal.

"What's up? What, you scared, nigga? Ain't nothin' gonna happen to you," Bilal said.

"Nah, I ain't scared of nothing."

"Then what's the hold-up?"

"I just gotta go pass my grandma's house for a minute."

"A'ight, we need to go put this food up anyway," Bilal said.

We walked over to my grandma's house, went in, and had something to eat. For some reason, every time Bilal came over, Grandma always offered him something to eat, and Bilal never declined.

While Bilal was downstairs eating, I went upstairs to my pops' old room.

Now, I'd been creeping in and out of Pops' room, going through his shit since I was nine years old. You could tell Grandma never went in there 'cause everything was always in its place. I knew where Pops hid one of his guns— the third shoebox to the left. I went into that shoebox and got the gun, but when I picked it up, I never realized that it was that fuckin' heavy. This was the first time I had ever touched Pops' gun. When I was little I never touched Pops' shit, I always just sat there and looked at it. Pops had a pretty-ass nickel-plated .357 Magnum with a rubber grip, which most gangstas called a bulldog. I looked into the revolver and saw it was loaded with six bullets.

I heard Bilal's voice from downstairs. "Hey, c'mon, man. We got things to do."

I tucked the bulldog down my pants and tightened my belt to make sure the heavy-ass gun didn't fall out.

"Okay, man, here I come," I called down to Bilal.

I put on my sweatshirt and changed my coat to the heavier one Pops had gotten me. It was a blue North Face ski coat. Bilal loved this coat, and since he only had one thin-ass jacket, I told him I'd give it to him.

When I came downstairs and Bilal saw me in the North Face joint, the first thing to come out of his mouth was, "Man, you're an Indian giver."

"No I ain't," I said to him.

"Man, yes you are. You said you was gonna give me that coat a long time ago."

"And I'm still gonna give it to you."

"When?" he asked, not believing me.

"Soon as we get back I'll give it to you and you can wear it home, since my other coat is over in Southeast."

"Thanks, Jovan. You the only friend I got besides Mal-Mal."

All the other kids around here were scared of Bilal, mainly because he was poor and the fact he always stayed in fights because people would tease him about Ms. Cookie.

"Hey, Grandma, I'll be back, okay?"

"Okay, baby. Don't be out all night. You know I gotta take you home so you can go to school tomorrow," she said.

"All right."

As Bilal and I were walking down the street, he said, "Damn, man, why can't you just move over here and go to school?"

"Man, Moms won't let me."

"Shit, I don't see why not."

"I think it might have something to do with my pops. I dunno."

"Whatever! Anyway, man, we're about to get paid. We can sell these belts for ten dollars apiece."

"What makes you think we're gonna get ten dollars when they only cost fifteen?"

"Shhhit, watch me work and we can sell the cologne for five dollars a bottle."

"Now I can see that, but the belts, I dunno."

"Okay, nigga, like I said, watch me work."

Bilal, for some reason, had hustling in his blood. He was determined that we were gonna sell those belts for ten dollars. On the other hand, I wasn't too much on the hustling tip, mainly because my peoples took care of me. We wasn't rich or anything, but my moms did have a job as a waitress at the NCO Club on Bolling Air Force Base and plus, whenever Pops came through, he would drop off a few dollars.

Even though Bilal didn't know I had the bulldog on me, our positions were set. He had the goods, and I had the protection. When we reached Ninth and I, the first person we saw was Fat Jimmy. Bilal knew Fat Jimmy from his moms. She used to deal with Fat Jimmy right after Bilal's pops was killed, but when Fat Jimmy realized that Ms. Cookie was only dealing with him to keep her habit up, he left her alone. That was what led Ms. Cookie onto the streets. She no longer had a man that could keep her with a steady supply for her habit, so she started going out stealing and tricking, selling her body to anyone who had some good dope.

"Hey, Fat Jimmy!" Bilal yelled as he saw the fat hustler pass bags of dope to one of his customers.

"What's up, man?" Fat Jimmy said. "Who dat, Li'l Bilal? What's up, youngin'? I ain't seen you in a while. What, you looking for your moms?"

"Naw, man, she's over at my aunt's house."

"Then what the fuck you doing on the strip, little nigga?"

"My man and me got some Pierre Cardin belts we trying to sell."

"Some belts?" Fat Jimmy asked.

"Yeah."

"Are they leather?"

"Yeah, man. Brand new joints, all different colors."

"Let me see 'em then."

Bilal opened his jacket and showed Fat Jimmy the belts.

"Damn, youngin', where y'all get all these fucking belts from?"

"C'mon, Jimmy, what kinda question is that?"

Fat Jimmy smiled at Bilal. "That's right, young nigga, you've been taught well, just like your father."

Even though Bilal's pops was a dope fiend, he still had a lot of respect in the hood. He was known as a cold-blooded killer. It was rumored that he used to rob a different bank every week. When people compared Bilal to his pops, he would get a real sense of pride, as if he one day would be reincarnated into his pops' image. That shit used to pump Bilal up.

"Who dat with you, Bilal?" said Fat Jimmy while watching my every move.

"Oh, this is my man Jovan. You probably know his pops too," Bilal said, pointing to me.

Now, I wasn't too happy running around braggin' on my pops and uncle, 'cause I knew they used to terrorize this hood back in the day. For all I knew they could have robbed Fat Jimmy.

"Who your pop, youngin'?" Fat Jimmy asked me.

"My pops' name is Winkle," I said to Fat Jimmy.

"Who, Winkle Price? Howdy's brother?"

"Yeah, man."

"Yeah, I know Winkle and Howdy. We used to go on capers together back in the day. How's your pops doing anyway?"

"He's a'ight."

"He still on the run for that bank robbery?"

"Nah, my pops ain't on the run for no bank robbery. He outta town on business," I said, defending my pops.

Fat Jimmy looked at me as if he realized he had let the cat out of the bag. It was obvious I didn't know about my pops' legacy in the gangsta world, so he quickly switched the conversation from my pops to my uncle.

"How your uncle Howdy doin'?"

"You know he down in Lorton max doin' fifteen to forty-five years."

"Yeah, I know. I got word he down there doing hard time. Youngin', you come from a vicious family; both y'all do, and I can just imagine how y'all gonna turn out. Give me one of them belts, Bilal. Let me see if they fit."

Fat Jimmy tried on all the belts, but he was too fat to fit them, so we ended up selling him three bottles of cologne for five dollars apiece.

"A'ight, Jimmy. Thanks, man," Bilal said.

"Anytime, youngin'. Whenever y'all get some shit, come see me first."

"Okay, we'll do that," Bilal said. "C'mon, Jovan, let's go over to Orleans Place and see if we can get rid of the rest of this shit."

Bilal and I walked from Ninth Street over to Orleans Place. When we entered the alley, there were so many customers I couldn't believe this spot was pumpin' this hard. Orleans Place was a powder coke strip. It attracted all kinds of people from prostitutes to politicians, and the man behind all this who would benefit and become a multimillionaire was Ray, a young, big-lip kid with a three-point jumper outta this world. Later in life he would become the biggest snitch in Washington, D.C.'s history.

Bilal and I approached our second customer of the day. He was laid back in the cut, watching over all his workers as they ran back and forth through the alley, handing him bundles of money. When I say *bundles*, I mean it. This dude was collecting so much money that he'd call one of his lieutenants over every time he got like ten thousand and tell him to put it up.

I would later find out that this lieutenant's name was John. Now, John was Ray's cousin, and he had just as much or maybe more respect than Ray did. John was like an enforcer-type dude, something I admired. It was rumored that he didn't play no games, and if you crossed him or anybody down with him, then you'd be dealt with immediately.

Bilal knew John from him coming around with his pops back in the day, and John also liked Bilal. He knew that Bilal was the only one taking care of Mal-Mal like a man, and he respected him for that. Bilal used to ask John if he could hustle for him, but John always lived by strong principles. Even though he knew Bilal needed money to take care of Mal-Mal, he still kept to his word that he would never employ juveniles in this drug game. Instead, he'd get Bilal to run a few errands to the nearest carryout or something and give him about twenty-five dollars for it. Shit, twenty-five dollars just to go get him a five-dollar fish sandwich. John was a good dude.

"Hey, John, what's up?" Bilal said.

"Who dat?" John said as he squinted his eyes, trying to see the two youngsters in the dark alley.

John didn't permit kids into his alley because it was way too dangerous. If anything was ever to happen to them, he'd feel responsible, so to avoid all the trouble, he made strict rules. The alley was off limits to juveniles.

"It's me, Bilal."

"Bilal, what I tell you 'bout coming in this alley?"

"Aw, man, my man and me here just trying to sell these belts and cologne we got."

"Some what? Belts and cologne?"

"Yeah, man."

John had a slight grin on his face. "Let me see what you got."

Bilal showed John the goods, and when John looked at the belts and cologne, he laughed so hard that Bilal and me felt a little ashamed.

"Why you laughin', John?" Bilal asked.

"'Cause, man, I don't wear this cheap shit. I wear two-hundred-dollar belts and cologne! This shit ain't nothing. I can't do anything with this.

"Damn, man," he continued, "tell you what; y'all go 'head and keep your shit. I'ma give you fifty dollars anyway, 'cause I know you gotta take care of your li'l bro. Take this stuff down the alley to one of my runners. They might buy it. They some Bammas anyway."

"Okay, thanks, John."

"Yeah, it ain't nothin'. You better start taking your butt to school, Bilal. Both you and your man here."

"But you don't even know me," I said.

"Yeah, but you hangin' with Bilal, so I know you ain't going to school either."

"Okay, thanks, John."

"Yeah, now hurry up and get your asses out of this alley," John said.

"A'ight," Bilal said.

When Bilal and I walked down to the end of the alley, we bumped into this hard-faced, dark-skinned dude with beady hair and pimples. He didn't look like no runner to me. He looked more like a fiend.

Bilal said, "Hey, man, you wanna buy some belts and cologne?"

The guy looked up and down the alley nervously before he answered, "Where they at and what you want for 'em?"

"Ten dollars for the belts and five for the cologne."

"Let me see 'em."

Bilal pulled out the goods and showed them to the dude.

The dude said, "Shorty, these mu'fuckin' belts cost fifteen dollars and this cologne cost eight dollars. What ya tryin' to do, get over on me?"

"Naw, man, we ain't tryin' to get over on you. We just tryin' to get paid," Bilal said.

"These fuckin' belts ain't worth no ten dollars," the dude said.

At that moment, I said something that I shouldn't have said. "Look, slim, if you don't wanna pay what we want, then give us our shit back."

"What you say? What you say, you little bitch-ass nigga? Nigga, I'll take this shit from y'all!"

Bilal then jumped up and said, "Man, you ain't taking shit from us!"

"What you gonna do, huh?" the fiend said as he still looked up and down the alley. "Nigga, this shit mine now. Get the fuck away from here 'fore I beat the shit outta both y'all!"

Bilal reached for the goods, and outta nowhere this mu'fucka hit Bilal in the face and kneed him in the stomach. Bilal went down on his knees, crying throughout all the commotion.

I didn't know what I was doing, but for some reason, I didn't feel nervous or scared. I felt like what I was about to do was justified. I looked at Bilal on the ground, and although I was angry, I still didn't replace logic for emotion. I knew that something had to be done and fast, so when the fiend turned toward me, I already had the bulldog pointed at his chest. I didn't hesitate or panic. I waited until his body was positioned directly in front of mine, and then I pulled the trigger two times.

Boom! Boom!

The impact of the bulldog damn near lifted me off my feet.

Bilal looked up at me in a state of shock and said, "What the fuck you do, Jovan?"

I never answered because it was obvious I was protecting us by any means necessary.

"Where the fuck you get that gun, man?"

"Shut up, man. Get the shit and let's go."

At that moment, everything in the alley stopped. The fiend was lying there dying in his puddle of blood; then we heard some voices saying, "Hey, what y'all doing?"

As Bilal and I took off running down the alley, we heard a woman scream and say, "Hey, come back here! What y'all do? They shot Boo-Boo! Call the police!"

We ran faster until we reached Sherwood Recreational Park, where we sat down and caught our breath.

Then came the question: "Man, Jovan, why the fuck you ain't tell me you was strapped?" Bilal said.

"I dunno, man. You probably would have told me I was scared and to take it back," I said.

"How the fuck you gonna know what I'ma say if you don't ask?"

"Man, the shit just happened. That nigga violated us and got what he deserved."

"What if he dies?"

"Then that's what he deserves."

Bilal was silent for a moment, then said, "Okay, where the fuck you get that gun then?"

"I stole it out my pops' room."

"Your pops got shit like that laying around the room?"

"Naw, man, I was sneakin' through his shit and found it."

"When he find out you got it, he gonna whip your ass."

"No he ain't, 'cause I'ma put it back tonight."

"A'ight, then let's go put that shit back, 'cause it's getting late."

"Hey, Bilal, you think anybody saw us?" I asked, scared.

"Man, them mu'fuckas don't know us. They coke heads, remember."

"Yeah, right," I said as I thought about what I'd just done.

"Hey, Jovan?"

"What is it now?"

"Hey, thanks, man, for not letting that mu'fucka stomp my head in."

"Slim, you my man, and I fuck with you from the heart. I ain't gonna never let nobody do nothin' to you and get away with it."

"Vice versa, nigga."

We both gave each other a hug and went into Grandma's house, which was directly across the street from the park. As soon as I came through the door, Grandma got right in my ass.

"Boy, where your ass been at? Didn't I tell you don't be out too late? I gotta take you home."

"Yeah, Grandma, but it's only nine o'clock."

"Nine o'clock my ass. Next time I'ma leave your butt standing out in the cold. Act just like your damn daddy. Don't listen for shit."

"I'm sorry, Grandma. You know I love you, baby girl," I said, hugging her tight.

"Go upstairs and get your things with your silly self," she said, giving me a light smile.

"Okay," I said.

"Hey, Grandma Price, can I use the phone to call my aunt before I go?" Bilal asked.

"Yes, go ahead, baby."

Bilal called and his aunt told him that Ms. Cookie had left Mal-Mal over there all day. She was pissed off because she had to get up and go to work in the morning.

"Okay, Aunt Gloria," Bilal told her. "I'ma come get him right now. I'm right around the corner."

I went upstairs to put Pops' bulldog back and pack my things. When I came back down, I had the blue North Face coat in my hand.

"Didn't I say I was about my word?" I said to Bilal.

"Yeah, so what's up?" he answered.

"Here, nigga. This coat still new, so don't fuck it up," I said, handing it to him.

"So it's mine now?"

"Yeah, it's yours."

"Then I can do what the fuck I wanna do with it."

"Give me my shit back, nigga."

Bilal and me were joking with each other as if nothing had happened earlier.

Grandma then yelled from the back of the house, "Hey, I hear you two out there. Y'all better stop that damn cursing in my house!"

"Sorry, Grandma."

"Sorry, Ms. Price." Bilal turned to me before he left and said, "Man, thanks. You the only friend I got."

I could see the sincerity in his eyes, as if he was about to shed a tear.

"A'ight, man. See you next weekend."

***

Bilal left and was on his way to pick up Mal-Mal from Aunt Gloria's house, which was on Twelfth and Wyle, a few blocks up from where the murder was put down. Just before Bilal could hit the corner of Twelfth Street, two police cars closed in on him. Both officers got out with their guns drawn.

"Freeze, goddamnit!" said one officer.

"Don't move, and put your hands in the air!" said the other officer.

Bilal was scared and confused as he placed his hands above his head, praying that they wouldn't shoot.

As one officer began to frisk Bilal, the other held him at gunpoint. Bilal almost fainted when he overhead the dispatcher on the officer's radio say, "Calling all cars. We now have the full description on the two suspects involved in the homicide on Orleans Place."

The officer holding the gun turned the volume up on his radio, while the other officer was still searching Bilal.

The dispatcher called out, "Suspects are two young black males between the ages of fourteen and sixteen, medium height. One of the males was wearing a blue coat with writing on the sleeve, blue jeans, and tennis shoes."

The officer frisking Bilal yelled out to the other office, "Does he fit the description?"

"Yeah, that's him. Lock his ass up!" the officer said.

Bilal was arrested and charged with murder. There was one witness who pointed out Bilal and stated that there were two people, but the one with the blue coat pulled the gun.

After hours of interrogation, Bilal never broke. He kept his silence. He remained loyal and was sentenced to a juvenile facility up until he was twenty-one years old.

This was the first time that the reality of the world Bilal was living in became completely visible to me. Bilal took the murder charge for me. Niggas nowadays would catch diarrhea of the mouth if they were caught. I would remember this and forever remain loyal to Bilal.

Sonya

"So now, Mr. Jovan whatever-your-middle-name-is Price," I said to him.

"Conrad, sweetheart. My middle name is Conrad."

"Okay, Conrad, it's my turn now to interrogate you."

As we looked each other in the face, I still couldn't believe how strikingly handsome he was. I hoped Jovan didn't have a girlfriend, wife, kids, or anything else that would make me get up and leave this place immediately.

"First, how old are you?" I said with a devilish grin.

"I'm twenty-four years old, but I'll be twenty-five next month."

"Hmmm, so you're a youngin'?"

"C'mon, Sonya, you only got me by less than two years. You act like you 'bout forty-something." We both laughed.

"Naw, I'm just joking with you. So when is your birth-day?"

"June third," he said.

"Oh, June third. That's my bro Tony's B-day."

"Yeah, he must be a good dude like me then, huh."

"Whatever, Jovan. You're sweet now, but you're proba-bly a li'l devil after someone gets to know you."

"Naw, boo, what you see here is what you get," he said, as he looked in my face, letting me know that he meant every word.

Damn, I hoped Jovan wasn't playing no games, 'cause if this was what I got, then I wouldn't want for nothin' else. Jovan Conrad Price was the perfect gentleman: a handsome, sharp, smooth, and intelligent young black man.

"Okay, so do you have a job?" I asked.

"Good question. You know most women nowadays don't even ask that question."

Shit, what did he mean by most women? I hoped he was not taking other bitches out to lunch on a regular basis.

"I've been questioned like this by a lot of women, but most of the women my friends date never even ask that question."

Whew, I was glad he cleared that up!

"Well, that's a very important question, because if you and a person are to become friends—and later on, who knows, you may end up falling in love or something—it's only right that each person knows what they're bringing to the table."

"I totally agree. Well, first of all, yes, I do have a job. I work for Rohon and Robinson, a law firm in the city. I've only been working there for a couple months, but I love it."

"What type of work do you do? I mean, are you actually a lawyer?" I asked.

"Well, yes and no. When I say yes, I say that because most of the legwork on cases is done by me. I find cases of law, place them in a motion, and format certain facts for the motion; then I give it to my boss, who is the actual attorney. He'll look over the motion, make a few changes, and bring it before the court to argue it."

"So you're the brains behind the machine?" I asked.

"Naw, I wouldn't call it that," he answered. "You can say that I'm part of a team and my position is unseen. I'm no lawyer yet, although I plan to finish law school. I only have two more year-long courses to take in order to take my bar exam. Right now I'm employed as a paralegal at the firm."

"What's a bar exam?"

"It's a test you have to pass in order to get your license to practice law in a certain state."

"So I guess you're taking yours in D.C.?" I asked.

"I haven't really decided yet. Shit, I gotta finish school first," he said.

"Are you still in school now?"

"Naw, boo, I took a rest so I could get a job and pay for my next two courses. I just got out of school six months ago. I took a two-year paralegal course."

Damn, it was so good to see a nice young black man with an education and intelligence, and to think of it, he wasn't even the preppy nerd type. This brother was smooth. I could tell that at one point in time he was a nigga in the streets but had enough sense to get his ass up and get an education and a job so that he wouldn't suffer the pains of death or prison like most of our young black males today. The world needs more people like Jovan.

"So, is that why you were in court today?" I asked him.

"Yeah, boo, it was hectic. We have a client who has come back on an appeal from thirty years, and the government wants to proceed with the case without giving us proper notice so that we could prepare briefs. Today my boss had to go and ask the judge for an extension of time in order for our firm to prepare and file briefs. I was just there as a backup to make sure that the judge and government act according to the law."

"Is that why you had that black notebook?"

"Yeah."

See, I knew he wasn't a criminal. I knew I had made the right choice in coming to lunch with him.

Jovan

When Bilal was sentenced to juvenile hall, I was crushed, because my true friend and comrade was gone for what seemed like forever. Since Bilal and I both were juveniles, there was no way that I could visit him, but at times, I would send him flicks of me and other bitches at the latest Chuck Brown or Rare Essence go-go club. To me it felt like I couldn't do enough for Bilal, the person who was doing time for a crime I had committed that only three people knew about: Bilal, me, and God.

As Bilal continued to do his time at Cedar Knoll Youth Division, I continued to keep the vow I made to him two years earlier, and that was to take care of Mal-Mal. Every time I went over to Grandma's house, I would go get Mal-Mal, take him to play video games or to the movies and get him an outfit and new kicks.

I was seventeen at the time and was hustling. For a seventeen-year-old, you could say I was getting it good. At that time, I was selling PCP. In D.C. we called it Boat— Love Boat, to be exact. There were also other nicknames for it, like John Hinkley, the fool who shot Ronald Reagan, or the most famous of all, That Butt Naked.

I was hustling on one of the most pumping and vicious strips in D.C., Whaler Place Southeast. Sometimes I would go on Galveston Street Soutwest and hustle with my man, Rose, or over in Maryland up around Glassmanor with my boys Li'l James and Ek-Dre.

Barry Farms was one of my spots also, but a nigga had to be real careful hustling in the Farms because people were getting killed and robbed almost every other week. I made sure that whenever I went into Barry Farms, I was always strapped, but it was cool, though, 'cause I was mostly dealing with one of my brother's old comrades, Li'l BB.

Li'l BB was a little brown-skin dude who went to school with my big brother. They was real close, and when my brother died, Li'l BB used to always look out for me. He had a blue 190E Benz, and he used to come past Galveston, pick me up, take me down Georgetown, and we'd get outfits for a night at the go-go club on Atlantic Street.

At that time I was pumping good. I had just bought my first car, a burgundy Nissan Maxima with burgundy sheepskin seats and five-star rims. At times, I used to go pick up Mal-Mal and take him out because Ms. Cookie was still on it like the Brown Hornet. Every time I saw her, she was getting smaller and smaller. At one time, she had lost so much weight that you could see every bone structure in her face.

Bilal was transferred from Cedar Knoll to Oak Hill Youth Center, which was a more treacherous joint than Cedar Knoll. When other dudes I knew would come home from Cedar Knoll, I'd ask them about Bilal, and everything I heard about him was good. They'd say, "Yeah slim, that nigga Bilal ain't goin' for nothin'! Slim go hard as a mu'fucka. He's on the boxing team down there. He run the store. He big as shit!"

Niggas used to jock Bilal so much that I stopped asking about him, 'cause I already knew what they were gonna say. When Bilal was transferred to Oak Hill, we lost contact, and the fact that I was out here getting money, fucking bitches, and going to go-go's didn't help either.

I also began to slack in my efforts in looking out for Mal-Mal because at times, he would page me and it would take me a few days just to get back to him. Whenever he needed something like video games or toys, I was the one who got it for him. The only thing about it was I was too busy to spend time with him. My world was moving too fast, and I couldn't see what was to come next.

In July 1988, I stopped hustling Love Boat and moved onto a more profitable drug called crack cocaine. At the time, crack in D.C. was at its all-time high. The demand for it was ridiculous.

I was copping from my boys Ek-Dre and Li'l James. These two brothers was getting it, and they both had a good reputation all over. Dre was a smooth nigga who loved to dress. He had all kinds of Polo, MCM, and Gucci shit. James was the hard one, more like the leader among his crew. They were some good niggas and was getting some major paper on the hill.

I was getting half a brick at that time, breaking it down in half ounces and ounces. I had runners up Glassmanor, Galveston Place, Wayne Place, Parkland, Fourth Street, Condon Terrace, and a few lames from Alexandria, Virginia.

I traded my Maxima in and bought a 1988 Nissan Turbo 300ZX with cream-colored leather, and I put some white deep-dish classic rims on it. My car was one of the tightest joints in the city, at least on the southeast side, 'cause them uptown niggas and them niggas on R Street Northeast was pushing 500EL Benzes and Convertible BMWs and shit. The type of bank I was getting was considered play money to them, because the niggas from around Bilal's way was super getting it. The Orleans Mob had 944 Porsches, convertible Jags, 300CEs, Range Rovers, the new Acura Legend and anything that cost more than fifty thousand.

On the Fourth of July, Mal-Mal paged me and I called him back.

"Hello," Gloria said, answering the phone.

"Yeah, Gloria, how you doing? This Jovan. Is Mal-Mal in there?" I said to her.

"Oh, hi, Jovan. Yeah, his li'l bad ass here. You coming to get him?"

"Naw, not right now, but I promised him I'd buy him some fireworks for tonight, and I'ma come pass and drop them off and come back later and light 'em with him."

"That's good, 'cause I gotta work tonight, and Cookie said she was gonna be here, but I ain't seen her ass yet," Gloria said, then she yelled, "Mal-Mal!"

"What?" Mal-Mal said.

"Boy, don't *what* me," Aunt Gloria said to him.

"Yes, ma'am."

"Get your butt in here. Somebody on the phone for you."

"Who is it?" Mal-Mal asked.

"Answer the phone and find out."

Mal-Mal came running to the phone and said, "Hello."

"Mal-Mal, what's up, youngin'?" I said to him.

"Hey, Uncle Jay. What's up, man? I thought you was gonna bring me some fireworks and light 'em with me tonight."

"I'm still gonna do that, Mal-Mal. I'm on my way over there to drop the fireworks off to you."

"You gonna stay, Uncle Jay?"

"For a little while. Then I gotta go do somethin', but I'ma come back and light 'em up with you, though."

"A'ight, Uncle Jay."

"Okay, young soldier."

As I was driving to Twelfth and Wyle Northeast to go see Mal-Mal, I got a page from this little freak broad out in Bowie, Maryland that I was staying with at the time. I didn't call her back right away, though.

When I pulled up onto Wyle Street, Mal-Mal came running out of the house.

"Uncle Jay, Uncle Jay," Mal-Mal said, running up to my car.

"What's up, youngin'?"

"Man, Uncle Jay, this your car?"

"Yeah, that's my joint."

"Man, this joint is tight! I bet it's fast, ain't it?"

"Yeah, it's fast."

One of Mal-Mal's little buddies came running outta Gloria's house. He was there to see the fireworks. Mal-Mal was always bragging about his Uncle Jay so much that his buddies would be just as happy as he was to see me pull up, but this particular kid was a little too grown. He always felt he was in competition with Mal-Mal, so when he noticed that Mal-Mal was fascinated by my car, he felt the need to say something just to make him mad.

"Hey, Mal-Mal, that joint ain't all that. My uncle got a Benz, and his joint is way tighter than that!" his friend said.

"Shut up, punk, 'fore I bust your nose again! That's why you ain't playing wit' my fireworks," Mal-Mal said to his friend.

"So? I don't care."

"Me either, punk."

That shit was funny, seeing two youngin's ready to wreck. If I wasn't in such a hurry, I would have taken both of 'em around back and let 'em fight. I was almost certain Mal-Mal would whip his ass, because Mal-Mal was eleven years old now and big as a house. He was also bad as fuck.

I kept getting pages from that broad out in Bowie, Maryland. This bitch was blowing my shit up with 911-911-911-911. She used to page me so much when I was out with other bitches that I ignored it when she put in 911 because most of the time, she'd just be trying to find out if I was with another bitch or not. Damn, she was getting on my nerves, but at the present time, I needed her. She had a nice apartment in Bowie, which was twenty minutes away from the city, and she had a nice job working for the Department of Labor, so I needed her credit.

She was the one who co-signed for the 300ZX, and when I got my bank right, she was gonna sign for a Mercedes 300CE for me. Plus, she was a stone freak in bed. She loved sucking my dick, and I loved it too. One thing about her I didn't like was that she was a Bamma-ass broad. She talked loud, she couldn't dress, and she wore cheap shit. Even when I'd try and buy her some fly shit, she still looked fucked up in it. She couldn't even rock it right. To add to all this, she had a two-year-old daughter by some punk-ass nigga that used to beat her ass.

As I looked down at my pager while Mal-Mal was still arguing with his buddy, I figured I'd use Gloria's phone to call her back. As soon as I entered through the front door, I could tell that Gloria was in a rush. She was running back and forth from the bathroom to the living room, as if she was in a hurry to go somewhere. She was fixing her hair and ironing her clothes at the same time.

"Hey, Gloria, can I use your phone real quick?"

"Yeah, go ahead."

Ring, ring, ring.

"Hello," a female voice said.

"Why the fuck are you blowing my pager up like that?" I said with an immediate attitude.

"Jovan, somebody broke into the apartment!" the female on the other end of the phone yelled hysterically.

"What?" I asked, not sure I had heard her correctly.

"They came in through the balcony."

"Is there anything missing?"

"I dunno! The furniture is all ripped up, the TV is broken. It doesn't look like they were trying to steal shit. It looks more like they vandalized the place. Jovan, I'm going to call the police," she said.

"No! Hell no! Don't call the police. I'm on my way," I said quickly.

"Jovan, please hurry up. I'm scared."

When I hung up the phone, Gloria could see that I was mad as hell.

"Is everything all right?" she asked me.

"Yeah, I'm cool. Look, I gotta go right now. I got something to do."

"All right, Jovan. You sure you're okay?"

"Yeah, yeah, I'm okay," I said, walking out the door.

When I came outta Gloria's house and walked toward my car, Mal-Mal came running down the street.

"Hey, Uncle Jay, where you going? I thought you were gonna stay and light the fireworks with me."

"I'll be back, Mal-Mal. Right now I've got something to do."

"Can I go with you?" he asked me.

"Naw, man, this is important; but I'll be back," I told him.

"Hurry back, Uncle Jay, 'cause it's almost dark now."

"Okay, youngin'."

As I pulled away from Wyle Street, I saw Ms. Cookie walking toward Gloria's house. She was walking real fast. I rolled down the window and said, "Hey, Ms. Cookie."

"Oh, hi, baby. Where you going?" Ms. Cookie asked.

"I've gotta go do something. Look, I brought Mal-Mal some fireworks, and I don't know if I'ma make it back in time to light 'em up with him. If I don't get back in time, can you do it?" I said to Ms. Cookie.

"Yeah, baby, I'll do that. I'm on my way to Gloria's anyway."

"Okay then, Ms. Cookie. See you later."

"Jovan, hold up for a minute."

"What's up?"

"Baby, you got ten dollars so I can get Mal-Mal something to eat from the carryout?" Ms. Cookie said.

"Yeah, hold up," I said, reaching into my back pocket where I kept a knot of ones and peeled off twenty dollars. I knew if I gave Ms. Cookie only ten, she'd just go cop a dime of blow, but with twenty she could get Mal-Mal something from the carryout and do whatever with the rest.

As I got on the highway to Bowie, all I could think about was my money. I had fifty thousand dollars over this bitch's house. My mind was racing. Who the fuck did this? I never brought anybody over there, and when I came home, I'd circle the parking lot a couple of times before I got out. I was always cautious not to put my bank in any danger. The more I thought about it, the madder I got and the harder my foot pressed on the gas.

As I turned off the highway onto the ramp, I reached under my seat and pulled out my black Beretta 9 mm. I always kept my pistol with me, especially when I was in Southeast, cause on that south side niggas ain't have no picks; they were always trying to kidnap and rob anybody who was getting some money.

Although the city was in an uproar around this time, I never had to use my Beretta. No one had given me a reason to. No one violated me like that dope fiend did back in '85, but tonight I felt violated, and whoever did this surely deserved two to the head. I'd killed before, and I would certainly kill again.

As I pulled into the parking lot, I didn't circle the block. I felt there was no need for my routine. I jumped out of my car holding my Beretta, hoping and wishing that the perpetrators were still around, Damn, all I could think about was my fifty thousand dollars. That was all I had: fifty thousand and my car. With that fifty thousand, I was going to cop two bricks and flip them over so this bitch and me could go to the nearest Benz dealer to cop my 300CE.

When I opened the door to the apartment, I saw that the place was a complete mess, and I knew my fifty thousand was gone. I ran toward the bedroom where I kept my money.

"Dee-Dee! Dee-Dee! I'm here. You a'ight?"

"Yeah, I'm fine. They just fucked my house up," Dee-Dee said.

When I went into the bedroom to check the vent where my money was, I saw that it was busted open. I knew my shit wasn't there, but I still reached my hands in to make sure. As I took my hands out of the vent, my whole fucking world was crushed, and I instantly developed a supreme hatred for all cruddy niggas in the game. From this point on, I was going to make it my business to find out all the niggas in the city known for robbing and kidnapping. I was also going to make it my business to know where they hung out and who was down with their crew.

Around 8:15 p.m., I got a page, and when I looked at it and saw that it was Mal-Mal, I remembered I had promised him I would light the fireworks with him. Even though I was fucked up and my money was gone, I still had to keep my loyalty to Bilal. I promised him that I'd take care of Mal-Mal, so I figured I'd go light the fireworks and sit over Gloria's for a minute and get my thoughts together. I didn't call Mal-Mal back. I figured I'd just pull up and surprise him.

"Dee-Dee," I said.

"What?" she said in a snappy way.

"Here's fifty dollars. Take a taxi over to your grand-mother's house," I said.

"For what? Where you goin'?" she asked.

"I've got something to do."

"Jovan, how the fuck you just gonna leave after something like this?" Dee-Dee asked.

"Just do what the fuck I said! Damn, your ass is always trippin' and getting on my fuckin' nerves!" I said.

"Well, if I get on your nerves that bad, you can just move the fuck on and don't ever come back!" Dee-Dee yelled.

That was all I needed to hear. My fifty thousand was gone, the apartment had gotten broken into, and my 300CE was nowhere in the near future. I realized I didn't need this naggin'-ass bitch no more. After all, I was only eighteen and she was talking about settling down. Shit, I hadn't even begun to live my own life yet. Plus, I was broke again, and I had to get back out there and grind on the corner. The last thing a nigga who was trying to get his grind on needed was a broad who didn't understand. So, I did what any nigga in my position would do: I packed my shit and left.

As I walked out the door, Dee-Dee called me a million no-good-ass mu'fuckas. "You ain't shit, Jovan. You too weak to have a strong woman like me! Fuck you, nigga. I hope you have bad luck all your life, you no-good, dirty bitch!"

As I got into my car and pulled off, I had a smile on my face. Although I was mad about my fifty thousand, I was happy as hell to get Dee-Dee outta my life.

On my way to see Mal-Mal, all I could do was think about how I was going to get back on. For one, I didn't want anybody to know that my bank had gotten taken. Also, I didn't want to get fronted nothin'. I liked to pay for my own shit. I wondered if I would have to sell my car and jewelry, because if I did, then niggas would put it out in the street that I was broke. Shit, I didn't know what to do. I needed some time to sit back and think.

As I pulled up onto Twelfth Street, I saw a bunch of flashing lights and a lot of people standing around. Some were crying, and others were just being nosey. The crowd was so thick that I couldn't make my turn onto Wyle Street, so I got out of my car and walked up the street. It was obvious something was wrong. When I hit the corner, all I saw were fire engines and ambulances. Aunt Gloria's house was going up in a blaze of flames. I was determined to know what had happened.

I saw Ms. Cookie on the ground, crying her heart out, screaming, "My baby, my baby!"

Instantly, I knew Mal-Mal was in that fire. Man, what the fuck had happened?

"What happened, Ms. Cookie? Ms. Cookie, what happened?" I said as my heart pounded inside my chest.

No one could hold me back. I was mad—mad at the world, mad at Ms. Cookie, and mad at myself.

Later, I found out that Ms. Cookie never went back to Gloria's when I gave her the twenty dollars. She went around Orleans Place to cop her some blow, and Gloria had to go to work and left Mal-Mal and his cousin, Gwenee, at home by themselves.

Mal-Mal wasn't but eleven years old, and Gwenee was only twelve. Anybody in their right mind would know you can't leave an eleven- and twelve-year-old home by themselves with a bunch of fireworks on the Fourth of July.

When the fire marshals finally put out the fire, they went into the house to investigate what had happened and to see if anyone was alive in there. Ms. Cookie was still crying, trying to pry her way through the police and firemen, but they held her back with all their strength.

"Get the fuck off me! My baby's in there! Oh my God, Mal-Mal! My baby, my baby! Please, God, not my baby!" Ms. Cookie screamed.

That's all I could hear was Ms. Cookie screaming. As for myself, I just stood in the middle of Wyle Street with no expression on my face. I had no feeling in my body. I don't even remember if I was thinking or not. I was in a complete daze, and my whole system had shut down.

The first body they brought out was Gwenee. The fire marshal had her in his arms, and her body was limp. She didn't have any burn marks on her or anything, so she must have died from smoke inhalation. Li'l Gwenee was Gloria's only child, and when Gloria arrived on the scene and saw the fireman holding her dead child in his arms, she went off.

"Give me my child! Give me my child!" she screamed, fighting with the police and fire marshal who were trying to hold her back. She cried in pain for her child, and then her cry became angry blame.

"Cookie, what the fuck did you do to my baby? What the fuck did you do?" She fell to the ground, scratching and kicking the police, screaming, "Get the fuck off me!"

The fire marshal then brought Mal-Mal out. The only way that I knew it was him was from the new Jordans he had on, because I had gotten them for him last week. His body was burned from head to toe. I was so fucked up at what I saw that all I could do was fall to my knees right there in the middle of the street and cry the loudest pain that I ever felt in my life.

Ms. Cookie fell unconscious and had to be hospitalized for a few days. All I could think about was Bilal and how he would take it.

I paid for Mal-Mal's funeral and wake because I had a little money from the niggas who still owed me in the street. I sold my 300ZX but kept my Rolex, and I had about twenty thousand to work with after the funeral and everything.

After we buried Mal-Mal, Ms. Cookie went into rehab, and I continued trying to get some money. I always felt in my heart that my life was indebted to Bilal for taking my murder rap, and I also felt somehow responsible for Mal-Mal's death. If I had only been there to help light those fireworks, Mal-Mal would never have tried to do it himself.

Sonya

"Okay now, Mr. Lawyer, tell me where you're from," I said.

Jovan started smiling, and for a minute I thought he was blushing.

"Well, I grew up all over Southeast. When I was young we used to live in the Farms."

"You mean Barry Farms?"

"Yeah, sweetheart."

"That's a rough neighborhood, isn't it?" I said.

"Yeah, it's rough, but it was cool coming up, because that's where I learned how to fight, how to pick and choose real friends, how to survive and peep the game. It's also where I learned how to express certain talents."

"Like what type of talents?" I asked.

"Music. I'm one of the original members of the Junk Yard Band. I used to play the buckets."

I immediately started laughing. "For real?"

"Yeah, sweetheart, I was the man on the buckets back in the day."

"Did you ever graduate to real instruments?"

"Yeah, I took up trumpet and piano in school."

"Damn, I never met a guy who knew how to play the piano," I said, impressed.

"There are a lot of things I know how to do that might surprise you," Jovan said, smiling.

"Stop being fresh. Remember this is our first date."

"So, you're calling this a date? That must mean I got a shot at seeing you again, huh?"

"No, I didn't mean it like that. I meant this is our first meeting, and if this goes well, who knows what may happen?" I said, smiling back at him.

"Now you're the one being fresh," Jovan said, laughing.

"So, where else did you live?" I asked.

"Oh, we moved from the Farms to the Valley."

"You mean Valley Green?"

"Yeah, sweetheart."

I wished he'd stop calling me that, because it was turning me on.

"Living in Valley Green was real rough, but somehow my mother found a way to keep me outta trouble. She sent me to the Number Eleven Boys' Club after school. That's where I played basketball, football, and took up boxing. On the weekends, she sent me over Northeast to my grandmother's house, and I liked going over there, 'cause that's where my best friend lived."

CHAPTER 3

"The Lawyer"

Ring, ring, ring.

"Law offices of Rohon and Robinson. May I help you?" Cindy said.

"Hey, Cindy, this is Mark. Is Jovan there yet?" Mark asked her.

"Yes. He's in your office, waiting for your call."

"Good. Plug me in," Mark said.

"Jovan?" Cindy said.

"Yeah, Cindy, what's up?" Jovan said.

"Mark's on line one."

"Okay, thank you," Jovan said, pushing line one. "Hey, Mark, what's the deal?"

"Well, it took you long enough to get there. I've been calling all morning," Mark said.

"C'mon, Mark, you called me at home at nine o'clock and it's now nine thirty-five. I came as fast as I could," Jovan said.

"Damn. Hope you brushed your teeth," Mark said, laughing.

"Good joke, Mark."

"Okay, enough of the funny stuff. Let's get down to business."

Jovan liked that in Mark; he knew when to joke and when to take care of business. Jovan guessed that was why they connected so well.

"Look, I need you to find me some cases on conflicts of interest, ineffective association of counsel, and illegal search and seizure."

"Are these the issues your client is putting forth?" Jovan asked Mark.

"Yeah, but not right now. I just need the cases beforehand in case the government wants to argue; then I'll already have my guns loaded."

Mark always stayed two steps ahead of the government, because whenever they presented something in the cut, he hit 'em right back with it.

After Jovan got off the phone with Mark, he went into Mark's private law library and looked up the cases that would fit his argument to a tee. The fact that this new client was his best friend made him work even harder. He Shepardized case after case, updated them, and faxed them straight to Mark.

Mark called back again.

Ring, ring, ring.

"Law offices of Rohon and Robinson. May I help you?" Cindy said.

"Cindy, plug me into Jovan again," Mark said.

"Jovan, line one. Mark again," Cindy said.

This time Jovan didn't pick up the receiver; instead he sat back in Mark's chair, placed his feet up on his desk, and pressed the intercom button.

"Yeah, Mark, what's up?" Jovan said.

"First of all, get your ass outta my chair. When you legally become a lawyer, you'll get your own desk and chair," Mark said.

"Yeah, right, besides yours, huh?" Jovan said, laughing.

"I don't know 'bout that one, buddy," Mark said.

"Hey, were those cases any good?"

"Yeah, they were damn good. The government's mad as hell," Mark said with a chuckle.

"What's next?" Jovan asked Mark.

"Well, my client only has one hang-up."

"What's that?"

"The government still has the statement from a witness during the grand jury testimony, and they're saying that this witness is still willing to testify," Mark said.

Damn, Bilal's shit was looking fucked up, so Jovan asked, "Did the judge grant a new trial?"

"No, not yet, but we do have some good news."

"Yeah, what's that?"

"Come to find out the officers who arrested my client never had a legitimate warrant for his arrest. They just had a personal vendetta against him, so they got some information from an informant and put together a bogus warrant and illegally searched his home."

"So, does he now have a good argument to drop all the charges?" Jovan asked hopefully.

"Yeah, but there is still one thing that fucks it up."

"What's that?"

"If the charges get dropped, the government is gonna reindict my client for conspiracy, and they will use the witness that was an informant for the police to testify against him and his grand jury statement, which I'm reading right now."

"Is his statement bad?" Jovan asked, needing to know because his best friend's life was on the line.

"Yeah, it's very bad. It says here that my client sold him at least five kilos of coke a week."

"Damn, they got him in a bind, huh?" Jovan asked.

"Yeah, this will fuck him up for good."

Bilal was Jovan's best friend, and he had to do something; he had to find some way to get him out of this bind.

"Mark, how much time do we have to work on this case?"

"I'm gonna ask the judge for an extension of time. I'll call you back and let you know how it goes," Mark said.

When Jovan got off the phone with Mark, he was in a state of confusion. How in the hell was he gonna get his man outta this situation?

Jovan

After Mal-Mal's death, I chilled out for a while, but I eventually got back into the swing of things. By the summer of '91, I was coping at least four bricks a week. My connect was from New York, and sometimes he would bring it down to me, but most times I had to go get it myself.

After a few months of dealing with my connect, we became real cool. He put me down on a lot of things in the drug game, and he taught me how to whip up bricks. I would take two bricks and cook them up with B1 vitamins and baking soda, and it would make three bricks out of two bricks. The coke would never come back Grade A, but on a scale from one to ten, I'd say it was a six.

I wouldn't sell these bricks to the niggas I fucked with regularly; I always kept them with good coke so they could make their money fast and buy more bricks from me. What I would do was serve it to them Virginia Bammas because they would buy anything as long as it was coke.

Virginia was pumping like that. Them Bammas would cop, like, two bricks a week from me, straight money not a dollar short. That was what scared me about those niggas. So when I served them, I made sure they brought their asses across the bridge to Washington, D.C. because if any funny business was to happen as far as the police was concerned, I'd have a better chance of getting away.

My connect also told me about the hydraulic stash spots, that James Bond shit. So what I did was go to the nearest Mazda dealer and buy myself a brand new MVP van. Then I sent it up to New York, and my connect had his man make me a spot that could hold at least eight bricks. That shit cost me ten thousand dollars, but it was worth it. I also bought a new silver 535 BMW with chrome BBS wheels.

At the time, I was renting a townhouse out in Clinton, Maryland, ten minutes outside the city, and everything was going good for me. I was anticipating my man, Bilal, coming home, and whatever I had was going to be broken down 50-50. Half of this shit was his. We'd both be getting money together, doing all the shit we dreamed about; but for right now, I was the man of the hour. I traded my old Rolex in for a new one, an 18K Presidential with a diamond bezel and diamonds flowing through the middle of the band. Bitches would go crazy when they saw me rocking that joint. I also had a three-carat earring that I rocked on occasion, and a plain Rolex band bracelet.

My style of clothes also changed. It was no longer Polo. I had switched to Gianni Versace, Gucci, MCM, and Ferragamo. I was getting too much money to be dressing like I was still some corner hustler. The more money I made, the less sweat suits and tennis shoes I wore. I started going to all the main events: fights, lavish parties, and social functions, and I was fucking the baddest broads in the city. I had more clientele than I could handle. I was holdin' around a hundred thou plus assets.

At the time, I was involved with the prettiest up and coming youngin' in the city. Her name was Barvette. She was brown-skinned with a milky complexion, nice hair, a nice body, and a walk that made her look sexier than she really was. The pussy was on one thousand. It was Barvette that hipped me to all the finer restaurants in the city. She also hipped me to all the boutiques on Wisconsin Avenue: Neiman Marcus, Gianfranco Feree, Versace, Gucci, and Everett Hall. In fact, I think the first time I ate at the Cheesecake Factory was with her—or was it with freaky Tracey? I don't know, 'cause I was fucking both of 'em at the same time.

We also went on trips together to Negril, Vegas, Cancun, and a couple of other places. Although she wasn't officially my girl, we were still cool as shit, so if there was anything I could do to help her out, I didn't have a problem with it—until she started asking for that Chanel shit. Now, that shit was costly. They wanted three thousand for a pocketbook, so instead of breaking her off a nice bank for that Chanel shit, I broke off the relationship. I hustled too hard to be giving up that much bank to a broad who wasn't officially my girl.

Damn, I wished Bilal would hurry up and come home. All I kept thinking about was how comfortable it was gonna be for him when he got there. I was Bilal's only family besides Aunt Gloria, and she was at the St. Elizabeth Mental Hospital. After Li'l Gweene died, Gloria wasn't the same, and Ms. Cookie had passed away a year ago.

When Ms. Cookie went into rehab, she discovered she had full-blown AIDS from shooting dope. I saw Ms. Cookie after she got out of rehab. She looked bad because the disease was killing her. I used to take her to the doctor and to the pharmacy to pick up her medicine, and sometimes I'd take her to lunch and we'd talk about Bilal and Mal-Mal.

Before Ms. Cookie died, she finally, for the first time, went to visit Bilal. I don't know how that visit went because right after that, Ms. Cookie was hospitalized and she went into a coma, and then two weeks later she died. I paid for the funeral and had her buried right next to Mal-Mal.

CHAPTER 4

"Only the Worst Could Happen"

It was October 1991, and Bilal was due to come home the next month. Jovan couldn't wait, but what he didn't know was that all his plans to welcome Bilal home would soon come to an end.

In early October, there was a coke shortage, and Jovan was still getting bricks, but not as many as before. The prices were sky high, and Jovan's connect had to divide whatever he could get with all his major clientele. The city was at its lowest point; only a few niggas had bricks stashed, and they wasn't servin' nobody who wasn't in their crew.

The only nigga out there who was still on top was Big Head Larry. Jovan didn't know Larry personally, but Bilal and he went to school together, and they were real cool back in the day. At the time, Larry was hangin' out with this New York nigga named Po, and Jovan didn't like Po because he came to his city when they were vulnerable and used it to his advantage. He got up under the most feared nigga in the city at the time, a nigga by the name of Big Silk. He knew he had to get Big Silk on his team, 'cause if he didn't, those niggas out there would have torn his ass to pieces.

In Jovan's eyes, Po was a bitch. He turned friends into enemies, he used real niggas for protection, and he hid behind a mask; but when that mask was pulled off, it was too late. Jovan found out that Po was down with the feds, and this bitch-ass nigga emptied his brain to the government and turned state's evidence on all those who held him in high regard. To Jovan, Po had committed the ultimate sin.

Niggas out there were hungry. Ounces were going for eighteen hundred a pop, and you couldn't find nobody selling anything for less than that. Then came the break Jovan needed—at least that's what he thought. His connect called him and told him he was back in action.

"Okay, slim, I'm on my way up!" Jovan said, excited to hear from him.

"Naw, money, you ain't gotta come up. I'm on my way down there 'cause I got a few more people I gotta see," Jovan's connect said.

"Shit, cool. C'mon, slim, I need you," Jovan said, needing to cop bad.

He told Jovan that he only had a few bricks and that he should try to cop as many as he could get. The price Jovan used to pay wasn't happening. It was a little higher, but not as high as niggas were paying out there. He was going to give 'em to Jovan for twenty-six. Out there they were going for thirty or better.

Jovan went to his townhouse in Clinton to count his stash, and all he had was a hundred and eighty thousand. He usually never copped with all his bread, but this time he had to, because he was gonna make a killing during this drought. He had enough to cop seven bricks, and his plan was to break 'em down to ounces and sell 'em for sixteen hundred apiece, two hundred lower than the going price out there.

Four hours later, Jovan's connect called him and said that he was staying at the Ramada Inn in Virginia, across from Pentagon City.

"Okay, slim, I'm on my way," Jovan said, about to hang up the phone.

"Yo, hurry up, money. They're going like hot cakes. I can't hold 'em for too long."

"A'ight, slim, I'm on my way," Jovan said, hanging up the phone.

Jovan packed the hundred and eighty thousand in shoe boxes and placed them in two big-ass Banana Republic bags. He got into his MVP and popped the hydraulic stash, placing the money in there, and then he headed to the hotel where his connect was staying.

When Jovan reached the Ramada Inn, he didn't bother to park his mini van because he was so anxious to be copping that he just pulled in front of the hotel, put his hazards on, and jumped out.

As he was walking into the hotel lobby, his pager was blowing up like shit. Everybody was trying to cop before the first of the month. Jovan was all smiles because this was going to be his big come-up. All he could think about was the money he was 'bout to get and how right his bank was gonna be when Bilal came home.

When Jovan got off the elevator and knocked on his connect's room, he heard two voices. Now, whenever Jovan used to cop from this dude, he was always alone. Although sometimes he would mention his partner, Shorty, he would still do business by himself.

When Jovan heard the two voices, naturally he was on his guard. He put the two bags of money into his left hand and kept his right hand free, close to his side, as close to his Beretta 9 mm as possible. He prayed this nigga wouldn't try to pull no move on him, because he already had a hate for cruddy niggas, and if they even thought about violating him, he guaranteed there would be two niggas in the hotel dead, and he wouldn't be one of 'em. He'd killed before, and would kill again if necessary.

When Jovan's connect opened the door, he had a smile the size of Texas on his face.

"Yo, money, what's up!"

"Ain't shit, slim. Still doin' my thang."

As Jovan entered the hotel, he got a glimpse of the other dude sitting on the bed counting money.

"Yo, Jovan, this is my partner, Shorty."

"What up, money? I heard a lot about you," Shorty said.

"Yeah, and vice versa," Jovan said.

After the introductions, Jovan and his connect got right down to business.

"Yo, Jovan, what you trying to get? You know I ain't gonna be in town that long."

"Slim, I'm working with one eighty."

Jovan connect's eyes got as big as shit when he heard how much Jovan had. Usually Jovan copped only four or five bricks at a time. Jovan guessed the sound of extra money excited him.

"Yo, this is what I'ma do: I got ten bricks left. I'ma give you eight, and you can owe me the difference until the next time you cop."

Damn, that was a sweet deal. Jovan immediately handed over the money and placed four bricks in each bag. He stood there for a second so that his connect could count the money, but it looked to him as if he was getting ready to pack up.

"You gonna count that?" Jovan asked curiously.

"Naw, money. I've been dealing with you for six months now. You ain't never been short. Your bank has always been right," Jovan's connect said.

As Jovan left the hotel, he felt like nobody in the city could fuck with him. All he kept thinking about was how much money he was gonna make.

His pager was still blowing up like crazy as he headed back to his townhouse as fast as he could to cook up and move this shit like a fat turkey on Thanksgiving. Jovan then started counting figures in his head. He had eight bricks at sixteen hundred an ounce. That would come out to at least three hundred and eighty thousand. He had his 535 BMW worth forty-two thousand and his MPV van worth twenty-five. All together that was four hundred forty-seven thousand. His jewelry was worth about four hundred eighty thousand, and with the little money he still had out in the streets that niggas owed him, he figured he was worth about a half a million dollars. He'd have more than enough when Bilal came home. He wished that bitch Dee-Dee could see him now, he thought, smiling to himself.

When Jovan got to his townhouse, he pulled his van in the garage, popped the hydraulic stash, retrieved the bricks, and went into the house to start cooking them up; but first he called all his clientele back and told them he'd be ready in a little while. Then he got the ceramic pie plate and baking soda out to cook the coke. He didn't bother to whip it. He wanted this shit to be Grade A butta! He wanted the city to know he had that bomb shit, and plus, he was selling it two hundred dollars cheaper than the going price.

When Jovan busted open the first brick, he could see that it wasn't the good shit he used to get. He didn't see them icy-looking snowflakes, and the smell was dull. When he placed the coke in the pan and waited for it to dissolve, the shit fell straight to the bottom. He stirred and stirred it, but it still never came together. Instantly Jovan started to get mad, and he grabbed the phone. He was about to page his connect but decided not to. He thought maybe it was just one bad batch outta the eight.

So Jovan went back into the kitchen and popped open the next brick. It was the same shit, and after opening all of the remaining bricks and seeing they were all the same shit, he came to realize this mu'fucka had sold him eight bricks of cement. This bitch-ass nigga had violated him, and he already hated cruddy niggas, and now it was his time to express that hatred.

Jovan grabbed his Beretta 9 mm, jumped in his BMW, and headed straight back to the hotel where those bitch-ass niggas were staying. He was going to kill both of them whores right there in the hotel.

He was so mad that he was running red lights, speeding, and not bothering to turn on his blinkers. As Jovan got on the 495 highway, he was still speeding, dodging in and outta traffic, and the only thing that was on his mind was murder in the first degree. To him, it was going to be justified. They had violated him, and they deserved what they were soon to get, just like that fiend in the alley on Orleans Place back in '85.

As Jovan dodged from the left lane into the right and back to the left, he didn't notice the red-and-blue lights flashing until he finally, for the first time since he had gotten behind the wheel, looked into his rear view mirror. Damn, the fucking police! As bad as he wanted to outrun them, he couldn't. Anyway, all he was doing was speeding. Plus, if he gave them a chase, he definitely wouldn't make it back to the hotel in time to kill those bitch-ass niggas, so he went ahead and pulled over, put his pistol under his seat, and grabbed his license and registration from the glove compartment. Jovan planned not to argue with the police. He figured he would just take his ticket and then go kill those bitches before they left town.

When the officer got out of his car, Jovan could see through his side mirror that he was saying something into the radio. After he finished talking into the radio, he unsnapped his holster and put his hand on his gun. When he reached Jovan's window, he asked him to turn the car off. Jovan did as he was told, and when he turned his head back to ask what he was being pulled over for, all he saw was the barrel of the officer's gun.

"Don't move! Put your fuckin' hands up!" the officer said to Jovan.

As Jovan was literally being arrested while still sitting in his car, another cop pulled up and blocked his BMW in.

"Get out of the car slowly," the officer said.

Both of these crackers had their guns pointed in Jovan's face, and for a second he thought they were gonna shoot him right there on the spot. When Jovan got out of the car, one officer put his hands behind his back and handcuffed him, while the other one searched his car. They found his Beretta, which he didn't have a license to carry, and that gave them more reason to go through his car. They sat Jovan in the back of one of their cars and continued searching his car for drugs or whatever else they could find. Jovan sat there for about an hour watching those crackers rip his BMW apart. They even called in drug-sniffing dogs. When they finally saw that there was nothing else in Jovan's car, they transported him to the D.C. jail.

Since he had been on an interstate highway, they had jurisdiction to charge him in federal court. Here Jovan was in the D.C. federal court. At trial, he was sentenced to five years for carrying an unlicensed firearm, and his man Bilal had just come home two weeks before his sentencing.

Sonya

Jovan's answers to my questions were interesting, but what I really wanted to know about Jovan was his family.

"Okay now, Mr. Lawyer, tell me about your mother," I said, because if he had a lot of respect for his mother, then I knew he had respect for women period.

Before Jovan could open his mouth to answer my question, the waitress came over and asked, "Would you two like anything else? Some dessert, a glass of wine or champagne, maybe?"

"No!" I snapped.

The waitress turned and walked away with a serious attitude. Jovan looked at his Movado watch to check the time.

"Hey, Sonya, why were you so mean to the waitress?"

"'Cause she keeps interrupting my interview."

Jovan smiled and looked at his watch again.

"Do you have something to do?" I asked.

"Naw, sweetheart," Jovan said.

I wished he would stop calling me that.

"It's only one-thirty. I've got all day. What about you?" he asked.

"I'm cool. I'm chillin', and if I get bored, I'll let you know." We both laughed, and then I went right back to my question. "So, Jovan, tell me about your mom," I said again.

"Well, my mother passed away when I was in school," Jovan said with a sad look coming over his face.

"Oh my God, I'm so sorry," I said.

"It's okay. Although I don't talk about it much, I do feel comfortable talking about it with you. I was in school taking my paralegal course. When I went to school, my mother was diagnosed with diabetes and she never told me. I don't know why, but I guess she didn't want me to mess up my education worrying about her condition. When she passed, I was at the end of my paralegal course, and I knew she would have wanted me to finish, so even though her death fucked me up, I still finished the course.

"She was a good woman, but I always thought she worked too hard. She was a waitress at the NCO Club on Bolling Air Force Base. She was loyal to my pops even after they divorced. I never saw my moms with another man."

Damn, Jovan's moms musta been strong or madly in love with his pops, I said to myself.

"She used to take me places and buy me all the latest gear. Even though we lived in the hood, Moms always had enough to get me the things I wanted. I mean, I wasn't spoiled, but I wasn't neglected either."

"Do you have any brothers and sisters?"

At that moment, when I looked at Jovan, I could sense something was wrong. I grabbed hold of his hand and said, "Hey, we don't have to talk about it if you're feeling uncomfortable."

CHAPTER 5

"The Lawyer"

Ring, ring, ring.

"Law offices of Rohon and Robinson. May I help you?" Cindy said.

"Cindy, Mark. Plug me in," Mark said.

"Jovan, Mark's on line one."

"Thanks, Cindy," Jovan said. "Hey, Mark, tell me something good."

"Okay, get your ass outta my chair."

"Man, I'm not even in your chair. I'm walking around here, pacing, trying to figure a way out for Mr. . . . . What's his name again?" Jovan asked, playing stupid.

"Davis. Bilal Davis."

"Yeah, that's right. I think I got something."

"Yeah, what?" Mark asked.

"Look, if you can get an extension for at least one week and get me a legal visitation pass, then I can interview this guy and possibly get some info on his witness that could contradict his testimony and maybe get an affidavit that could free him."

"Well, I've got good news and bad news. Which one you want first?" Mark asked.

"Give me the bad first," Jovan said, not really wanting to hear it.

"Well, I can't get you that pass because you must be a licensed lawyer."

"Damn," Jovan said, disappointed.

"But I can get you in with me on a temporary pass seeing as how you're my assistant, and anyway, I'll be interviewing another client at the same time, so you'd have at least an hour alone with him," Mark said.

"Shit, that ain't no bad news, Mark, but I think I'm a little scared to hear your good news now." We both laughed.

"Jovan, let me put you down on some inside law shit."

"What's up?"

"As long as you know the law, how to work it, how to get around it, and fuck it the right way, you'll never have any bad news. Bad news to a lawyer is another way of saying it's time to lie."

"So what's the good news then?"

"Jovan, good news will always be good news," Mark said, laughing.

"Okay, I will ask you once again: What's the good news?"

"Hey, man, I got the extension a half hour ago."

"That's great, Mark. You're always two steps ahead of the game," Jovan said, proud to be working with Mark.

"Thanks, and you're getting good at it too, Jovan. You're also on the right track. Keep it up and when you become a lawyer, you'll always stay two steps ahead also."

CHAPTER 6

"School of Hard Knocks"

Jovan

I was sentenced to five years in federal prison with no outside support from no one. I had a few broads that used to come and see me every now and then, but I wasn't focused on them. My main concern was how was I going to get back home and get a lawyer to do my appeal because once again I was broke. Well, not flat broke.

When I got locked up, I had Keda, who was my female gangsta at the time, go past my townhouse and get my jewelry and the MPV van and take them over to my grandma's house before the landlord found out he wouldn't be getting his eleven hundred dollars a month no time soon.

My BMW was seized by the government because it was used in a crime. I could have gone to court and tried to get it back, but I didn't want to risk the chance of them investigating how I paid forty-two thousand dollars cash and drove it straight off the lot, so I just took it as another loss.

The only person I was in contact with the whole time I was locked up was my grandma. I used to call her a lot, but since my father was nowhere to be found, I knew that Grandma couldn't keep paying for all those collect calls on her Social Security check. I slowed down on the calls and wrote letters and sent her cards occasionally.

Soon after I was sentenced, they transferred me to Lewisburg Federal Penitentiary. As the bus drove up to what looked like Castle Gray Skull and two of the biggest iron doors I've ever seen in my life opened, the first thing that came to my mind was, *How the fuck did I get here, and why are they putting me in a maximum security facility with niggas serving three life sentences?* I would be lying if I told you I didn't care where they sent me. Shit, I only got five years. I wasn't supposed to be in there.

After being processed and given my federal prison number, 20518-016, I was given a bedroll and sent to J block. When I got to my cell, I didn't bother to look around to see if I recognized anyone, because I was so tired that I just made up my bed and went to sleep.

The next morning when I woke up and went to the chow hall, the first nigga I saw was my man Mack from R Street. I knew Mack back in '88 when he had a convertible BMW. He was always cool with me. We never did business with each other, but we always acknowledged each other's presence.

"Hey, Jovan, that you?" Mack said.

"Yeah, what's up, Mack?" I said.

"What's up, Joe?" When Mack spoke, he always expressed the word "Joe." To the homies in D.C., "Joe" is our slang for main man or slim, dude or whatever. For D.C. niggas, it was different doing time in federal prison than doing time back home, because we made sure that we all got along with each other. It wasn't anything like our state prison, Lorton, where homies robbed, killed, and stole from each other. The homies in federal prison stuck together mostly for territorial reasons, so whatever beef a homie had with another homie that wasn't outside the limits of death was immediately squashed once they entered federal prison. We held back on any serious aggressions until it was time to go to war with others.

D.C. had an image to protect, and homies rolled with homies no matter what.

Mack came over to me and gave me five and a respectful hug that is only reserved for real niggas.

"What's up, Joe? Why the fuck you down here? Last time I saw you, you were pushing a BMW with a bad-ass bitch beside you going down Georgia Avenue."

"Yeah, slim, that same BMW got me these five fuckin' years," I said.

"All you got is five years?" Mack said with a surprised look.

"Yeah, man."

"Damn, Jovan, what the fuck you doing in Lewisburg? You're supposed to be in a camp, or at least a low security facility, man!" Mack said.

"I dunno what type of games these people playin'."

"Yeah, you got to holla at your counselor about that tomorrow. Anyway, c'mon so I can introduce you to the homies."

Mack introduced me to all his co-defendants first. Some I already knew, some I didn't, but as I grew to know these niggas, every last one of 'em was real. He also introduced me to Li'l Nut, and we became super cool. Nut, Mack, and me worked out regularly. It was these niggas that helped me get a six pack, triceps, biceps, and a chest that needed to be in an *Ebony* magazine centerfold. After six months in Lewisburg, my body went through a complete change. I lifted weights; not heavy weights, just light reps. I did pull-ups by the twenties and dips by the thirties. I did five hundred crunches in the morning, five hundred at count time, and five hundred before I went to bed. I turned myself into the ultimate physical machine, and then it was time to work on my brain.

I read all kinds of literature and books, mostly by Dr. N. Akbar, and I read a few by J.A. Rogers, Dr. Frances

Cress Welling, Carter G. Woodson, Jerome Bennett, Noble Drew Ali, and Elijah Muhammad, but my favorite one of all was the Holy Quran.

There was something else missing in my life that I needed bad, real bad. It wasn't a female friend. I had plenty of those to call if I wanted to get freaky and tell 'em to play with their pussies while I listened, but I was beyond that. It wasn't money, although I could use some. It was something else that was holding me back, and when I passed the library, I knew just what it was. I needed to learn how to get outta there. I needed to learn the law, the same law that gave me five years. I needed to learn about it because who knew? I could one day give it right back to someone else.

By the end of the first week of trying to learn the law, I was frustrated. It seemed like every book I read didn't make any sense or went straight over my head. I stopped working out with Mack and Nut and focused all my attention on my legal situation. I still would do a thousand push-ups and crunches every day to keep my body toned, but mostly I was reading the Federal Criminal Code and Rules book.

One morning on my way to the law library, I walked by some new inmates, and I didn't look any of them directly in the face. I just glanced at them as they walked by me with their bedrolls, headed to their new blocks. As I turned toward the library, I took another glance, and suddenly I saw someone very familiar. I looked one more time to make sure my eyes weren't playin' tricks on me. Yep, that was him: that nigga Shorty, one of the bitch-ass niggas who had violated me. Now it was his turn to be violated.

I bent my head down and walked by again just to really make sure it was him, but after I heard someone yell his name, I knew for sure that this was my man.

"Yo, Shorty, you in that block over there," said another inmate.

"Okay, thanks, money."

Same name, same accent. Finally I would get a chance to get my due justice. I went straight to my cell. I didn't move fast; I just acted normal and calm. I sat in my cell and began to put my plan together. I thought about the time I had, only five years, but this nigga had violated me. I had to get him, but I also had to get away with it.

Think, Jovan, think! The only way I could get this nigga was to get him in one of the TV rooms when nobody was there, or at least when a lot of people was in there, 'cause it was dark as shit in them TV rooms, and when that joint got packed, you couldn't see or move.

It was Friday, the day they showed the latest movies, so this was my chance to give it to a nigga who really deserved it. When my cellmate, Parker-Bey, came in the room, it was almost time for the movie. My celly was from Detroit, and he was in the Moorish Science Temple. He was the one I used to get all the positive literature from.

"What's up, Jovan?" Parker-Bey asked.

"Ain't nothin'," I said.

"You gonna go up tonight and check out the movie?" he said.

"Naw, I think I'ma lay back and finish reading this damn law book," I said.

"Yeah, you doin' the right thing trying to get outta jail, something a lot of these unconscious brothers should be doing, but instead they'd rather stay in jail and kill each other," Parker-Bey said.

I was thinking to myself, *Yeah, you got that right. Well, at least part of it, 'cause I'm definitely trying to kill a mu'fucka, but I ain't trying to stay in jail.*

"I'll holla at you later, Jovan. I'ma check this movie out."

"Okay, Parker-Bey," I said, turning back to the law book I was pretending to read.

When Parker-Bey left, I waited a good five minutes before I started working on my plan. *Damn, I pray this shit goes right. It's a must that I kill this nigga, but it's an absolute must that I get away with it.*

First thing I did was put on my khaki uniform and black boots. Then I put my gray sweatshirt on over top, making sure you couldn't see the uniform underneath. I looked at myself in the mirror, but the more I looked, the more I felt I needed a better disguise. I put on one of my celly's gray kufi and a pair of those shades they sold in the commissary. As I looked at myself in the mirror again, I was now completely happy with what I saw, I looked like a militant Black Panther type dude. No one would know who I was, so no one would be able to identify me, and no one would know how vicious a killer I was but me.

I reached into my mattress and pulled out the eight-inch flat blade that Mack had given me when I first got there. I tucked it in my pants, took a deep breath, and headed to the TV room to kill my second victim, a nigga who truly deserved it. As I walked down the hallway, I could tell that I had on the ultimate disguise, because when I walked by Mack and Nut, they didn't even recognize me.

As I walked by, I could hear them talking. Mack said, "Man, where Jovan at? I ain't seen him in about a week."

"He's probably in the law library working on his case. Slim must really be trying to go home," Nut said.

"Yeah, I can respect that."

When I entered the TV room, it was just like I pictured: dark, loud, and smoky from the cigarettes and Black and Mild cigars. The atmosphere was perfect for my plan.

I walked to the back of the room and saw Shorty and another dude sitting there, talking and kicking it about old times. He probably was telling his man how he got a free hundred and eighty thousand back in D.C., but little did he know that money was gonna cost him his life.

I took a seat directly behind Shorty. There were three other dudes sitting in my row with me. They didn't talk loud. To me it looked like they were minding their own business, like all convicts were supposed to do. Sitting in the row with Shorty was his man and two homosexuals sitting together.

As the movie was about to start, I reached in my pants slowly, making sure no one saw me, and held the knife in the palm of my hand so tight that it felt as if I had dipped my hand in Super Glue. I wasn't scared or nervous; I was calm and collected. I peeped my surroundings one more time, and then came the golden opportunity I was waiting for: the TV went blank for about five seconds. I reached my left hand up under Shorty's chin and pulled back with all my strength, exposing his whole neck and throat to the blade. My first blow was vital, but my second blow was much more vicious. I drove the blade so hard through Shorty's neck that the tip of the blade was poking out the back of his head. Shorty died instantly. He didn't have a chance to scream or fight back. He didn't even get a chance to tell on me. He was through!

When the TV came back on, Shorty's friend was quiet, and I could see that he was involved with one of the homosexuals sitting next to him. When he was finished and looked over at Shorty and saw that he was dead, he never even looked behind him. He just got up and left. In prison, when someone just gets up and leaves without saying a word, that means something just happened or was about to happen, and if you're not involved, then you get up and leave also. So once Shorty's man got up, everybody else got up.

While niggas were trying to get outta the TV room as fast as they could, I laid back for a second, took off my sweat suit, balled it up, and left it in the corner along with the knife. I folded my celly's kufi up and put it in my pocket and threw the shades in the trash. Now I looked like the average inmate with khakis ironed and pressed, boots shiny, and shirt buttoned up and tucked in.

When I came back to my cell, I saw that my celly was already in there.

"What's up, Parker-Bey?" I said.

"Hey, what's up, young brother? I thought you were staying in tonight to work on your case. You wasn't up in the TV room, were you?"

"Naw, I went down to the law library to read up on a few things."

"Good," Parker-Bey said.

"Why you say that?"

"'Cause I think something happened in the TV room tonight. I was just making sure you were a'ight."

"Oh, you ain't gotta worry 'bout me. I only got five funky-ass years, and I'd be a damn fool getting into some shit," I said.

"That's right, young brother. Your main concern is to get home to your loved ones," Parker-Bey said.

"Yeah, right, and that's exactly what I plan to do."

CHAPTER 7

"Welcome Home, Bilal"

While Jovan was in Lewisburg trying to get these five years up off him, Bilal was at home doing his thang. Jovan always knew that Bilal would be the perfect hustler. He had it in his blood; plus, he was alone with no family and no place to go.

In February of 1992, Bilal Davis had the whole city on lockdown. When Bilal first came home, he got with Carlos Gonzales, a Spanish nigga he was down at Oakhill with. Carlos and Bilal became good friends while they were locked up, and they always promised each other that they would get together when they got out. Carlos fronted Bilal two kilos of powder for twenty-five thousand as a coming home present, and he went right back around his old neighborhood and started hustling. Niggas knew Bilal from when they were little, but mostly they remembered him killing Boo-Boo in the alley back in the day. At least that's what they thought he did.

Bilal took over the Northeast with an iron fist. Orleans Place was abandoned after John got locked up, and the fiends wasn't on powder no more. They wanted crack. Bilal did the first thing that came to mind: he got together the most vicious youngin's from around the way—Li'l G, Cat, Soup, and Shortdog—and he paid them to take out every major nigga that was sellin' crack. That way, when it came time for him to open shop, every dime in the Northeast would be his.

Bilal cooked both kilos up raw because he wanted his shit to be the best coke out there. Although it was the only coke out there, he still wanted to attract customers from other neighborhoods.

When Bilal opened the alley back up on Orleans Place, it was jumping even harder than it did back in the day. It was rumored that Bilal was making at least thirty thousand a day selling dimes.

After about a month, Bilal had more money than Carlos, but regardless of that fact, they remained partners and they put their money together, copped thirty kilos from one of Carlos's uncle, and then Bilal had shit on almost every major strip in D.C. The last spot Bilal re-opened, the legendary Hanover Place Northwest, was the spot that was going to put him into multimillion-dollar status. It was rumored in prison that Bilal collected at least a hundred thousand a day from Hanover Place alone.

As Bilal's organization grew bigger, his stash grew just as big. Carlos and Bilal went to Mexico to meet a new connect because Carlos's uncle could no longer meet their demand for more bricks. He ended up introducing them to his connect in Mexico. They went there and ended up with the deal of the century. The connect agreed to sell Bilal and Carlos ninety-percent cocaine for seventy-five hundred a kilo, but under one condition: when they purchased, they had to buy no less than two hundred kilos at a time. Bilal and Carlos immediately agreed and started doing business with the Mexican one week later.

Here Jovan was stuck in Lewisburg Penitentiary with five years and no way to get in contact with his man, his true friend, his comrade for life, Bilal Davis, the new king of D.C.

CHAPTER 8

"Come on Home"

As the months went by, Jovan spent every free hour that he had in the law library. He wouldn't go to chow, watch TV, get on the phone, or anything. All he wanted to do was learn about the law. The more he stayed in the law library, the better he got. He also met some real niggas while working on his case that helped him out. Some showed him how to format motions; others showed him how to read cases. Big Linwood, Cashwell, Cookie, and Young Rico aka Ali Katabb all taught him how to fight the government with its own weapon. After he learned as much as he could about the law, he became known around the prison as Jovan the Law Fiend, Jovan Cochran, or the Jailhouse Lawyer .

Jovan had been locked up for almost two years now, and the judge finally answered his appeal. At the 4:00 p.m. stand-up count, Jovan's counselor told him to come into his office and sign the priority mail book.

"What's up, Stevens? Somebody sent me some money priority mail?" Jovan asked.

"I don't think so, Price," Stevens said.

"Then what is it?"

"I think it's some legal mail here for you. Just c'mon down and get it after the count," Stevens said.

During the whole count time, Jovan couldn't stop from wondering what this legal mail was. He paced the floor back and forth, trying to figure out what it could be. He was hoping it was the answer to his appeal that he had put in about eight months ago.

He hadn't asked for a new trial. He asked that the whole charge and indictment be dropped on the basis of illegal search and seizure and racial profiling. The officer on his case never said he pulled him over for a traffic violation. He never wrote a ticket; he just placed him under arrest and searched his car without his consent. He also did not have any reasonable suspicion to search his car. He just saw a young black man driving a BMW doing about seventy in the left lane. The only thing he was supposed to do according to law was give him a ticket and go on about his business.

After the count was clear and the cells popped open, Jovan raced to his counselor's office.

"Stevens, you got that mail for me?" Jovan asked.

"Yeah, Price, it's right here, but first sign the log stating that you received it."

Jovan signed the log and grabbed the mail. He couldn't wait to read it, so he opened it up right there in Stevens' office. It read:

The United States District Court For the District of Columbia

In the instant matter of the United States vs. Jovan Conrad Price, the District Court grants appellate's motion, reverses the conviction, and drops all charges.

The Petitioner is to be released from Federal custody IMMEDIATELY.

At that moment, Jovan almost fainted. He rushed to his cell to retrieve all of his personal belongings and went to call his grandma to tell her the good news.

Ring, ring, ring.

"Hello?" Jovan's grandma said.

"This is a collect call from Jovan. If you wish to accept this call, please press five now," the operator's voice said.

Grandma pushed five and said, "Hey, baby."

"Hey, Grandma, how you doing?" Jovan said excitedly.

"Oh, I'm doing okay. I would be better if you or your daddy was here," she said.

"Well, Grandma, I don't know about my daddy, but I'll be there soon."

"How soon, baby?" Grandma asked.

"Sooner than you think, Grandma. I just won my appeal!" Jovan said, jumping for joy.

"Stop playing, boy!" Grandma said, screaming.

"Grandma, I ain't playing. I'm dead serious."

"Well, that's good, baby. When you leaving?" she asked.

"I think tomorrow morning. You gonna come pick me up from the bus station?"

"Yeah, baby, I'm so glad you're coming home, because now you can get that damn van from in front of my house. It's been sitting here for almost two years." We both laughed.

"I'll call you in the morning, Grandma," Jovan said.

"Okay, baby. Love you."

"I love you too, Grandma."

"Oh, Jovan," Grandma said before hanging up.

"Yeah."

"Did you read about your friend Bilal in the newspaper?"

When Grandma said that, instantly Jovan thought Bilal had been killed.

"Naw, Grandma, what happened, and when was he in the paper?" Jovan asked her, afraid she was getting ready to tell him Bilal was dead.

"About two days ago, baby. It said something about him being a drug kingpin and being arrested with a whole lot of money in his possession."

When she said he had gotten locked up, Jovan was relieved to find out he wasn't dead.

"Did they catch him with any drugs on him?"

"I dunno, baby. It didn't say anything about drugs, just money, and a whole lot of it, too. I hope he'll be all right. Bilal's a good boy. He's just been through so much."

Jovan wondered if Bilal ever came by his grandma's while he was away.

"Hey, Grandma."

"Yes, baby?"

"Did Bilal ever come over there while I was locked up?" Jovan asked her.

"Oh yeah, baby. He came over a few times. I was supposed to give him your address, but every time he came over I couldn't find it," Grandma said.

Damn, Jovan thought, *my man was out there getting all that money and he was still loyal. I bet if Grandma had given him my address, my account would have been fat as shit. Now this nigga gets locked up and I'm on my way out the door.*

CHAPTER 9

"A New Beginning"

On December 31, 1993, Jovan was home free. The first thing he did when he got home was call Peppa over to his Grandma's house. He fucked her all night long. He fucked her so hard that when she got up in the morning, she couldn't even walk straight.

"Damn, Jovan, you act like you ain't never had no pussy before," Peppa said when she woke up the next morning.

"It ain't that, Pep. It's just that I ain't had none in two years."

"Shit, I know you was in there playing wit' that thing."

"Yeah, I jerked off a few times, but it ain't nothin' like the real thang," Jovan said, laughing.

Jovan didn't have to make love to Peppa, because she was a hood rat, so it didn't matter if he fucked her like a ho or caressed her like a gentleman. She was gonna fuck with a nigga like him regardless, because she already knew his status and capabilities of getting money again, so giving him that pussy any way he wanted it was more like an investment to her.

After Peppa left, Jovan went outside to check on his van. He popped the hydraulic stash and saw that he still had his P13 .45 automatic. He closed the stash back and took his van to the nearest detail shop, and after his van was done, he went back home to spend some time with his grandma. She had cooked a nigga so much food that when Jovan got up from the table, he almost threw up. Jovan kicked it with his Grandma for a while, talking about what he was going to do with his life.

The next morning, Jovan decided to get his tags renewed along with his license. He got together all his old clothes—well, not old, because most of the shit he had was still brand new and the tags were still on 'em. He still had a nice wardrobe, mostly Versace and Armani, and you know that shit wasn't going outta style for a minute, plus most of the Versace shit he had he bought from California on Rodeo Drive. He had shit niggas hadn't seen yet.

Jovan was glad Keda went back to his townhouse and got his shit for him when he got locked up, 'cause if she hadn't, he'd really be fucked up.

Jovan hadn't seen Keda yet, but when he did, he was gonna let her know how much respect a nigga had for her. The whole time he was down, outta all the bitches he had, Keda was the only one that kept it real. She'd send him a few dollars, some cards, and a couple of flicks of herself with thongs on. Although he wasn't too impressed with that at the time, he still recognized real when he saw it.

After Jovan left the Department of Motor Vehicles, his next plan for the day was gonna be hard. He had to get a job. Yeah, Jovan C. Price, outta jail with a paralegal diploma trying to find a job at any law firm that would accept him.

The first place Jovan went to was the Law Offices of Rohon and Robinson. As he was parking his van in front of the office, Mark was just pulling up in his green 535I BMW. Perfect timing, he thought as he grabbed his diploma and hopped out of the van. Just as Mark was getting outta his car with a flimsy briefcase full of motions, Jovan greeted him.

"What's up, Mark? How you doin'?" Jovan said.

"Hey, my main man, Jovan. What's up? What brings you by the office? You caught a new case or something?" Mark asked.

"Naw, the life of crime is over for me. I came to ask for a serious favor."

"Well, if you want me to represent one of your friends or something and they don't have any money, then I can't do that for you, but I'll work with you if you can pull a rabbit out your hat and drop me a few Franklins," Mark said, laughing.

Jovan laughed at Mark's slick way of telling him "if your bank ain't right, you better get outta sight."

"Naw, Mark, it ain't like that. It's a little more important."

"Tell you what, Jovan; I've got a few minutes before I have to go back to court. Come in my office so we can talk."

Mark's office had changed a little since the last time Jovan was there. He also had a new secretary that was phat as hell. She had booty like J-Lo. Her name was Cindy, and she looked all right to be a white girl.

"I see you made a few changes, huh?" Jovan said.

"Yeah, the more money I get, the better the office looks. Now, what's your problem and how can I help you?"

Jovan told Mark everything he needed to know. He told him how bad he wanted to be a lawyer and how bad he needed a job so he could pay for his next two years at Howard University. To his surprise, Mark accepted his plea.

"Look, Jovan, I'm going to hire you and teach you as much as I know, but for a thousand dollars a week, you're gonna have to bust your ass for this law firm. We don't lose many cases, and for the ones we do lose, we end up winning on appeal. Another reason I'm hiring you is because I know you know a lot of these fools that keep getting locked up, and you may have a better approach to them than I do. So yeah, I'ma need you, but you're gonna have to work hard," Mark said.

"Thanks, Mark. I'll never forget this. When do I start?"

"Is there someplace you gotta be right now?"

"No," Jovan said.

"Well, you can start as of this moment. Here's some cases. Look them up and copy them for me."

Jovan picked up the cases and was about to go straight to work.

"Oh, Jovan," Mark said as Jovan was about to leave his office.

"What's up?"

"I see that you're casual today. You think you could dress like that often?"

"Oh, don't worry 'bout that. All my clothes are casual—expensive but casual. I haven't owned a pair of Nikes since 1991."

Mark laughed at Jovan's remark, but it was true. He didn't wear sweat suits and tennis shoes anymore, except if he was working out. He was a fly nigga, always was and always would be.

CHAPTER 10

"6 Months Later"

Jovan was still at Mark's office, learning as much as he could. This day, Mark was in court representing his best friend, Bilal Davis. Mark didn't know that Bilal and Jovan were best friends, and Jovan intended for it to remain that way. Bilal got arrested on some bullshit charge of a one-count conspiracy with no co-defendants, no drugs involved, and no murders. He was charged with conspiracy because of the amount of money they found in his stash house. They confiscated 3.5 million of Bilal's money.

The house wasn't in Bilal's name, and he wasn't on the lease. The only way they connected Bilal to the money was from a suitcase full of expensive clothes and two plane tickets to Paris in his name, along with his passport. Bilal was going away to take a break from the streets, and he was taking some broad he messed with to Paris for a month.

Come to find out that one of Bilal's customers was caught with a couple of bricks down Southwest, and in turn for his freedom, he agreed to be an informant for the Sixth District police. The officers at this precinct hated Bilal. They wanted him bad but could never get anything on him, until they got a hold of Fat Mike.

Fat Mike hustled down Southwest on Delaware Avenue, and Bilal used to look out for this nigga. Mike always bought only two kilos, but Bilal used to give him five and let him owe him the rest later. Bilal always looked out for niggas that he thought had that hustle in 'em.

On the morning Bilal was going to Paris, he made one mistake by serving Fat Mike at one of his stash houses on Florida Avenue. The only reason why that much money was in that house was because Carlos was supposed to come over first thing in the morning and send it down to Mexico for shipment. After Bilal served Fat Mike, Fat Mike went right around the corner and told the police that Bilal was in the house, never telling the police that Bilal had just sold him his last five bricks. Fat Mike was a bitch. He figured he'd pay for only two bricks and get Bilal locked up so he wouldn't have to pay for the other three.

The officers that were waiting called the precinct for backup. They didn't even get a legitimate warrant. They just busted into Bilal's joint, locked him up, and later he was sentenced to thirty years.

Bilal hired Mark, and Mark's motion for a new trial was so strong because of the newly discovered evidence indicating that the warrant that the officers used was bogus and not signed by a judge. The judge immediately called Bilal's case back for a new hearing.

CHAPTER 11

"Long Time Coming"

On May 10, 1994, Jovan was granted a temporary pass as an attorney's assistant. As Mark and Jovan went upstairs, Jovan chose the first conference room, and Mark chose the one across from him. Jovan had to do that so Mark wouldn't look over and see Bilal and him smiling and talking like they knew each other. Plus, he wanted to see Bilal first and give him the eye so he wouldn't come out all loud trying to hug a nigga, blowing Jovan's cover.

The first inmate they brought out was a little dude Mark was representing because he got caught up in a foolish carjacking with some friend while high on PCP. His people had a little money, so they hired Mark. As Mark started interviewing his client, the C.O. brought Bilal into the conference room.

Jovan hadn't seen Bilal in almost nine years. He was big as shit, ripped up like Mike Tyson! He had on his blue D.C. jail jumper, blue kufi, a pair of Versace glasses, and a pair of new blue-and-white Versace tennis shoes. Damn, even in jail Bilal was giving it to them. You could tell everyone in the prison respected him and that he was fucking the C.O., 'cause the C.O. that brought him in whispered something in his ear and felt his dick while patting him down.

When Bilal turned around and saw Jovan sitting in the conference room, his eyes got big as shit. Jovan placed his fingers to his lips to let him know not to let the cat outta the bag and then got up and reached out his right hand.

"Mr. Bilal Davis, I'm Jovan Price, paralegal assistant to your lawyer, Mark Rohon. I'm here to talk to you about a few things."

Bilal had a slight grin on his face as he shook Jovan's hand. When the C.O. left and closed the door to the conference room, the first thing that came outta Bilal's mouth was, "Nigga, what the fuck you doin' here?"

"I come to pay my loyalty to my only friend," Jovan said as he held back the tears with all his might.

Bilal sat back in his chair, looked at Jovan, and shook his head as if in a state of shock.

"Man, Jovan, we got a lot to talk about," Bilal said as Jovan noticed he, too, was holding back years of unshed tears.

"Yeah, I know, but first we gotta get this shit together 'cause I only got a hour with you," Jovan said.

"Man, don't tell me you're a real lawyer."

"Naw, I ain't no lawyer yet. I'm a paralegal."

"Get the fuck outta here," Bilal said, still shocked.

"Naw, slim, this is real."

"How the fuck did you become a paralegal?"

"Long story, Lal. I'll fill you in later." Jovan smiled and said, "What's up, Lal?"

"Ain't nothin'. I'm just sitting here trippin' the fuck out because my fucking best friend who I ain't seen in nine years becomes my lawyer."

"Nigga, I told you back in '85 that I'll never let no one do nothin' to you."

"And I told you vice versa," Bilal said, glad to see his friend.

"Bilal, you already proved that. Now it's my turn to show my loyalty. Now, look and listen carefully," Jovan said, ready to get down to business.

Jovan filled Bilal in on everything from the time he got locked up in '85 all the way up until now. Bilal dropped a few tears then hurried up and wiped them away. They told each other that they loved one another and would forever remain loyal, and that from this point on they'd never lose contact again.

"Look, Lal, you're gonna win your case next week. We only got an extension of time for one week," Jovan told Bilal.

Jovan told him everything about Fat Mike. Bilal never knew Fat Mike was the one who gave him up. He always thought that the police had came up into his spot and found the 3.5 mil on a humble.

"Damn, Bilal, them people took a lot of money from you, slim."

"Yeah, Jay, they hit a nigga's head, but I'm still cool though. I still got like 3.5 mil that Carlos is holdin' for me."

"How much you payin' Mark?" Jovan asked inquisitively.

"He didn't tell you?" Bilal said.

"Naw, I didn't ask him."

"I gave him two hundred thousand and told him if he could guarantee he'd win my case, I'd give him another fifty."

"You paying this mu'fucka all that money?" Jovan asked, shocked.

"Jovan, that ain't shit compared to my freedom. Shit, a nigga like me is worth two hundred fifty million."

"Yeah, I feel you on that one, Lal."

"And, nigga, when I get out, you're going to get a piece of the action too."

"Man, you know I can't hang with you when you get out. Them people's gonna be watching you."

"No, they ain't; not if I play it right. Jovan, this all I know. I don't know nothin' else. I'm a born hustler just like my pops," Bilal said sadly.

Jovan knew one day Bilal would think that he had turned into his pops. He also knew what Bilal said was true, that this was all he knew. Personally, Jovan thought, with 3.5 mil he'd quit and do something else, or at least try to wash that shit up.

"Look, Bilal, your hearing is next week, and if somehow Fat Mike doesn't walk up in that courtroom, you'll be walking out."

Bilal came closer, lowered his voice, and said, "Jovan, look, this is what I need you to do."

"What's that, Lal?" Jovan asked.

"Okay, do you remember Li'l G from around Orleans Place?"

"Yeah, I remember shorty. I hear he's out there killin' everything that moves."

"Yeah, that's right. He's the li'l youngin' I fuck wit'. Look, go around Orleans Place and tell Li'l G I said to lay the demonstration down on Fat Mike ASAP, and that I got fifty thousand for that move. If it's done nicely, I got an extra thirty thousand as a bonus."

"Damn, Bilal, giving up eighty thousand for Fat Mike's head. That's a nice start-up bank," Jovan said. "Okay, Lal, you got that. I'll get on top of that as soon as I leave here."

"Yeah, Jay, and next week when I get out, you and me are going somewhere and talk. I don't care what you're doin', nigga. You my family, and some way you're gonna be a part of my team and play your position. You got that, nigga? Forever I remain loyal," Bilal said seriously.

"Look, Bilal, when we get up, just shake my hand. Don't try and hug me, because we still wanna keep Mark in the dark."

"Okay, Jay."

When Mark signaled to Jovan that it was time to go, Bilal and Jovan stood up and shook hands. This time when Jovan shook Bilal's hand, he saw the tattoo on his right forearm. It was a tombstone with flowers around it, and it read: *In Loving Memory of Mal-Mal, My True Love.* As Jovan looked at the tattoo he felt guilty, because for some reason, he always felt responsible for Mal-Mal's death.

Mark and Jovan left the jail. Mark asked him, "Hey Jovan, I'll see you in the office tomorrow or what?"

"Yeah, but first I gotta try and find this witness to see if he's gonna sign this affidavit," Jovan said. He had to find Li'l G.

"Okay, call me if you find out anything."

Jovan had been up all day without anything to eat, so before he went around Northeast, he stopped somewhere and ate something. Normally, he didn't eat fast food because he tried to keep his figure tight. Right now he was 178 pounds of all muscle. Today he had to break one rule; he drove around the corner on Pennsylvania Avenue and pulled into the Kentucky Fried Chicken drive-thru and ordered a baked chicken dinner. After pulling off, Jovan looked at his watch and saw that it was 6:00 p.m.. He hoped this youngin' was out there.

Jovan drove around Orleans Place and saw two dudes he didn't know. He didn't bother to ask them where Li'l G was because Li'l G be killing so much they'd probably think Jovan was trying to do something to him. As he continued to drive down the street and before he got to the intersection of Orleans Place and Sixth Street, he saw Omar pull up in his Pathfinder. Jovan rolled down his window to signal for Omar to pull over, and it looked like he was reaching for his gun, until he saw Jovan's face.

Omar rolled down his window and said, "What's up, Jovan? Damn, nigga, where you been at? I ain't seen your ass in a long time."

"Yeah, I know. I just been chillin'."

"You heard what they did to Bilal? Them people smashed him with thirty years."

"Yeah, I know, but I'm looking for Li'l G. I gotta holla at him about something," Jovan said.

"You a'ight, Jovan? You ain't got no problems or nothin', do you?"

"Oh, naw, I just need to holla at shorty about something important."

"Check around back. They're probably behind Wilson's playing craps," Omar said.

"Okay, slim, thanks."

"Anytime. It's good to see you again, man," Omar said. "Start coming around more often. For a minute I thought you was one of them niggas trying to get at me, and I was 'bout to put this glock to your head."

"Yeah, Omar? I'll see you later," Jovan said, laughing.

As Jovan drove around back, he could see Short Dogg, Cat, Dre, Soup, and one-eyed Sean shootin' craps. It was obvious these niggas was beefing hard as shit, 'cause soon as Jovan pulled up, they all pulled their shit out.

Dogg had a MAC-11, Cat had a Glock 40, Dre had a Beretta, and Soup had the prettiest Smith and Wesson .45 Jovan had ever seen. He didn't see one-eyed Sean pull anything out; he guessed he felt safe knowing these niggas were strapped.

When Jovan got out of his van, the first nigga who said something was Cat. "Who dat?"

"It's Jovan," Jovan said to him.

"Who?" Cat asked.

"Jovan, Bilal's man."

As Jovan walked up closer so Cat could see who he was, the first thing he said was, "Nigga, where the fuck you been hidin' at?"

"Slim, you know I don't do no hidin'."

"What's up?"

"Ain't shit happenin'. I see you niggas still the same way; ain't letting a nigga just walk up on you."

"Oh, hell naw. You know we ain't going for it!"

Everybody put their straps back in their dips but Short Dogg. For some reason, this li'l nigga was on point. He was Li'l G's young protégé, and if he didn't feel comfortable, he showed it.

"Man, Jovan, what'cha doing around here? You back in action or what? 'Cause we do need a connect. Ever since Bilal went in, we've been fucked up, and you know that bitch-ass nigga Carlos ain't trying to do nothin' with us. He's scared we ain't gonna pay him. That nigga's a ho. I don't understand what Bilal see in him."

Jovan wanted to say to Cat that what Bilal saw in Carlos was millions of dollars that Cat couldn't get, but instead he asked the question that he went there for.

"Naw, Cat, I ain't back in action. I'm looking for Li'l G," Jovan said to Cat.

When Jovan said that, Short Dogg looked at him as if he said he wanted to kill Li'l G. This li'l young nigga was on point. He knew Jovan never did business with Li'l G before, so Jovan could understand why he had his antennas up.

"Jovan, man, come here for a second and let me holla at you in private," Cat said.

"Yeah, what's up, Cat?"

"Look, man, whatever you looking for my man for, I know it must be a good reason, but for real, slim, we don't even know where he's at. You know homicide been around here all week looking for shorty. They're trying to pin some shit on him, so when he got whiff of that, he jetted. Shit, that's my man and he ain't even tell me where he was going."

"Damn, Cat, I needed to talk to him bad."

"Slim, ain't too much I can do, but you can give me your number, and if he calls or comes around, I'll give it to him," Cat said.

Jovan gave Cat his pager number and a special code for Li'l G. "Look, Cat, as soon as you talk to him, tell him I've got a hell of a proposition for him, and it would be in his best interests to get back at me ASAP."

"Okay, Jay, I'll do that."

"A'ight, I'll holla at ya later."

"Okay, Jovan, take care."

As Jovan got back into his van, he looked through his rear view mirror and watched Short Dogg stick his MAC-11 into his pants and he just shook his head. Damn, these young niggas was out there going hard as shit, but in all actuality, they didn't know that Jovan had killed at the age of fifteen, way younger than they were.

CHAPTER 12

"The Next Day"

Jovan woke up the next morning and checked his pager to see if Li'l G had paged him, but he didn't see the special code that he had given his man. Damn, he had to find this youngin'. Fat Mike had to be dealt with before the hearing, which was only five days away.

When Jovan went back around to Orleans Place, it was about one o'clock, and he didn't see anybody but some crack heads looking for coke, trying to trick anybody for a hit. Jovan drove all through the neighborhood, and there was still no sight of Li'l G. Damn, this shit was fucked up. He had to get Bilal out of jail. He rode around a few more times until he saw Cat and Soup in front of the liquor store on Sixth and K. He pulled up and got out.

"Hey, Cat," Jovan said, pressed and determined to find this nigga Li'l G.

"What's up?" Cat said.

"You hear from youngin' yet?"

"Man, Jovan, I've got some fucked up news for you. Shorty got locked up last night as soon he came around here. He called me this morning and said they got him out in Maryland, the Upper Marlboro jail. He said they're trying to charge him with three bodies out there."

"Damn, that's fucked up!" Jovan said, looking disturbed.

"You a'ight, slim? You sound like you're more fucked up 'bout my man than I am. What, he owe you some money or something?" Cat asked curiously.

"Naw, Cat, I just needed him. Does he have a bond?"

"You know them people ain't giving a nigga like Li'l G no fuckin' bond. They're gonna try and fry his ass," Cat said.

"Okay, slim. Damn."

When Jovan got back in the van, all he could do was think about his man. He had to get Bilal out. He couldn't let his man stay in jail. This nigga done took a murder rap for him, and in some way he still felt responsible for Mal-Mal's death. He owed Bilal his life. Bilal was his best friend, his truest comrade, and his family.

Even though he was a paralegal now and trying to get his shit in order, somehow this game always knew how to pull a nigga back in. Jovan had killed before, twice to be exact, but those mu'fuckas had violated him and deserved it. Bilal was his family, and he had made a vow to him nine years ago that if anyone violated Bilal, they violated him. Jovan would remain as loyal to Bilal as Bilal had remained to him. He had to put the demonstration down on a nigga who truly deserved it. He had to kill Fat Mike, but the main thing he had to do was, just like in Lewisburg, he had to get away with it.

CHAPTER 13

"The Plan"

Bilal's hearing was only two days away, and Fat Mike was still breathing. Jovan had spent the day before scoping out all of Fat Mike's moves: what he drove, what time he opened and closed shop, how many runners he had, and most of all, did he carry heat? He knew that Fat Mike carried a gun when he saw him stashing it as the police drove by.

Jovan parked his van on the opposite side of Delaware Avenue and watched Fat Mike's every step. Since his windows were tinted, he had all day without someone peeping him out.

Jovan saw that Fat Mike had about four runners, at least three friends, and one young nigga holding the stash. He also saw that he opened up shop around two o'clock. Mike was kinda smart, because this was the time that the police department changed shifts, so when he had that two o'clock rush, he'd be able to get as much sales as he could without worrying about the jump-outs.

Jovan couldn't just run up on Fat Mike, 'cause he'd be ready. Mike stayed strapped, and the young dude with the stash stayed strapped also, so even if Jovan did run up on Mike and blast him, he'd have to get the other one also, and most likely it would come out a big mess. He'd be either at the morgue or on the five o'clock news, and for sure he didn't want any of that.

As Jovan was sitting in his van trying to figure out a way to eliminate Mike and get away with it, he noticed a Pepco meter. He could see from a distance that the meter was broken, and he wondered if there was another meter. Most of the time there would be another one close by, so he looked toward the side of the building and there it was—the other meter, broken just like the one on the other side. Jovan immediately drove off and went to the nearest Sunny's Surplus store.

CHAPTER 14

"Forever Loyal"

Jovan couldn't sleep all night. He stayed up pacing back and forth, trying to figure out what he was going to do. Bilal's hearing was the next day at 2:45 p.m., and Fat Mike was still alive and breathing, willing to get on the stand and empty his brains on Jovan's best friend. To him, snitching was the ultimate sin. He hated that more then he hated cruddy niggas, and we know how much he hated cruddy niggas, so putting the demonstration down on Fat Mike would not only be doing a favor for a friend, but it would also, in his eyes, be doing justice by giving it to a nigga who truly deserved it.

Jovan left the house around eight o'clock that morning and went to the office to check on some cases and to see if Mark needed him for anything, but his main purpose for going to the office this early was to try to get Mark to get Bilal another extension.

Jovan got to the office about fifteen minutes before Mark did. Cindy was already there, and Jovan wondered if she had ever been fucked by a black guy, because she was phat as hell for a white girl. He contemplated whether he should try to fuck Cindy, but as soon as he built his courage up to approach her, Mark came running through the door.

"Hey, Cindy," Mark said.

"Hello, Mark," Cindy said.

"Hey, Jovan," Mark said.

"Good mornin', Mark," Jovan said.

"Jovan, what are you doing here so early?"

"Nothin' really. I was just checking up on some cases for today's hearing."

"Good. Did you ever find that witness?"

"Sure didn't. I don't even think he lives in D.C. anymore."

"Well, let's hope not, 'cause if he does, Mr. Davis is in a lot of trouble."

Damn, Mark acted like he didn't even give a fuck about Jovan's man, and he was getting paid two hundred fifty for his services. Man, Jovan felt like killing Mark instead of Fat Mike.

"Look here, Mark, if the witness comes in, what kinda argument do we have?"

"We really don't have an argument. My job was to get Mr. Davis's charges dropped on the illegal search warrant, and I've done that—well, not officially, but at 2:45 p.m. today, my services are done. Now, if the government brings Mr. Davis up on new charges of conspiracy, then that's a whole new different case, and we'll have to talk figures with Mr. Davis about that," Mark said.

Damn, Mark's a cruddy mu'fucka, but this is the game lawyers play and this is how they get paid, Jovan thought. So Jovan had to respect Mark's position as a lawyer because, in all actuality, he was right.

"Hey, Jovan," Mark said. "I've got a hearing to go to this morning at eleven o'clock for this young kid in a carjacking case. I want you to come along with me and take some notes so you can see how I work my shit. Like I told you, Jovan, I'ma teach you everything you need to know about being a lawyer. Besides, you have on the perfect outfit. Who knows? You may meet one of those freaky-ass prosecutors who likes to fuck in the office."

"Naw, I'll leave that part up to you," Jovan said, but what he really wanted to say was that he'd rather fuck Cindy right there in Mark's office.

CHAPTER 15

"Perfect Timing"

Jovan went into the courtroom with Mark and watched him lie and manipulate the court into dropping the carjacking charge down to an unauthorized use of a vehicle charge. The youngster's family was happy. Although he would still have to do six months, it was a whole lot better than doing sixty years.

To Jovan, Mark was one of the best lawyers in D.C., although there were other lawyers who were just as good. For instance, his partner, who was a black woman by the name of Michelle Robinson, was real good. Her specialty was homicide cases. She could get a nigga off even if he was caught with the smokin' gun in his hand. There was also Kenny Roberts, whose specialty was conspiracy cases. He was known for getting major drug dealers outta fucked up situations, but he had started falling off after he lost a case and some niggas went to his office and shot his ass. To Jovan, Mark was the best, but maybe that was because he was his protégé.

After the hearing was over, Mark told Jovan to go back to the office because he was going to lunch with the prosecutor in the youngster's case.

"Hey, Mark, I see you made a deal with the devil." Jovan said, laughing.

"Yeah, now I gotta fuck this fat bitch in order to get the charges dropped," Mark said.

"Whatever happened to your sharp-ass lawyer skills?"

"This is one of 'em. You'll learn, Jovan. It's just gonna take some time," Mark said.

As Jovan was on his way out of the building, this was the moment he locked eyes on Sonya. Bilal's hearing wasn't for another couple of hours, and besides, he really didn't want to go back to the office. To buy himself some time, he figured he'd make contact with this lovely woman and hopefully be able to take her out to lunch. He carried himself like a true playa disguised in a gentleman's quality. His approach was so smooth that there was no way she could refuse his offer.

Sonya

When I held Jovan's hands and felt his palms, they were warm and smooth, just like his approach. I wanted to take his hands and kiss his fingers then gently rub them over my hard nipples, but it was way too early for that. Plus, Jovan would have to wait a minute before I would ever give myself up to him.

"Hey, Jovan, you don't have to talk about your family anymore. We can move on to another subject," I said.

"No, it's okay," Jovan said, looking at his watch again. I began to wonder if he had someplace else to be.

"Well, to answer your question—yes, I did have a big brother, and his name was Derrick. When I was eleven years old, he was killed.

"Derrick was a hustler who used to run Barry Farms back in the day. He had a lot of money, and whenever I wanted something, he'd get if for me. He bought me bicycles, go-carts, took me to the movie and King's Dominion Amusement Park. He did everything a big brother was supposed to do. I looked up to him and loved him very much. He used to always tell me he was gonna buy Momma a big house way out in Maryland in one of those nice neighborhoods and we'd have all kinds of toys and stuff. I looked forward to that day, until somebody stole that joy from me.

"One day my brother was found duct-taped in his Benz with one shot to the head. The police never found out who killed my brother, but they said the motive most likely was robbery," Jovan said, his voice filled with pain.

"Oh, Jovan, I'm sorry to hear that. I'm so sorry."

Damn, I really felt for Jovan. As he was talking, his eyes began to water. Although he didn't let a tear drop, I knew it was painful for him to talk about his brother.

Jovan looked at his watch again and said, "Sonya, I got a conference call to make to my boss, because he has a hearing in about an hour and I need to brief him on a few things. Can you excuse me for about ten minutes?"

"Sure. Take your time. I'll be right here."

I knew Jovan was hurting about his brother, and he probably wanted to go somewhere for a couple minutes to let it all out—or maybe he really did have to call his boss. Damn, it felt good to finally meet a smooth brotha with a job, and a good job at that.

Jovan

As I was telling Sonya about my brother, the pain grew deep. Thinking about him gave me that hate: the hate that I have for all cruddy niggas, the hate that I couldn't wait to express on a nigga who truly deserved it. I looked at my watch and saw that it was about 1:45 p.m., perfect timing.

As I got up and was on my way out the door, I saw the same white waitress looking at me, so what I did was fake like I was going to the bathroom. As I walked by her I said, "Excuse me, miss. My watch seems to have stopped. Do you have the exact time?"

"Yes, it's one forty-six p.m.," the white waitress said.

"Okay, thank you very much."

As she walked away to attend to other customers, I slipped past the bathroom and out the door. I jumped into my van and headed to Delaware Avenue, which wasn't even three minutes away from the restaurant. As I pulled up on the opposite side of the street, I could see that Fat Mike was just about to set up shop. I figured that he'd hurry up and make a quick ten thousand on the two o'clock rush, then head down to the courthouse and catch diarrhea of the mouth by crossing a nigga who had been good to him.

I drove my van around the corner and parked by the dumpster on the side of the building. I popped my hydraulic stash, got my 16-shot .45 automatic and the new blue zip-up jumper with the Pepco Gas Company logo on it, along with a blue hat with the same logo. I had bought them the day before at Sunny's Surplus. Then I grabbed my black notebook, which was stuffed with about 150 sheets of blank paper. I pulled the hat down tight, looked in the mirror on my sun visor, and checked out my disguise. I wasn't satisfied with what I saw, so I reached in the back seat of the van and grabbed a pillow that I had left in there the day before when I was scoping the scene. I undid my belt and tied the pillow around my stomach then zipped up my jumper and looked in the mirror again. I was now satisfied with my disguise. I looked like a little chubby Pepco gas meter inspector.

As I got out of the van, I looked around to make sure no one saw me then I proceeded around the corner to where Fat Mike was telling everybody what positions to play. There were three fiends and two other younger dudes with him. Damn, the day before there were only three fiends and one youngin'. Shit, I couldn't turn back now, because Bilal's hearing was in less than an hour, so I walked up to the first meter with my notebook and began to fake like I was jotting down some notes.

One of Fat Mike's youngin's came over and said, "Slim, what'cha doing around here?"

"Oh, excuse me, young man. I work for the gas company." I said with an experienced look, as if this had been my job for years.

Fat Mike came over and said, "Who that, Lump?"

"It ain't nobody but the Pepco man fucking with the meters."

"Hey, Pepco man, I sure hope you can fix that shit, 'cause my people's gas is fucked up. One day it's working, and the next day it's not," Fat Mike said.

"Yeah, I know what you're saying. It's a little messed up, but it ain't nothin' I can't fix. Hey, there's usually another meter around here, and from looking at this one, I can tell this isn't the main meter. If I can find the other one and fix that first, then it won't be a problem getting this old raggedy thing back to normal. Do you know where it's at?"

Fat Mike fell right into my trap. "Yeah, it's right around the corner. C'mon, I'll show you. Lump, watch that shit. I'll be right back—and tell everybody to get ready because it's almost two o'clock."

"Okay, Mike."

"C'mon, Pepco man. Hurry up so I can show you this shit. I've got something to do within the next hour."

"Okay, thanks, my man."

As Fat Mike led me around the corner, I looked around and peeped the surroundings to see if anyone was in sight. I saw no one. So far, my plan was working perfectly. I wasn't anxious, nervous, or scared; just calm, cool, and collected. Just like with my last two victims, I felt like what I was doing was justified. I was about to give it to a nigga who truly deserved it.

As Fat Mike walked closer to the meter, I pulled out my .45 automatic, and when he turned around, my .45 was stuck right between his eyes. Before he could say anything, let alone blink, I pulled the trigger two times— *boom, boom!*—and Fat Mike's body hit the ground with force. I then took out my handkerchief, wiped the gun, and threw it down next to his body.

As I was walking away, I looked around to make sure no one saw me. My van was parked alongside the trash dumpster. I took off my disguise and threw it in the trash, got in my van, put the pillow in the back seat, and fixed my clothes. I didn't stay to see if Fat Mike was dead, because I already knew he was.

As I drove back to the restaurant, all I was thinking about was my man Bilal because his hearing was at 2:45, and if everything went well, he should be a free man today. From that point on, nobody was gonna be able to stop us.

When I got back to the restaurant, I didn't go straight in, I peeked through the window to make sure Sonya was still there. Yeah, she was still there, looking lovely as ever. Hopefully she wasn't mad because I had taken so long, but I was only gone for fifteen minutes.

When I walked back into the restaurant, I saw the same white waitress, and again she was smiling at me. She came over to me and said, "My God, you've been in the bathroom all that time. Are you okay? Was there something wrong with the food?"

"Something got caught down my throat. I'll be fine, thank you. Oh, by the way, what's your name?" I said.

"Kathy, and yours?"

"Jovan."

"All right then, Jovan. I hope the next time I see you you're by yourself and not with a nice-looking lady friend."

"Who knows? I may come back tomorrow all by myself." Then I gave her a wink and left.

As I was walking up to Sonya on the patio, I pulled out my cellular phone and acted like I was talking to somebody. I said, "Okay then, Mark. I pray everything goes well. You're the best lawyer I know." I then pretended to end my conversation and hang up my phone.

I turned to Sonya and said, "Sorry, sweetie, that I took so long."

"It's okay. You've only been gone fourteen minutes," Sonya said, smiling.

"Damn, sweetheart, were you timing me?"

"No, baby. While you were gone I was sitting here thinking about how wonderful a person you are and that I have never met a man like yourself."

"Is there something wrong with me?"

"Oh no, Jovan, not at all. you're just different from any other man I've met."

I started laughing, but inside I was shaking my head, saying to myself, *Baby, you just don't know that I just finished blowing a nigga's brains out ten minutes ago.*

Sonya

Finally Jovan came back, and as he was walking toward the table, I could see he was on his cellular phone, still in conference with his boss. Jovan was one cool-ass nigga, and the whole time he was gone, I was thinking about him. A sista like me could get used to having a brotha like Jovan in her life. For one, he wasn't thugged out, but he was aggressive. Two, he was handsome as hell, and three, from the way he walked, it looked like he was packing, and boy did a sista need that. He also had a good, legitimate job, and he was trying to go back to school to further his education. What more could a woman ask for? I hoped he didn't have anybody else, because I'd be one mad bitch if he told me he had a girlfriend.

"Well, Jovan the attorney . . ."

"C'mon, Sonya, I told you I'm not an attorney yet," Jovan said, cutting me off.

"But you will be soon," I said.

"How you know that?"

"'Cause I can the see ambition in you, Jovan."

"So you're saying you can tell the future?"

"Maybe," I said, smiling, and Jovan smiled also.

"So tell me this, Ms. Psychic."

"Tell you what?"

"Where is this little lunch date gonna take us?"

I gave him a smile and a sneaky grin and said, "That's for me to know and you to find out."

"How am I supposed to find out?"

I took out a piece of paper and scribbled my home and work numbers on it and passed it to Jovan.

"Here's my numbers. It's up to you to use them, because that's the only way you'll find out," I said, handing him the piece of paper.

"Don't be so mean, sweetheart," Jovan said jokingly.

"I'm not being mean. I'm just being a strong black woman. By the way, I hope you don't have a girlfriend or anything else that may get in the way of us getting to know each other better," I said seriously.

Jovan laughed and said, "If that's your way of asking if I've got a girlfriend or any kinda baby momma drama, then my answer is no, sweetheart, but it would be nice to have someone compatible to my wants and needs."

I liked the way Jovan put that. He had a smooth way of getting his point across.

"So, Jovan, it's almost two forty-five and we've been here all day talking."

"You're just gonna leave me here?" he asked with a devilish grin.

"No, not at all, baby," I said.

"I was just playing. I know you probably have something to do, and I have to be at the courthouse by three o'clock to meet my boss. So what time should I call you?"

"Call me whenever you think about me."

"Okay, then by the time you get home, you should have about fifty messages from me." We both laughed.

"Jovan, you have such a good sense of humor. It was so nice meeting you," I said sincerely.

"It was nice meeting you too, Sonya. You just don't know how much you made my day," Jovan said, meaning every word of it. "C'mon, let me walk you to your car."

CHAPTER 16

"Untouchable"

When Jovan got to the courthouse, it was three o'clock on the dot. He rushed into the building, got on the elevator, and headed to the second floor where Bilal's hearing was being held. As he was getting off the elevator, he assumed that the hearing was already over and that his plan must have worked because Mark, Bilal, and a female that looked like she came straight out of a magazine were walking out of the courtroom headed his way. They all had big-ass smiles on their faces. The female looked like a Hawaiian or something, and she and Bilal were hugging so hard that it was obvious that this was his girlfriend. Damn, Bilal had a nice bankroll and a fine-ass bitch to go along with it.

"Hey, there's my assistant. Bilal, you remember Mr. Price, don't you?" Mark asked once they reached me.

"Yeah, I remember him. He's the one who worked so hard on this case. How you doing, Mr. Price?" Bilal asked, pretending like he didn't know me.

"Fine, Mr. Davis. Glad to see that everything worked out for you," Jovan said.

"Yeah, the government was trying to put shit in the game, but Mark batted that shit down."

"So, Mark, what did you do this time?" Jovan said, acting as if he didn't know what was goin' on.

"Well, I just went in there and showed my ass. I think the judge is pissed at me."

"Why's that?"

"'Cause the government kept talking about they had a witness, but he never showed up, so I got up and asked, 'Where's the ghost?'"

"He got mad at that?"

"No, I think he got pissed because the whole courtroom was laughing," Mark said, laughing himself.

Bilal said, "Yeah, Mark, you did your thing like a real pro." Little did Bilal know that Mark didn't do a fucking thing. The reason why he was standing there was because of Jovan's work, and Jovan planned to tell him that later on.

"Mr. Price, let me introduce you to my fiancée, Meeka."

"Hello, Meeka, nice to meet you." Damn, she was a pretty-ass bitch Jovan said to himself.

"You too, Mr. Price," Meeka said with a slight grin.

Meeka looked at Jovan as if she already knew him or had heard about him from Bilal. Jovan hoped Bilal wasn't putting this broad down about him, 'cause he didn't want nobody to know his business but Bilal and him.

As they continued to walk down the hallway, a little white man with some tight jeans and a Penn State sweatshirt came over to them.

"Bilal Davis, you think you got away, but let me tell you something, man. I'ma be on your ass day in and day out, and the next time I get your ass, I'ma make sure I catch you good," the man said.

"Yeah, well, thank you, detective, but let me inform you about something. Investigating me won't do nothin' but waste your time."

"We'll see," the detective said, walking away. Damn, he sounded pissed.

"Who was that, Mark?" Jovan said with an inquisitive look.

"Oh, he was the detective who wrote up the bogus warrant to go into Mr. Davis's house," Mark said.

"Well, Mr. Davis, it looks like you gotta keep your nose clean," Jovan said.

"Huh? My nose is clean, Mr. Price. Always was and always will be," Bilal said.

"Jovan, you coming by the office or what?" Mark asked.

"No, I think I'ma head on home and get me some sleep."

"Okay, see you later."

"A'ight, Mark. You too, Mr. Davis, and congratulations on your freedom."

"Thank you, Mark. Thanks for everything. I'll have somebody drop the rest of that off to you tomorrow," Bilal said as he eagerly wanted Mark to hurry up and leave.

"Sounds good to me, Mr. Davis."

With that, they all got on the elevator and headed out of the courthouse to where their cars were parked.

"Bye, see y'all later," Mark said as he headed off to his car first.

As soon as Mark got in his car and left, Bilal jumped out of nowhere and said, "What's up, my nigga!" He then gave Jovan such a tight bear hug that he almost lost his breath. "Meeka, this here is my best friend Jovan I've been telling you about."

"I kinda figured that, boo. So, Jovan, I heard a lot about you. You know Bilal loves you like a brother. I can never get him to stop talking about you," said Meeka while she looked at Jovan as if she knew things about him that she shouldn't.

"Yeah, well, I hope it was all good stuff."

"Believe me, Jovan, it was."

Jovan wondered if Bilal had told this broad everything. *Naw*, he thought, *Bilal's too sharp for that. He's a real nigga.* Jovan knew that he kept his females out of his business. He probably just talked about some childhood shit to her; that's about it.

"Look, come on with me. We got a lot to talk about," Bilal said.

"Bilal, I thought you and me were gonna be alone tonight," Meeka said, whining.

"Meeka, this is my family, my only family, and he's coming with me whether you like it or not."

Meeka was so mad that Jovan could sense the jealousy as she stormed off to get into Bilal's silver 850 BMW.

"Look, Lal, go 'head home with your woman. We can talk tomorrow. Go get some pussy, nigga," Jovan told Bilal.

"Man, fuck that. I got all year to fuck. Plus, I'm getting tired of her ass anyway."

"Bilal, that's a bad piece you got. You'd be a fool to let her go."

"She's a'ight, but I've had bitches who looked way better than her. The only thing about it is she's real, and she's the only one who pulled through and stayed down with the ole boy when I got that thirty years, so I owe her."

"I can respect that. A nigga always need a soldier in his corner."

"What you driving, Jovan?"

"I still got the MPV I had back in Ninety-one."

"Damn, you still pushing that bullshit?" Bilal asked, amazed.

"Yeah, but the real reason I've still got it is because it has a hydraulic stash that can hold eight bricks," Jovan told Bilal.

"Yeah, you better keep that joint. It might come in handy. Look, go get your van and follow me out to my house so we can talk," Bilal said then asekd, "Oh, Jovan, how's my baby Grandma Price doing?"

"She's a'ight, but her legs fucking with her though. You know she got arthritis," Jovan said sadly.

"We're gonna have to get her to one of those expensive hospitals so she can get rid of that," Bilal said, as if it would make me feel better.

"Yeah, Lal, I feel you."

Jovan followed Bilal and Meeka to their house, which was about a 45-minute drive out to Potomac, Maryland. This spot didn't have nothin' for under $600,000. All types of celebrities lived out there: Sugar Ray Leonard, Chris Webber, Juwan Howard, Peabo Bryson, Johnny Gill, and a few other no-names with a rack of bread.

As Bilal and Meeka pulled up into their driveway, Jovan couldn't believe that this was their house. The last time Jovan saw a house this big was when they interviewed Puffy, the owner of Bad Boy Records, in his home on MTV. Now he was witnessing the truth behind all the lavish jailhouse stories he had heard about his best friend while in Lewisburg.

In the front driveway, there was a black Range Rover, a green Lexus coupe, a white 600SL, and in his garage there was a blue Mercedes V12 600S coupe, the new joint, plus the silver 850 BMW they were in. Here Jovan was stuck with this old fucking van, but for what he did earlier, this van had come in handy.

When Bilal and Meeka got out of the 850, he told her to go in the house.

The first thing Jovan said was, "Nigga, I see why you got locked up. What the fuck you doing with all this shit layin' on your lawn?"

"Oh, Jay, this ain't nothin'. The Lex and SL is Meeka's. The rest of that shit is my toys."

"Your toys?" Jovan said.

"Yeah, nigga, my toys. In case you haven't heard, Jay, I got the city locked. Ninety-four is my year. Better yet, our year, 'cause whatever I got, you got," Bilal said as he looked at Jovan with all sincerity. This was the same look he had given him nine years earlier when he first talked about makin' this dream come true.

"Damn, it feels good to be a part of some real cash, but for real, whatever position I play, it's got to be low key, 'cause I ain't going back to jail," Jovan said as he admired his best friend's lavish lifestyle.

Bilal showed Jovan around the house. He started with the living room; then he took him see to all seven bedrooms, the kitchen, and then downstairs, where he had a miniature movie theater, pool tables and all. This nigga had Versace curtains, bedspreads, and paintings. He even had Versace dishes lying in the china closet.

"Damn, Lal, I see you went Versace crazy. I thought I loved the shit, but after seeing all this, you must own the store," Jovan said, laughing.

"Naw, Jay, Meeka did all this crazy-ass shit. When we moved in, I gave her a mil to play with and the bitch went crazy," Bilal said, laughing also.

"How long you've been fucking with her, Lal?"

"Shit, ever since I came home off the juvenile life bit."

When Bilal mentioned the juvenile life, Jovan felt a little fucked up. He had never thanked Bilal personally, but he knew where his heart was at, and Lal must have sensed it also.

"Hey, Jovan, c'mon out back on the court. We need to sit down and talk. Meeka," Bilal called.

"Yes, sir master?" Meeka said sarcastically.

"Cut that shit out, girl."

"Okay, what's up, baby?"

"Get us a bottle of Cristal, will you, baby?"

"Like I said at first, yes, sir master," she said as she stomped off.

"Damn, Bilal, why she acting like that?" Jovan asked him.

"You know how they get. Shit, Jay, the bitch ain't had no dick in almost eight months."

"Well, from the way she's acting, I think you need to hurry up and give her some."

"I'll deal with her later, slim. Right now I'm wit' my man."

When Bilal and Jovan went outside to talk, Jovan saw that he had a full court basketball out back, weights, and a pool with a Jacuzzi. "Hey, Lal, how much you pay for this house?" Jovan asked him.

"With all the accessories, about a cool four mil."

At that, Jovan started counting Bilal's bank in his head. He had lost 3.5 mil in the raid, and he told him he still had 3.5 mil plus four mil for the house, and at least one mil for the cars. Jovan hadn't seen his jewelry, but he guessed that may be worth about a mil or half at least. Bilal had to have had at least thirteen million at one time. Damn, this nigga really was the king of D.C.

"Damn, Bilal, I see you spend a lot of money."

"What's the use of having it if you can't spend it?"

"You got that right, slim, but you know you gotta find a way to wash that shit."

"We'll worry 'bout that when we get there. Right now I'm broke."

"Broke! How the fuck you broke and you still got three point five mil?"

"Jay, half that shit isn't mine. Half of it belongs to Carlos."

"Yeah, I heard about Carlos. Give me the reading on him," Jovan said, wondering what Carlos was really like and how Bilal got hooked up with him.

"Well, Carlos and me were down Oak Hill Youth Center together. Carlos ain't no sucker, but you know he's

Spanish and niggas used to try him all the time. I taught Carlos how to box, and after that we became cool."

"Yeah, I heard you were down there on the boxing team knocking niggas out."

"Yeah, I was like that at one time. A nigga a li'l rusty right now, but believe me, I still know where my ass at."

"Finish telling me 'bout Carlos."

"Well, Los and me became real close."

"Like you and me?" Jovan said, knowing deep down inside that no one could ever take his place. He just wanted to hear it come outta Bilal's mouth.

"Naw, Jay, there will never be another you. Anyway, some uptown niggas put a vicious press game on Los 'cause they knew he was getting some money. Los wasn't going for it, but he was outnumbered. One day they came in his room, about six of 'em, pulled knives on him, and they had him, too. They were 'bout to burn his ass up. I peeped the move and busted in the room before they could do anything and knocked three of 'em the fuck out. When I did that, the other three flunky-ass niggas ran. I hear these same niggas down Lorton right now getting fucked."

"For real, Lal?" Jovan asked him.

"Well, not all of 'em; just two of 'em. Two are behind the wall going hard, and the other two got killed when they came home."

"Damn," Jovan said as he thought about Bilal and how hard it was for him growing up in the system.

"Well, ever since that day, Carlos vowed to me that he'd never forget that, and that whenever I came home, he had a spot for me on his team. So when I came home, he gave me two bricks for twenty-five thousand, and I have never looked back. Jay, Carlos is a good dude, I want you to meet him," Bilal said as he looked Jovan in the eyes.

"Naw, that's a'ight, Lal. I ain't really trying to meet too many new niggas," Jovan said.

"He ain't just no new nigga, Jay. He's my partner—our partner," Bilal said.

Jovan could tell from the way Bilal was looking that he was beyond serious.

"In that case, I guess I do have to meet him. Look, Bilal, I gotta tell you something. I never could find the dude Li'l G. I searched everywhere for him, but come to find out he got locked up out in Maryland for three bodies," Jovan told Bilal.

"Yeah, so who you get to lay the demonstration down?" Bilal said, curious as to why Fat Mike never made it to court.

At that moment, Jovan looked Bilal straight in the eyes and said, "I did it."

Bilal laughed and said, "Get the fuck outta here!"

"Yeah, slim, I gave it to him good like the bitch-nigga he is, or better yet, was."

"How you do it, Jay?"

"Man, I had the perfect plan. I laid on this nigga, peeped his every move, then went to Sunny's Surplus and bought a gas uniform."

"What!" Bilal said, looking surprised.

"Yeah, nigga, I was disguised as a gas meter inspector," Jovan said, smiling.

"Get the fuck outta here!"

"Man, listen, I laid this shit out so tight, covered all my tracks, and then went about my daily routine."

Bilal was shocked by how Jovan put his murder game down. "How the fuck you think about being a gas meter inspector?"

"Lal, I'm a paralegal, and if I'ma commit a crime, I've got to know how to get away with it. And guess what? You ain't gonna believe this shit."

"What?" Bilal said, looking at Jovan as if he wasn't telling the truth.

"It's hard for me to believe this, but I did all this while taking a broad to lunch at Phillips Seafood restaurant," Jovan said, smiling as he thought back to his lunch date with Sonya.

"Hell, nigga, you ain't that tight. You've been in jail reading too many Donald Goines books!" Bilal said, laughing.

"C'mon, Bilal, how the fuck a Donald Goines book gonna teach a nigga how to contemplate a murder like that?" Jovan asked.

"Yeah, you right, but damn, Jay, this shit is unbelievable. What broad did you take down to Phillips today?" Bilal asked, amazed.

"I met this bad-ass broad in the courthouse this morning. We went to lunch and I kicked it with her for a while. She's got a good head on her shoulders. She's an assistant producer at BET and bad as fuck, slim. Man, this the baddest broad I've seen in years."

"How you get away from her to go lay your demonstration down?" Bilal asked, still finding Jovan's story hard to believe.

"I faked like I had a conference call from Mark."

"Damn, nigga, I ain't never heard no story like that. You tight as shit, Jay. Outta all the killers I know in the city, I ain't never heard a nigga put it down like that. That's some professional Mafia-type shit. Damn, now you've got two bodies under your belt."

"Naw, Lal, now it's three bodies," Jovan said.

"What!" Lal yelled as his eyes opened wider.

"Yeah, I had to punish a New York nigga while I was up in Lewisburg," Jovan said.

"You killed a nigga in jail and got away with it?" Bilal asked, totally shocked by this new admission.

"Yeah, Lal, I had to."

"Okay, let me hear it. I'm dying for this one," Bilal said with a smirk on his face.

Jovan told Bilal every detail of how he killed Shorty, and Bilal was in such a state of shock that he didn't believe Jovan.

"So you on some old James Bond shit, huh?"

"Naw, slim, I just learned my lesson nine years ago. If you gonna kill a nigga, make sure you do it right so no one but the nigga you kill suffers."

Bilal put his head down and said, "Jay, what you did nine years ago was outta love, nigga."

"What I did a couple of hours ago was still outta love, and there's one thing I wanna say to you that I wasn't able to say in nine years," Jovan said as he held his head down, not wanting Bilal to see his eyes water.

"What's that?" Bilal asked.

"I'm sorry for not telling you I was strapped, and I thank you from the bottom of my heart for taking the beef."

"Jay, you ain't gotta thank me for that shit. Back then was outta love, and until the day my casket drops, everything I do for you is outta love."

Bilal and Jovan gave each other a strong hug, just like they had nine years ago.

"Look, Jay, what'cha gonna do? You gonna get this money with me or what?"

"Man, for real, you know I ain't too good at hustling. Every time I hustle and get a few dollars, something always go wrong," Jovan said, thinking back.

Jovan told Bilal about his fifty thousand getting stolen back in '88, and he told him about his New York connect and how shit went wrong.

"Face it, Jay, the hustling thing ain't me. Plus, I'm tryin' to go to law school and get my license so I can represent niggas like you and get a free two hundred fifty thousand for doing nothin'," Jovan said, laughing.

"Yeah, right. I forgot you're supposed to be some lawyer. Damn, picture that: a lawyer/killer. Jay, you a mu'fucka. You're the tightest nigga I know."

"Go 'head with that shit."

"Naw, Jay, I'm serious. This is the move, and you've got to be a part of this team. I do all the hustling and you do the killing; the same position we played nine years ago. You can still do the lawyer thing. I like that shit, but when it's time to lay a demonstration down, I'ma need you," Bilal said seriously. "Jay, you know I ain't never killed nobody. I ain't saying I won't, but from hearing your stories, I don't think I'm that smart to be pulling moves like that. Plus, Li'l G is locked up, and even if he was still home, I wouldn't fuck with him on that tip no more 'cause he ain't shit compared to you."

"Yeah, Lal, I'm flattered," he said, laughing. "But for real, I ain't trying to be no killer for hire. You ain't gotta pay me to put in no work. If a nigga fuckin' with you and I see that I can help, then I'm there, slim. I owe you. You're my best friend. But one thing, Lal."

"What's that?"

"Man, you know we can't be hangin' together in the streets. The feds is gonna be watching you now; especially the one that was in the courthouse today."

"Yeah, he's a piece of shit, Detective Tony Bridges. That white mu'fucka wants me bad."

"You've got to do your thing on the low, Lal."

"Yeah, I understand. Hey, c'mon in the house. I've got something for you."

Bilal went downstairs for a minute and came back with a gym bag.

"Here, nigga," he said as he threw the bag at Jovan.

"What's this?" Jovan asked.

"Open it."

When Jovan opened the bag, all he saw was stacks of money.

"How much money is this, Lal?" Jovan's eyes damn near popped outta his head at the sight of all this money.

"That's only two hundred and fifty thousand. I really can't hit you off like I want to yet. You know Los and me only got three point five mil and our connect won't sell us nothing under two hundred bricks."

"Damn, slim, what the fuck was Los doing while you were in?"

"He held shit down, got rid of the remaining shit, and laid low for a minute. The fact that I was locked up had niggas trying him, and we got one nigga now I'ma have to go see tomorrow. I gave this nigga thirty bricks before I got locked up, and when Carlos went to holla at him about the money, he started acting shady, talking 'bout he only dealt with me."

"Yeah, you've got to get that up off him. Thirty bricks is a lot of money," Jovan said, instantly calculating the price in his head.

"Yeah, I'ma see slim first thing in the morning. Jay, where you staying at?" Bilal asked.

"I'm chilling with Grandma for a minute."

"Man, I wanted to get Grandma Price a house so bad, but I didn't know how to ask."

"I'm glad you didn't ask, because she probably woulda cursed you out. You know she's been living there ever since my pops was born, and she ain't going nowhere," Jovan said, laughing.

"Yeah, Jay, what's up with your pops anyway?" Bilal asked.

"I dunno. I ain't seen him, and I'm not trying to, either."

CHAPTER 17

"Sky's The Limit"

Jovan went back home to his grandma's house and kicked it with her for a while. He wondered what Grandma would say if he asked her if she wanted a new house. Since she was in a good mood, he figured now would be the proper time.

"Hey, Grandma," Jovan said.

"Yes, baby?"

"What would you say if I told you I wanted to buy you a new house?"

"Well, baby, first thing I'd tell you is that you must be crazy and that I've been living in this house for almost forty-five years. This house is sentimental, and it is the landmark for our family. This is home, Jovan; always was and always will be. Second, I'd tell you to keep your money and put it to good use to buy some business or something, and after that, if you have some money left over, then you could give me some so I can fix up this raggedy-ass house that we call home," Grandma said.

At that, Grandma and Jovan both laughed so hard. It was cool chilling with her because after all the shit he'd been through today, she sure knew how to make a nigga feel good.

"Hey, Grandma, it's getting late and I'm a little tired, plus I gotta go to work tomorrow. I'm going up to bed now."

"Okay, baby. You want me to wake you up in the morning?"

"Naw, Grandma, my alarm is already set."

"Okay. Oh, Jovan, your daddy called today. He asked about you and told me to tell you he loves you."

"Okay, Grandma, next time he calls, tell him I said what's up."

"Okay, baby."

"Oh, Grandma," Jovan said before going upstairs to bed.

"Yes, baby."

"I love you, baby girl. You know you my world!" Jovan said, kissing her on the cheek.

"Boy, take your silly butt upstairs and go to bed," Grandma said, hugging Jovan.

Grandma loved whenever Jovan expressed his love for her, because it always made her day. He went upstairs to his bedroom, then sat and thought for a moment about his life and what he just committed himself to do. Bilal had pulled him right back into the streets, right back into the game. Well, not really Bilal, but standing on his principles of his loyalty to Bilal had pulled him back. Plus, he still felt responsible for Mal-Mal's death, which in turn made him feel obligated to his best friend, and besides, there was a whole lotta bank involved.

Jovan opened up the gym bag full of the money Bilal had given him. This was the most money he'd ever had at one time: two hundred fifty thousand. The sight of it made his dick hard, but this wasn't shit compared to what Bilal had. Even in his broke stage this nigga was still rich.

Before Jovan went to bed, he checked all his pants pockets to make sure he didn't have anything in them before he sent them to the cleaners the next day. He reached in his right pocket and pulled out a piece of paper with Sonya's work and home numbers on it, placed it on his dresser, then lay back on his bed and began to think about her. Damn, she was pretty. He wondered if their friendship would blossom into something special. He wondered if she liked him or not. He looked good and dressed well; he had a job, and now he was two hundred and fifty thousand dollars richer. What the fuck did he have to do to get this broad? He fell asleep thinking about Sonya.

Sonya

Damn, it was 10:00 p.m. and I still hadn't gotten a call from Jovan. I wondered if he liked me, because most niggas I met and gave my number to called me at most an hour later. I hoped I wasn't too much for him that day at lunch. I had told him about my past—well, not everything—but I was sure our conversation went well. I wondered if I had said anything wrong, or maybe he didn't like the way I looked. Why hadn't this man called me yet? I wondered as I lay back on my bed, thinking about Jovan. How was I going to get to this man? I decided he must not have wanted me because if he did, he would have given me his number.

Ring, Ring, Ring.

"Hello!" I said into the phone, praying it was Jovan.

"Damn, girl, you answered the phone like you just won the lottery."

"Oh, hi, Germain. I thought you was somebody else," I said, disappointed that it wasn't him.

"Somebody else? Girl, who's gonna be calling you at ten o'clock at night? Ain't like you got a man or nothing," Germain said, laughing.

"Fuck you, Germain. And why are you calling me this time of night anyway? You couldn't wait to see me at work tomorrow?" I asked her.

"Girl, my husband and I had an argument tonight, and his stupid ass stormed outta the house like a fucking kid."

"So what am I supposed to be, some marriage counselor or something?" I asked Germain.

"Shut up, silly. Just talk to me until he gets back."

"Look, Germain, I'm not gonna be on this phone all night long, but I'll talk to you for a while. You know you my girl."

"Good. So what's up, and why weren't you at work today?" Germain said, prying.

"Now you wanna be my mama. Well, if you must know, I had an appointment at the courthouse today."

"What did you have an appointment at the courthouse for?"

"None of your business, nosey."

"Okay, go ahead with you li'l secretive self."

"Anyway, while I was at the courthouse, I met this fine-ass brotha."

"What, you finally gave somebody the time of the day?"

"Yeah, girl, and we went to lunch together and had a nice time," I said, smiling, remembering our lunch date.

"What's his name? Who the hell is this mystery man?"

"His name is Jovan."

"Jovan?"

"Yeah, girl, he's tall, light brown, with dark wavy hair, physically fit, he dresses nice, and guess what, girl?"

"What?"

"He's got a job."

"Stop lying!" Germain yelled.

"Yeah, and he's got a good job too."

"What does he do?"

"He's a paralegal, and he works at this big law firm. He's gonna go back to law school and finish up so he can become a lawyer and get his own office," I said proudly.

"Damn, girl, how old is he?"

"He's twenty-four."

"So you got yourself a youngin'?" Germain said, laughing.

"No, girl, I only got him by less than two years."

"Damn, Sonya, twenty-four with a job like that. That's wonderful. So did he call you yet?" Germain asked.

"No, actually when you called, I thought it was him."

"Hold on, Sonya. My stupid-ass husband just walked in the door. Where the hell you been?" Germain asked her husband.

"None of your fuckin' business!" Kevin, Germain's husband, said.

"What? Sonya, let me get off this phone before we get to fighting up in here. I'll see you tomorrow at work."

"Germain, you need to stop acting like you a nun and give that man some pussy," I said, laughing.

"Mind your business. This is married life, and when you get married, then you can say something. Until then, keep your damn mouth shut," Germain said.

"Girl, you so silly. I'll see you at work tomorrow."

"Okay. Bye-bye, Sonya."

"Bye, Germain."

Jovan

When I woke up, Grandma was already downstairs cooking breakfast. She had made egg and cheese omelets, toast, grits, and hash browns.

"Jovan," Grandma called from downstairs.

"Yeah, Grandma," I answered, sitting on the side of my bed.

"You up, boy?"

"Yeah, Grandma, I'm up."

"Come on down here and get this breakfast."

I went in the bathroom, got myself together, and went downstairs.

"Good morning, baby girl. What'cha cook for the ole boy?" I said, giving Grandma a kiss on the cheek.

"Sit down and eat your food with your silly self. You act just like your damn daddy."

Grandma loved it when I joked with her. I just wished she would stop throwing my pops all up in my face, but I knew why she did it. Grandma missed him, and the fact that I resembled him so much made her happy and sad at the same time.

"Grandma," I said.

"Yeah, baby."

"Remember last night when we talked about a new house?"

"Yeah, and I told you no."

"Well, look, I've got a few dollars tucked away so you can go ahead and fix up the house," I told her.

"Oh, no, baby. Keep your money. You need it for law school."

"Grandma, believe me. I've got enough money for school."

"Well, then, why aren't you in school yet?" Grandma asked me.

"'Cause."

"'Cause what?"

"'Cause right now I like my job, and I'm learning more working with Mark than I would if I was in school. When I get it all down pat I'ma go to school and come out two steps ahead of everybody in my class."

"Well, it sounds good, but keep your money, baby."

"Grandma, you must not have heard me. I've already got enough money for both of us."

"Okay, baby, but it may cost a lot to get the basement redone and my ceiling fixed," Grandma said, still not sure

I would be able to afford to pay for school and get her house fixed.

"Whatever it cost, you got it. Just call the people today and get an estimate and let me know." It felt good to be able to give Grandma some money.

"Okay, baby."

I went back upstairs to get myself ready for work. Today was nice, not too hot or too breezy. It felt good. I went into the closet, pulled out some cream-colored Armani slacks I had never worn. I then grabbed a cream-colored Armani mock neck T-shirt. I had bought it one size bigger so it wouldn't be fitting all tight like them gay mu'fuckas be wearing their shit. I also grabbed a pair of light tan soft-bottom Caesar Picotti slip-ons with a matching belt.

I took myself a good long shower, brushed my hair to let the waves pop out, put on some Giorgio Armani cologne, and got dressed. I reached on my dresser to put on one of my watches. I had three: a Movado, an 18k white gold Cartier, and a Rolex. I chose the Cartier, and I also put on my 18k white gold bracelet.

As I was reaching for the bracelet, I saw Sonya's number. I put it in my pocket, went downstairs and kissed Grandma, then headed for the office.

I got to the office at least ten minutes early. As soon as I came through the door, I saw Cindy in a tight-ass plaid skirt looking phat as hell.

"Hey, Cindy," I said.

"Morning, Jovan. You look nice today."

"Thank you, Cindy. You look nice yourself."

Lately Cindy had been complimenting me on my style. I think she wanted a nigga to put some dick in her. I didn't fuck with white girls, but if she offered me the pussy, I wouldn't turn it down.

"Hey, Cindy, is Mark here yet?"

"No, he hasn't gotten here yet. You know he might be late being as though he doesn't have to go to court today," Cindy said. Then mark came through the door. "Hold on, Jovan. Speak of the devil; here he comes now."

"Morning, Mark," she said to him.

"Morning, Cindy. Look, Jovan, we don't have much to do today but knock off a few briefs. Most likely we'll be done around noon. After that you can take the day off," Mark told me.

Yes, I loved my job. Work for half a day and still get paid for a full day.

"Cool. Just tell me what you need," I said.

"Well, I need two motions drawn up, one for faulty and deficient indictment. This kid got convicted for a gun that wasn't even in his indictment."

"Okay, that should be easy."

"The other is for a Brady material violation. The government didn't give the defense the fingerprint lab's report on the gun before trial started."

"All this is on the same case?" I asked Mark.

"Yeah."

"Oh, that's light. I should be finished in about an hour or so."

"I already know that. That's why I told you you could take a half a day," Mark said sarcastically.

"So you're telling me you know my work like that?"

"Don't flatter yourself, Jovan. You're good, but you're not a lawyer yet."

Mark was always letting me know when I was advancing, and I could tell he was proud of me. Almost every motion that was filed and came out of that office had my name on it right under Mark's. It read: On the brief for Appellate, Attorney Mark Rohon and Paralegal Specialist Jovan Price of Rohon and Robinson law firm. Mark's partner, Michelle, already told me how Mark would be down at the courthouse braggin' on me, telling other lawyers that I'd be taking their business soon.

After I finished the briefs, which took me way more than an hour, more like two and a half hours, I took them straight to Mark for him to go over them.

"Here you go, Mark," I said, handing him the motions.

"So you finally finished, huh?"

"Yeah, it took me a minute to put up a good argument for the Brady violation."

"Sit down, Jovan. Let's go over them right now."

Mark read my motions then placed them on the desk, leaned back in his chair, and crossed his legs. He was silent for a moment.

"What's wrong? You don't like the briefs?"

Mark pulled his chair to his desk and looked me straight in the eyes and said, "No, I don't like the briefs, Jovan; I love 'em. Look, I'ma give it to you raw. Most of the work you do for me is better than some lawyers who've been practicing twenty years. Jovan, you gotta get into law school and finish up so you can take your bar exam. There's a lot of money out here waitin' for you. You'll be the perfect lawyer; you're young, smooth, and plus you know some of these fools who keep going to jail. Face it—you'd be the perfect attorney. Shit, if I got into some trouble, I'd hire you."

"Why, thank you, Mark. So if I pass the bar exam, does that mean I can get a partnership in the firm?"

"Don't flatter yourself, buddy. A partnership is out of the question, but you better bet there will be an office here waiting for you."

Damn, Mark sure knew how to make a nigga feel good.

I wondered what Bilal was doing. I went into Michelle's office to use her phone to call him while she was in court.

Ring, Ring, Ring.

"Hello," Bilal said as he picked up the phone like he was anxiously waiting for a call.

"Damn, nigga, you answering the phone on the first ring like you were waiting for my call," I said.

"What's up, Jay? I thought you was this nigga that owes me that bank. I've been paging his ass all fucking morning," Bilal said.

"He ain't called back yet?"

"Fuck no. I hope this nigga ain't playin no games. Where you at anyway, Jay?"

"I'm at work."

Bilal instantly burst into laughter at the thought of his best friend really taking this lawyer shit seriously.

"What you laughing for, Lal?" I asked, knowing he was indirectly teasing me.

"'Cause, man, I can't believe this shit," Bilal said, still laughing.

"Believe what shit?"

"You being a lawyer, man. For real, Jay, I'm just fuckin' with you. Look, I gotta go meet Carlos up on Kennedy Street. Call me back later on so we can go out or something."

"Look, Lal, I told you we can't be doin' it like that."

"I know, Jay, but I'ma bring Carlos so you can meet him."

"Okay then, Lal."

I hung up the phone, sat back, and imagined what this nigga Los was like. I wondered if Bilal would tell him about all the work I put in. Even though he and Bilal were cool and shit, I still didn't want no one but Bilal to know my work. You gotta keep that shit quiet to the fullest degree, 'cause that's how niggas be getting locked up, braggin' about the shit they did. I refused to go back to jail.

It was almost 11:30 a.m., and I had the rest of the day off. As I was wondering what I should do, I reached in my pocket and looked at Sonya's number, I hesitated for a second then said "What the fuck?" I dialed Sonya's work number.

Ring, Ring, Ring.

"BET Studios, may I help you?" a female voice said.

Damn, I had forgotten Sonya's last name. "Uh, excuse me," I said, stuttering.

"Hello," the female voice on the other end said again.

"Yes, may I speak with Sonya?"

"Sonya who, sir?"

"Sorry, I don't know her last name, but I—" I started to say, but the voice on the other end cut me off.

"Jovan, is that you?" Sonya said.

"Yeah, who's this? Sonya?" I said.

"Yeah, crazy, it's me. You call my job and you don't remember my last name," Sonya said, laughing.

"I'm sorry, but I don't think you ever told me your last name."

"Well, if I didn't, it's Duncan, and soon to be changed, 'cause these people here are getting on my last nerve."

"Oh yeah?"

"Yeah, and why didn't you call me last night?" Sonya said with a slight attitude.

"Hold up, sweetheart. We just met yesterday and you demanding calls already? You're real persistent, aren't you?" I said jokingly.

"Yes, I am, and if I had your number, I woulda called and cussed your ass out."

"You wouldn't do that to a brotha like me, would you?"

"Try me, mister."

We both laughed. I liked Sonya's little act of aggressiveness. It only showed me that she was really diggin' me.

***

While I was on the phone talking to Sonya, Bilal and Carlos were meeting uptown on Kennedy Street. Los was a short, chubby, light-skinned Puerto Rican, and he drove a blue four-door 600S Mercedes-Benz. As Lal pulled up in his 600S coupe, Carlos got in and immediately they began talking business.

"Los, what's up with this nigga Petey? He's owed us three hundred fifty thousand for like eight months now. Why you ain't get it from him yet?" Bilal said angrily.

"'Cause every time I went around Trinidad the nigga was kinda acting funny," Carlos said.

"Funny how?" Bilal said, his anger building up even more.

"I asked the nigga 'bout the bank and he was like, 'Los, I do business with Bilal and Bilal only, so when Bilal come around, then he'll get his money.'"

"Yeah, this nigga knew I had thirty years, didn't he?"

"That nigga knew. He just wasn't try'na pay me. He thought you had thirty years and you was washed up."

"Why you ain't get somebody to punish his ass? You know the nigga Li'l G locked up in Maryland on three bodies, and I don't fuck with the rest of his crew. Them niggas cruddy."

"Yeah, I know, and I couldn't do it myself 'cause every time I came around he had the dude Chicken Wing wit' him, and them niggas kept touching their shit just to let me know they were strapped," Carlos said.

"Man, I don't believe this nigga Petey. As much as I looked out for this dude, and it ain't like he don't got the money, this nigga pumpin' like shit. Did he ever put something down on that thirty?" Bilal said.

"Yeah, three hundred thou. So he owe three fifty. He gotta have that by now."

"Yeah, his ass got it. He just thought he got away with some free money when I got locked up. I've been paging this nigga all morning too. C'mon. We're going 'round Trinidad to see if this nigga out there," Bilal said.

"Oh yeah, Lal," Carlos said.

"What's up?"

"You know that nigga Fat Mike got his head hit."

"Yeah, I heard. Who did it?" Bilal said as if he didn't know already.

"Word on the street is that the dude Li'l Dog from Southwest put it to him."

"Li'l Dog. Yeah, I know youngin'. That's one of Big Silk's protégés. Good li'l dude, but he's got a vicious gambling problem."

Damn, Jovan really was tight, Bilal thought. He killed Fat Mike and had Los thinking somebody else did it.

As Los and Bilal pulled up on Sixteenth Street around Trinidad, Petey and Chicken Wing were sitting on their cars in front of Petey's stash house where he kept all his bricks. Petey had a green convertible Mercedes, and Chicken Wing had a black 928S4 scarface Porsche with chrome BBS wheels.

When Los and Bilal pulled up, Petey and Chicken Wing both pulled out their straps.

Lal rolled down the window and said, "Nigga, it's me. Put that shit up."

First thing Petey said was, "Man, what you do to escape?"

"Naw, I ain't escape, nigga," Bilal said as he grilled his face at Petey.

"Then how you get out?" Petey said, looking nervous.

"I won my appeal. Look, Petey, all that shit is neither here nor there. I need to holla at you in private."

Bilal got out of his car, and Petey and he walked a couple of steps away.

"Look, Petey, I need my money," Bilal said, getting right to the point.

"Bilal, hold up," Petey said as he tried to stall the conversation.

"Petey, I ain't try'na hear no bullshit. You owe me three hundred fifty thou, and I need it like now."

"Man, Bilal, shit's a little fucked up for me right now."

"Fucked up? How, nigga? You got a brand new convertible Benz that cost like seventy-five thousand, and your man got a Porsche worth 'bout sixty-five. I know you ain't get that shit with your last."

Carlos got out of the car and walked over to Bilal and Petey. "What's up with you not paying my man here? He said he came 'round here like three different times," Bilal said, pointing to Carlos.

"Man, Lal, this nigga came 'round here on some different shit, like he was pressin' me or something."

"How he pressin' you for something that's his, Petey?"

"Man, you knew Bilal had thirty years. You just wasn't try'na pay me," Carlos said as he looked at Petey with eight months of built-up hatred.

"Like I said before, Carlos, I dealt with Bilal when I got them thirty bricks. I put three hundred thousand in Bilal's hands, not yours, nigga," Petey said, attempting to break bad with Carlos.

"Petey, who the fuck you think you talking to like that?" Carlos said.

"I'm talking to you, Carlos. You don't even know me like that to be coming at me."

"Nigga, you owe me three hundred fifty thousand and you sayin' I don't know you like that? Fuck that. Where my money at?" Carlos yelled.

"You bitch-ass nigga, you wait for Bilal to come home and try to get some heart."

At that time, Chicken Wing got up and started walking toward Petey.

"Hold up. Look, Los and Petey, y'all cut all that bullshit out. It's obvious you two niggas can't get along. Like you said, you dealt with me. Well, I'm here now, so where my dough at?" Bilal said as he peeped Chicken Wing about to pull out his strap.

"Look, Lal, come around here tomorrow. I'll have your money then," Petey said.

"Yeah? You know I've been paging you all morning. Why you ain't call me back?" Bilal said.

"Man, I left my pager over my baby mother's house last night."

"Petey, I suggest you have it on you at all times from now on."

"Yeah, okay, Lal."

"A'ight then," Bilal said before going back to his car with Carlos and driving off.

"Man, Lal, that nigga lying like shit. He was just looking at his pager when we pulled up," Carlos said.

"Yeah, I know. I just wanted to see how he looked when he lies. Los, how much money we got?"

"Three point five mil still, plus about one point five mil still in the streets."

"Damn, what was you doing while I was gone?"

"I wasn't fuckin' with the connect, 'cause I was a little skeptical about coping with our last. You know we can't buy no less than two hundred bricks."

"Who where were you getting shit from then?"

"I was fuckin' with the dudes from cross town, and they'd give me like twenty-five bricks here and there."

"Was the number high?"

"Fuck yeah. Them niggas want all of theirs."

"Okay, when you come by the house tonight, bring that money with you."

"Okay, Lal."

Jovan

Sonya and me talked for a little while, laughing and having a good time. It was around 11:45 a.m. and I didn't have anything to do. My day at work was practically finished, so I popped the magic question.

"What you doing for lunch?"

"I dunno. My friend Germain and me might go down to Houston's in G-Town or something. Why?"

"Who's Germain?" I said curiously.

"Germain is a female," Sonya said, chuckling.

"Oh, okay, 'cause for a minute . . ." I stopped before I said I thought Germain was a man.

"What was you gonna say, Jovan?"

"I wasn't gonna say anything. I just wasn't gonna call anymore."

"Damn, Jovan, you wouldn't have given me a chance to explain? Shit, I coulda had a uncle or cousin named Germain," Sonya said.

"Well, you don't," I said.

"And how do you know that?"

"'Cause you woulda told me."

"Jovan, you're crazy," Sonya said, laughing.

"Yeah, crazy 'bout you, Sonya," I said, smiling.

"Yeah, whatever, and why did you ask me what I was doing for lunch anyway?"

"Obviously I was gonna ask to take you out to lunch."

"Well, Mr. Jovan Price the Lawyer, it's still not too late to ask me."

"So you're not going to lunch with your friend?" I said, glad that she was willing to change her plans to have lunch with me.

"No, not if you're still considering taking me to lunch," Sonya said as she smiled at the thought of having another lovely afternoon.

"So when will you be ready to take your lunch break?" I asked.

"In like twenty minutes," Sonya said.

"Perfect. I'll be out front waiting."

"No, Jovan, just come on in to the front desk."

"Okay."

When I got off the phone, I began to think about where I should take Sonya for lunch. The weather was nice, my bank was right, and I was dressed for the occasion. Wherever we went it had to be outside. Maybe I would take her down to Tony & Joe's and eat out on the deck, or Sequoias, or the Cheesecake Factory on Wisconsin Avenue. I didn't know where, but I would think of something.

Mark came into Michelle's office, saw me sitting there, and said, "Hey, Jovan, you'd better get your ass outta Michelle's office. She'll be back in a few minutes."

"That's all right. I'm 'bout to leave anyway."

"You going home?"

"Naw, I'm gonna take this nice female I met yesterday out to lunch."

"Oh, you met a new bun," Mark said jokingly.

"Bun? Mark, you're silly. Yeah, man, I met this girl yesterday and it already seems like I've known her for years."

"Damn, that's the sign."

"The sign?"

"The sign of love."

"Man, ain't nobody say nothin' 'bout love."

"No, Jovan, that's just how it was when I met my wife."

"Yeah, which one?" I said with a sarcastic grin.

"You know, you can be a pain in the ass sometimes," Mark said, grinning at my comment.

"Go 'head, Mark." We both laughed. "Look, I'll see you tomorrow. Tell me how it goes with those briefs."

"Okay. Oh, hey, Jovan."

"Yeah, Mark?"

"You taking that girl out in your van?" Mark asked.

"What else I'ma drive?" I said.

"Here. Take my car. Just bring it back unscratched," Mark said, throwing me the keys to his brand new BMW. I had one before, back in '91, but this one was a new joint, fresh off the lot.

I went into my truck and got a few things and headed for the nearest deli. When I got to the deli, I bought a turkey and cheese sandwich on rye, a tuna fish on wheat, some potato chips, a freshly made fruit salad, two Evian waters, and a freshly squeezed grapefruit juice.

I pulled up in front of Sonya's job, looked in the mirror to make sure my appearance was cool, and got out of my car—well, Mark's car—and headed inside to the front desk. There was a chubby young woman at the desk. She was cute, but she was too much on the heavy side.

"Excuse me. May I help?" she asked me.

"Yes, I'm looking for a Sonya Duncan," I said.

"Hold on a second."

When she got on the phone to page Sonya, I got the feeling they must have known each other, because I was ear hustling and I heard the girl say, "Sonya, girl, it's this fine-ass man down here asking for you. Yeah, girl, he looks too good in his cream outfit and jazzy shoes. Okay, I'll tell him you'll be right down."

She hung up the phone, turned to me, and said, "Excuse me, sir. She'll be right down."

"Okay, thank you."

"Anytime," she said while she looked me up and down with a devilish grin as if to say, "You can fuck me too."

When Sonya came downstairs, there was another woman with her. She looked like she was whispering in Sonya's ear.

"Hey, Jovan," Sonya said.

"Hey, sweetheart."

"This here is my coworker and friend, Germain."

"How you doing, Germain?" I said to her friend.

"Hello, Jovan. I've heard a lot about you," Germain said, smiling.

"Oh yeah?"

From what Germain just said, it made me wonder what Sonya was saying about me. Shit, after all, I had just met her only two days ago.

"All right, Germain, you've met Jovan. Time to go now. Bye," Sonya said, grabbing my hand to leave.

"God, Sonya, you ain't even let me say nothin'," Germain said, looking mad.

"You said enough. Bye. We gotta go. See you later."

"Okay, Germain. Have a good day," I said to her.

"I will if you keep her with you and don't bring her back," Germain said, laughing.

"I just might do that," I said as I looked at Sonya out of the corner of my eye, waiting to see her expression. Sonya stuck her tongue out at Germain, and Germain gave her the finger.

When we got in the car, Sonya started talking first. "Jovan, you look very nice today. You're dressed real jazzy to be a paralegal."

"Thank you. You look nice yourself, Sonya. More like a model than a assistant producer," I said as my eyes pierced her whole body.

"Jovan, where are you taking me?"

"I figured since the day was nice we'd go somewhere outside and chill."

As we were driving, I put on a Sade CD and went straight to the song "Cherish the Day." Sonya lay back in her seat, looking good as shit. You could tell she was into the music 'cause her feet were moving and her head was bobbing as she closed her eyes.

When we pulled up to this secluded area at Rock Creek Park, Sonya opened her eyes and said, "Oh, Jovan, I haven't been here since I was a little girl. What are we doing here?"

"Well, sweetheart, I thought it would be nice if we just had a little picnic, just you and me chilling. Is something wrong with that? You wanna go someplace else?" I asked, afraid she was not pleased with my choice.

"No, a picnic is perfect. It's just that I've never been on a picnic with a man before."

"Well, boo, you're going on one today."

I took the blanket and pillow outta my van, along with the food from the deli, which I had put in a basket, and found us a nice spot under a tree. I laid out everything then went back to the car to get Sonya.

"Jovan, I have on heels. How am I gonna walk on that grass?" Sonya asked me.

"Tell you what; just get out of the car."

Sonya got out then asked, "What are you gonna do?"

At that moment I lifted Sonya up in my arms and carried her across the grass. She held onto me tight as if she didn't want to let go as I placed her down on the blanket.

"Jovan, that was fun, but I must say I was a little surprised by your actions. I do not know of any man who would have done what you just did. If only there were more men like you these day. Was I heavy?" Sonya said.

"No, sweetheart. You wasn't heavy. I could carry you forever." I sat down beside Sonya, and she began to take her shoes off.

"Here, let me do that for you." I took off each shoe slowly and began massaging her feet.

"Oh, Jovan, that feels so good. You sure know how to treat a woman."

"Sonya, you've got the prettiest feet I have ever seen," I said as I admired her perfectly manicured feet.

"Thank you, Jovan, and you are the most romantic person I have ever dated," Sonya said, looking deep into my eyes.

"Now, how you gonna say that when this is only our second time with each other?" I said, grinning slyly at her.

"Yeah, you're right. I may be speaking too fast," Sonya said.

We both laughed. I then got our food out of the basket and placed it on the blanket.

"Well, Sonya, I wasn't sure what you liked, so I got a turkey on rye and a tuna fish on wheat," I said, placing both sandwiches in front of her for her to choose.

"I'll take the tuna. What's that over there?" Sonya asked, pointing to the container of fruit.

"Oh, this is a freshly made fruit salad."

"Umm, it looks good."

We ate and talked about almost everything. She had this way about her that put my soul at ease. I had just met her and I was digging her style already. This shit had never happened to me before. I mean, I'd had a lot of women before, but not one like her.

"Jovan," Sonya said, bringing my attention back to her.
"Yeah?"

"Come over here closer to me." As I moved closer, Sonya began to massage my back and neck. "Jovan, do you work out?" she asked as she continued massaging my neck.

"Yeah, baby, I do. I go to the gym three times a week," I said, enjoying her soft hands as they massaged my neck.

"I can tell."

Sonya was rubbing my back and neck so good that my dick started getting hard. After she had massaged me, I returned the favor as we continued talking.

"Jovan," Sonya said.
"Yeah?"

"I wanna taste that fruit salad."

"Well, the only way you can taste it is if you let me feed it to you," I said, opening the container of fruit.

"I'm cool with that."

I fed Sonya strawberries, watermelon, cantaloupe, and all the other fruit that was in the salad. The way she closed her eyes and held her tongue out made my dick even harder. I started imagining how she'd look while we were making love. After I fed her the fruit salad, she fed me a few strawberries, and I did the same thing she did: closed my eyes and held out my tongue.

Suddenly something sweet, soft, and warm touched my tongue, but I didn't bother to open my eyes because I realized that Sonya was kissing me. I kissed her back. The kiss itself was explosive, and I could have kissed her all afternoon.

"What was that for?" I asked after she had stopped.

"Just a little something to let you know how much I appreciate you doing all this for me. Jovan, you've made me feel special today. I've never had no one take the time out to do something like this," Sonya said seriously.

"And I've never had no one to take out like this until I met you."

"Yeah, right. You've probably got women crawling on their knees trying to be with you."

"I was just thinking the same thing about you."

"No, baby, you don't have to worry about that," she said.

"Vice versa. So are you sayin' we can see each other again?" I asked hopefully.

"You damn right. Every chance we get, Jovan."

"So I take it you're feeling me right about now, huh?"

"Men like you don't just fall out the sky, so when I find one, I gotta grab hold to him."

"I'm thinking the same thing about you."

"C'mon, baby, I gotta get back to work," Sonya said, getting up off the blanket.

I got up and carried Sonya back to my car, packed everything, and drove her back to work. When we pulled up to Sonya's job, I gave her my number and a light kiss on the lips.

Before she got out of the car, Sonya said, "Jovan, again, thank you for today. I had a wonderful time, and by the way, your ass better call me tonight or else."

"Or else what?"

"Don't call and see what happens."

"So you're threatening me now?"

"No, that's not a threat, baby. It's a promise."

As Sonya was getting out of the car, Germain and another female were standing out front waiting for her. Germain and me waved at each other, and as Sonya closed the door, I could hear her say to Germain, "Damn, y'all so nosy!"

Sonya

Jovan and I had a nice time at the park, and to tell you the truth, he romanced the hell outta me. Most niggas didn't even think about doing shit like that. They thought they had to show their money off to get somebody to like them.

It was wonderful being with Jovan just looking at the sky, trees, and all of nature. I was on a natural high with him. He gave me inspiration because he wasn't like other guys I'd dated. He had an aura about him that made me smile and made my pussy get wet all at the same time. I guess that was why I kissed him like that. I couldn't hold it back. Jovan made my day, and I knew if I continued seeing him, eventually he'd make my world.

Jovan

After I dropped Sonya off, I went back to the office and gave Mark his keys.

"Hey, Jovan, how did it go?" Mark asked me.

"It went real cool. I laid it down like a true playa supposed to," I said and then told Mark what happened.

"Man, Jovan, you're smooth. I might have to try that one."

"Naw, you couldn't do that. Your shit would be in the newspaper on the front page: *Lawyer Fucks Prosecutor in Public Park.*" We laughed.

"Jovan, you're crazy, man. Look, I'll see you tomorrow," Mark said.

It was about two o'clock, and I had a lot of time before I had to go to Bilal's house. I had about two thousand in big bills on me, so I decided to go down to Georgetown to Solbiato and get a few shirts and some shoes.

I got down to Georgetown and parked on the opposite side of the store. I looked at all the cars in front of Solbiato. It looked like a car show. There was a Lexus LS400, Benz Coupe VI2600, Benz 500SL, Infiniti Q45, and a Range Rover. This was where all the players in the city shopped, and believe me, the joint was flooded with bitches.

When I came in the store, I saw D and Ant, two dudes I knew from the southeast side. I shoulda known all that big shit outside was theirs and their crew. These niggas were getting it. They were the only niggas in the city that wasn't copping from Bilal.

When I came through, the first person that made contact with me was D. We were cool back in '91 when I had a few niggas on the south side movin' ounces like welfare cheese. We never did business together, but we always respected and acknowledged each other, I guess mainly because our styles were similar. The nigga was smooth just like me, and he wore top flight shit and kept a bad bitch with him.

When I was locked up in Lewisburg, I used to hear good things about him, about how he stayed loyal to his man Ant when he was down Lorton and how he broke him off something real nice when he came home; sorta like Bilal and me, but the only thing different was that Bilal and me didn't hang out together or hustle together.

"Hey, what's up, Jovan?" D said, coming over to me.

"What's up, D?"

"Ain't shit going on. Damn, Jovan, I ain't seen you in a while. Where you been at?"

"I was in the feds for a minute," I said.

"How long you've been home?" D asked.

"About eight months now."

"Yeah, so what you doing?" D said as he checked me out to see if he could notice any signs of me getting back into the hustling game.

"I'm a paralegal now. I work for Mark."

"Who, Mark Rohon?" D asked, surprised.

"Yeah, I've been working for Mark for the past six months now."

"Damn, Jay, I was 'bout to ask you was you tryin' to get down. I know we ain't never did business before, but I do know your hustling skills, and I'd love to have a nigga like you on my team," he said, eagerly wanting me to accept his proposition.

"Naw, man, I ain't fucking around no more. I'ma do this paralegal thang."

"If that don't work out for you, you know you can always holla at me," D said. "So what, you getting ready for that party tomorrow?"

"What party?" I said, thinking about all the lavish parties I went to back when I was hustlin' real good. Damn, that shit was fun.

"The Madness Connection is giving a hair show and an after party downtown at the Sphinx Club," D said.

"The Sphinx Club. That's off of Fourteenth Street, ain't it?"

"Yeah. You going?" he asked as he watched me fumble through the shirt racks.

"Naw, I doubt it. I'm just here try'na find a couple shirts or something," I said, continuing to look through the shirt racks.

"They got some a'ight shit in here, but I already got most of this shit. Jovan, you know me. I gotta go up to Wisconsin Avenue to the V shop and get that signature Versace shit. I'ma holla at you, slim. Take care," D said.

"A'ight, D. Keep your head up."

Damn, if I ever wanted to ever hustle again, I had the biggest opportunity in the world.

I checked out a few shirts. I didn't see anything I liked, but I did see some shoes. I bought a pair of Versace soft-bottom shoe-boots, some Caesar Picotti slip-ons, and a pair of nice-ass Salvatore Ferragamo lace-ups. All together it came to eleven hundred dollars.

As I was leaving, I saw this gray Hugo Boss sweat suit. Now, I don't wear sweat suits, but this joint was hitting. I had to get it. The sweat suit was six hundred dollars.

I left and went to Grandma's to see if she had gotten those estimates to get the house fixed. As soon as I came through the door, I heard Grandma hanging up the phone.

"Hey, Grandma, what's up, baby girl?" I asked her.

"Jovan, I wish you would have came in a little earlier. You would have caught your daddy. That was him on the phone, and he asked about you. He wanted to talk to you."

"Oh yeah. Grandma, did you call and get the estimates on how much everything will cost?" I said, quickly changing the subject off my pops.

"Yeah, baby, but I dunno if you got that kinda money."

"C'mon, Grandma, how much is it?"

"They want seven thousand for the basement and three thousand for the ceiling."

"I got that for you, baby girl."

"Jovan, where you get that kind of money, boy?"

"It fell out of the sky, Grandma."

"Fell out the sky my foot. You better not be out there doing nothing illegal," Grandma said seriously.

"C'mon, Grandma, I'm a lawyer's assistant. What I look like breaking the law?"

"Yeah, you better not, 'cause if you do, I'ma be breakin' my foot off in your ass."

"Go 'head with that, baby girl," I said to her, laughing.

"You so damn silly. Did you eat yet?"

"Naw, Grandma, I ain't hungry."

I went upstairs to get ten Gs out for Grandma and came down to give it to her. It was about 6:30 p.m., so I decided to call Sonya. She had been on my mind all day since our picnic.

Ring, Ring, Ring.

"Hello," Sonya said.

"May I speak to my wife?" I said, happy to hear her voice.

"Your who?" Sonya asked, thinking the person had the wrong number.

"My wife," I said, smiling.

"Who is this?"

"Who do you want it to be?" I asked her.

"Jovan, is that you?" Sonya said after realizing it was me.

"Yeah, baby, what's up?"

"Boy, you crazy," Sonya said.

"Crazy 'bout you, that is."

"Yeah, right. I see you finally called."

"Yeah, I was getting scared. I didn't want you to call me and cuss me out."

"Whatever, Jovan," Sonya said, glad that I had called her.

We both laughed. Man, it seemed like I already knew Sonya. Outta all the broads I'd been with, ain't none of 'em made me feel like she did.

"So, Jovan, what did you do the rest of the day?"

I told Sonya everything I did, and she told me how her day went and how she bragged to her friends at work about our lunch date. She asked about my grandmother and when she would meet her. We talked for about two hours like teenagers in high school.

CHAPTER 18

"A Way Out"

It was about 8:30 p.m. when Bilal called.

Ring, Ring, Ring.

"Hello," Jovan said, answering the phone.

"Jovan, you're supposed to be at my house," Bilal said.

"Nigga, you never gave me a time."

"Okay, well, I'm on my way home, so hurry up and come over," Bilal said.

"I'm on my way," Jovan said.

"You eat yet, Jay?"

"Naw, Grandma cooked but I wasn't hungry."

"Cool. I'ma have Meeka cook something for us."

"A'ight then."

After Jovan got off the phone with Bilal, he put on his tan Armani summer jacket and headed for the door. As he was leaving, he called out, "Grandma, I'm going out."

"Okay, baby. What time you coming back?"

"C'mon, Grandma, I'm a grown man now. You can't be putting your press game down on me like that."

"Boy, shut up wit' your crazy self. I wanted to know if I should wait up for you so we could talk."

"Naw, you ain't gotta wait up. I might be out for a while," Jovan said, giving her a hug.

"Okay, baby. You be careful out there," she said, kissing him on the cheek.

"Always, baby girl." *Damn, Grandma always be putting me on a serious guilt trip,* he thought. *I wanna get out and get my own place, but it would probably break her heart. I guess I'll give it a little time before I roll out.*

On Jovan's way to Bilal's, he listened to the whole Scarface CD, *The Diary*. His favorite song was "Never Seen a Man Cry." For some reason, that joint and the other joint "Jesse James" fit his lifestyle. Both of them joints used to put him in a zone, mainly because there was so much truth in 'em.

When Jovan arrived at Bilal's house, as usual all that big shit was sittin' on his lawn. You woulda sworn Mike Tyson lived at the joint. There was an extra car that wasn't there the last time he was there, a 600s 4-door Benz, and he figured it was Carlos's joint.

As Jovan came to the door, Meeka was right there with much more attitude than the last time.

"Hi, Jovan. C'mon in. The fellas are downstairs in the game room. Jovan, I'm cooking. You don't eat beef, do you?"

"Naw, Meeka, I don't eat red meat."

"Good then. Tell them the food will be ready in a minute."

"Okay, Meeka," Jovan said, heading downstairs, where Bilal and Carlos were playing pool.

"Hey, my mu'fuckin' nigga Jay. What's up, slim?" Bilal said, coming over to give him love.

"What's up, Lal?" Jovan said, returning the love.

"Los, c'mon here. Jay, this Los; Los, this Jay," Bilal said, making the introductions.

"What's up, Jay? As you already know, Bilal speaks very highly of you. I've been hearing your name come out of this nigga's mouth since Oak Hill," Los said.

"Yeah, I heard a few things 'bout you also, and finally we meet," Jovan said, shaking his hand.

"And from here on you niggas is family," Bilal said, butting in.

"That's already understood," Jovan said, giving him a stern look.

When Jovan looked over to his right, he laid his eyes on the most money he had ever seen in his life: stacks and stacks of dough, along with four money counting machines.

"Damn, y'all niggas got a lot of money layin' around!" Jovan said, amazed at all the money.

"We just finished countin' that shit, Jay. Well, I just finished countin' it 'cause this nigga was upstairs playin' house with Meeka," Los said as he looked over at Bilal and laughed.

"Go 'head with that shit, Los. How much money is that?" Bilal said.

"A little more than five million. About five point three," Los said.

"Man, Lal, that's a lot of dough," Jovan said, not taking his eyes off the money that looked like stacks of cinder blocks.

"Nigga, a percentage of this shit is yours, so go ahead and kiss it," Bilal said.

"Naw, I'm a'ight. What's up? Give me the rundown on what you plan to do with all this money," Jovan said curiously.

"Look, Jay, this is the plan: we got five point three mil. We're gonna cop with three point five mil. After we get finished pumpin' all this shit, I'ma sell the house and most of these cars, head down to Atlanta, and turn all this shit legit, get some kind of business, maybe a few car lots. After we cop and move everything, we're gonna come out ten million strong, and after I sell the house and cars, we're gonna have like seventeen million altogether.

"Los is going back to Puerto Rico, and I'm going to Atlanta, and, Jay, you're going to law school to get that license, 'cause we're gonna need a way on how to legitimize this shit. Jay, I want you to go to Atlanta with me, get yourself a law firm, and we can enjoy this money together, 'cause like I said, a percentage of this shit is yours."

"Yeah, Jay, Bilal talking some serious shit. You know the feds gonna be closing down on us soon, so we wanna be legit when they come, and from what I'm hearing from Bilal, you're the lawyer that can make that shit happen," Carlos said, smiling.

"I ain't no lawyer yet," Jovan said to Carlos.

"Well in two years you will be, and by this time next year, we'll be finished with seventeen to twenty million strong, divided three ways. So what's up, Jovan? You wit' it or what?" Los asked.

"I'd be a fool not to be, nigga."

"You were wit' it ever since we were fifteen years old. You just ain't believe me when I told you we were gonna be rich," Bilal said with a big smile on his face.

"Yeah Lal, this here is surely a dream come true."

"Los, how much money we got left in the streets?" Bilal said.

"Not that much. Petey still owe that three hundred fifty thousand,; Li'l Manny owe me like two hundred thousand. He just called me a minute ago and told me come get it," Carlos said. "Yeah, and I'll go get that from Petey tomorrow at one o'clock."

"Y'all know the Madness Connection is giving a party tomorrow, and since I ain't been nowhere in eight months, I'm try'na go. What's up, Los? You wit' it?" Bilal asked.

"Yeah, I'll go, Lal."

"Jay, what's up? You gonna roll or what?"

"Man, Lal, I told you we can't be hangin' out together. I don't want the feds seeing your face next to mine, nor do I want any of these bitch-ass niggas out here knowing that you and me are best friends. That's the only way we're gonna come out this game on top," Jovan said to Bilal.

"Yeah, you right, Jay. You're the lawyer, and you know the law and how funky they play."

"Damn, this shit reminds me of some old *Godfather* movie," Carlos said, happy to see Jovan join the team.

"Shut up, Los. You a fool, man. C'mon, let's play some pool," Bilal said, going over to the pool table.

"Jay, you know how to shoot pool?" Carlos asked.

"Yeah, I know how to play a li'l bit."

"How much money you got?"

"Something light, 'bout five hundred."

"Put it up then, nigga. Money on the wood make the game go good," Carlos said, laughing.

"If that's so, Los, then where your bank at?"

"I got something special for you if I lose."

"Okay, rack 'em then."

"Los, go easy on him. He ain't got but five hundred dollars," Bilal said.

"Damn, Los, you must be good like that, huh?" Jovan said.

"Yeah, and I'm 'bout to punish you!" Carlos said, racking the balls on the table.

"Damn, since you 'bout to punish me, you might as well let me bust 'em and get the first shot."

"Okay, go ahead, Jay. I really ain't try'na embarrass you in front of Lal."

"Whatever, nigga."

They all laughed. Jovan grabbed the heaviest pool stick, chalked it up, and bust the balls. His first shot he hit in two balls; then he put in two more, and then two more. He didn't even give Los a chance to get on the table. Bilal and Los were looking at Jovan in shock.

"What's wrong, Los? I thought you were gonna punish me," Jovan said, laughing at the look of shock they both had on their faces.

Lal was laughing hard as shit as he said to Carlos, "Nigga, you always jumpin' out there losing on that pool table!"

"Fuck you, Lal, and fuck your funky-ass pool table!" Carlos said.

Jovan shot the last shot, and the eight ball went into the corner pocket, straight down the pipe. As soon as that happened, Los threw a set of keys onto the table.

"What the fuck is this?" Jovan asked him, looking at the keys.

"You won the game. They're yours," he said.

"Fuck you talking about?"

"The silver 850 BMW sitting out front—that's yours, nigga. Ain't nobody ever drove it but Meeka, and that was the other day when she picked Lal up from the courthouse."

"Yeah, Jay, Los was gonna give that to you as a present, but I guess he wanted to get a good game of pool outta you first, or better yet, a bad game of pool," Bilal said, still laughing.

Carlos did not find Bilal's statement funny. He said, "Fuck you, Lal! Look, Jay, the joint got a hydraulic stash spot too. It's small, though. It hold like two guns. I'll show you how to work it later."

"A'ight, and thanks, Los," Jovan said, picking up the car keys.

Meeka came downstairs and said, "Y'all food is ready."

"Okay, Meeka, we'll be right up."

Carlos then said something to Meeka in Spanish. Jovan looked at Lal as if to say, "What the fuck is going on?" Lal just laughed and said, "Oh, Meeka is Los's cousin. He introduced us back in Oak Hill, and we've been together ever since."

"Now I understand why she gets a million dollars to play with. She helped build this shit and was with you when you had shitty underwear."

"I dunno about shitty underwear, Jay, but she been with a nigga from rock bottom, and we're getting married after all this shit is over. We're gonna do it in Atlanta, and I want you to be my best man, Jay."

"Always was and always will be, Lal. Forever I remain loyal."

"Vice versa, nigga."

They went upstairs to eat, and afterward they went outside to talk.

"Damn, Lal, Meeka can cook her ass off," Jovan said, still savoring the taste on his tongue.

"That comes from our family. All of us can cook," Carlos said.

"Los, stop lying. Only thing you know how to cook is crack."

"Fuck you, Lal!" Carlos and Bilal started play wrestling and Jovan could tell they loved each other. Jovan thought Bilal looked at Carlos as his little brother, like he could fill the void of Mal-Mal's place in his life.

Los taught Jovan how to work the hydraulic stash in his new BMW. That joint was brand new, silver with light gray leather interior.

"Lal, I'ma keep this over here 'til I find somewhere to park it," Jovan said to Bilal.

"A'ight, Jay."

"Look, I'll see y'all tomorrow."

"Jay, be over here at eight o'clock tomorrow. We got something for you."

"Okay, fellas."

Jovan gave both of them hugs and went back to Grandma's house. It was about eleven o'clock when he got in, and he went upstairs to get himself ready for bed when the phone rang.

Ring, Ring, Ring.

"Hello."

"Hello, may I speak to Jovan?"

"Yeah, this me," Jovan said, realizing it was Sonya on the other end.

"Why didn't you call me?" Sonya asked.

"What's up, baby? You miss me already?"

"Don't baby me, and yes, I do miss you, but like I said before, why didn't you call?" Sonya said again, this time with a serious attitude.

"What, you beefin', Sonya?" he asked her, not sure where the attitude was coming from.

"Yeah, I'm beefin', Jovan. I've been thinking about you all day," Sonya said, this time with less attitude.

"Me too, baby. You've been on a nigga's mind like shit. It seems like we've known each other for years."

"Yeah, I know. You sure we haven't met in another lifetime before?"

"I dunno. We might have."

"Jovan, am I gonna see you tomorrow or what?"

"You better say ain't a day gonna pass that I don't see you."

"Don't make promises you can't keep, Jovan."

"Baby, all I got in this world is my—" I started to say, but Sonya cut me off.

"Hey, you better not say that. I saw *Scarface* before!" she said, laughing.

We laughed and talked for about an hour before I went to bed.

CHAPTER 19

"No Way Out"

Jovan woke up feeling good. The night before, after he talked to Sonya, Jovan had laid back and thought about what Bilal was saying that night. Atlanta was cool—a new identity, legit money, and plus you could get a million-dollar home down in Atlanta for like three hundred thousand. It sounded real good. Yeah, Jovan thought Bilal's suggestion was a smart move for everybody. Seventeen to twenty million strong divided three ways, couldn't go wrong.

Jovan arrived at the office kinda late and ran right into Mark.

"Hey, Jovan, you're late," he said.

"I know, Mark. I had a long night."

"With who, your new girl? You mean to tell me you got some already?" Mark said, smiling.

"Naw, I had a few things to take care of."

"Okay, but now that you're here, we've got a lot of work to do today."

"Break it down to me."

Mark had Jovan doing more work that day than he had done since he first started working for him. That was just how this legal shit was: one day you were busy, the next day wasn't nothing happening.

***

Carlos called Bilal about twelve o'clock. "Lal," Carlos said.

"Yeah, Los."

"Look, I'm on my way 'round Georgia Avenue to go pick that money up from Li'l Manny."

"I thought you did that last night," Bilal asked.

"Naw, when I left your house I picked this li'l freak up and went to the hotel out in Crystal City," Carlos said.

"Where you at now?"

"I'm on Seventh Street, getting ready to cross Florida Avenue."

"Okay, slim. Call me after you pick that up. I'm on my way 'round Trinidad to go see Petey," Bilal said.

"Did you page him again?" Carlos asked.

"Yeah, I paged that nigga like three times."

"Man, I think we may have some problems outta Petey. Plus, I don't trust them niggas. You know how they got on in the first place," Carlos said.

"Yeah, they were supposed to rob the dude Chink for like three hundred thousand," Bilal answered.

"Yeah, after this I ain't fuckin' wit 'em no more."

"Okay, slim, meet me around Orleans Place after you get that from Li'l Manny," Bilal said.

Carlos met Li'l Manny at the McDonalds on Georgia Avenue, and he gave Carlos the two hundred thousand. Li'l Manny wanted to know the next time he would be able to get down.

"Sometime next week, Manny, and I'ma do something real nice for you, 'cause after that I'm finished," Carlos said.

"Okay, Los," Li'l Manny said.

Manny got back in his Corvette and rolled out. As Carlos was putting the money in the trunk of his car, two dudes walked up on him with .45s pointed at his dome.

"Get back in the car, Los," one of the dudes said to him.

Carlos turned to see who it was, and when he saw Petey and Chicken Wing, he said, "Petey, man, you ain't even gotta do this."

"Shut your bitch ass up and get in the car!" Petey yelled to him.

Carlos got back in his car with Chicken Wing in the back seat and Petey on the passenger's side. They both had their guns on Carlos.

"Look, Petey, I've got two hundred thousand in the trunk, this Rolex, and about four thousand in my glove compartment. Man, just go 'head, take that shit, and let me go," Carlos pleaded.

Petey smacked Carlos upside his head with his pistol and yelled, "Shut the fuck up, nigga. I'm doing the talking. Now drive!"

"Where to?" Carlos asked.

"Go up Georgia Avenue," Petey said.

Carlos drove up Georgia Avenue, still not knowing his fate.

Chicken Wing started talking, "Los, where the money at? And don't play no games. I ain't talking 'bout that punk-ass two hundred thousand in the trunk either. Take us to y'all stash."

"Slim, we ain't got no more money. The feds got everything when Bilal got locked up," Carlos said.

Carlos knew that if he told them where the five point million was at, then not only would he be dead, but Bilal and Meeka would also die.

"So you ain't try'na give that shit up, huh?" Petey said.

"Man, slim, that's the truth. I swear to God on everything I love that's all we got," Carlos said, pleading for his life.

"Pull over in this alley," Petey said as he kept his gun stuck in Carlos's rib cage.

"Man, Petey, don't kill me. I swear that's all we got, man!" Carlos pleaded with tears in his eyes.

"Shut the fuck up and pull in the alley!"

Meanwhile, Bilal went around Trinidad to pick up his money from Petey. When he drove up to Petey's stash spot, he didn't see Petey or Chicken Wing's car. There were only two dudes out front talking.

Bilal rolled down his window and said, "Hey, what's up, youngin'? Y'all see Petey?"

"Naw, we waitin' on him now," one of the dudes said.

"How long you've been waiting?"

"We just got here, slim."

Bilal parked his car and figured he'd wait for Petey. Since he had his clientele out front waiting on him, he knew Petey wouldn't be that long; but usually when Petey wasn't around to serve these niggas, then Chicken Wing would.

Bilal paged Carlos, and when he didn't call him right back, Bilal sensed something was wrong. Usually when he paged Carlos, he would call him right back. Why the fuck wasn't Carlos callin' him back? He hoped that dude Li'l Manny wasn't wit' the feds.

Bilal paged Carlos again, and after about forty-five minutes of waiting on Petey and Carlos to call back, Bilal grew impatient. Petey's customers left, and Bilal went looking for Carlos.

First Bilal went around Ninth Street, where Carlos's runners were. He pulled up on Li'l Kenny and Raymond.

"Hey, Kenny," Bilal called out to him.

"What's up, Bilal?" Li'l Kenny said.

"You seen Los?"

"Naw, he ain't come through yet, and I have been paging him all day."

"Look, when you see him, tell him to call me."

"Okay, Bilal."

Bilal then drove around Orleans Place, where he was supposed to meet Carlos after he picked up the money. Bilal pulled up around back and saw Cat, Soup Bone, and Li'l Short Dog.

"Y'all seen Los come through here?"

"Naw, Bilal, but I saw him earlier when I was coming out the Madness Shop. He was going up Georgia Avenue, and he had Petey and Chicken Wing wit' 'im," Short Dog said.

"Petey and Chicken Wing?" Bilal said with a disturbed look on his face.

"Yeah, slim."

"You sure it was Petey and Chicken Wing?"

"Yeah," Short Dog said.

Bilal instantly got nervous, and as he headed toward Georgia Avenue, all he could think about was Carlos and how he loved him like a little brother. He knew that if he was with Petey and Chicken Wing, something was wrong. Plus, Carlos had never called him back. As he raced up Georgia Avenue, tears started forming in his eyes. If something happened to Carlos, then those niggas was gonna pay with their lives.

Bilal looked up and down Georgia Avenue, but there was no sign of Carlos's car. When he turned onto Webster Street, he passed an alley, and as he was driving by, he caught a glimpse of a car sitting there. Bilal put his Benz in reverse, pulled into the alley, and saw that it was his friend's car.

He got out with tears welling up in his eyes and looked in Carlos's car, saw that it was unlocked, and opened the door. Carlos's keys were still in the ignition. Bilal knew something had happened to Carlos. Bilal took the keys outta the ignition and went straight to the trunk of his car. When he opened the trunk, he saw Carlos's body curled up like a baby, with two holes in his head the size of a half a dollar. Instantly Bilal dropped to his knees.

Ring, Ring, Ring.
"Hello, law offices of Rohon and Robinson," Cindy said.
"I'd like to speak with Jovan Price," Bilal said.
"Please hold," Cindy said. She then buzzed Jovan. "Jovan," she said. "You have a call on line one."
"Jovan Price here," Jovan said, answering the phone.
"Hey, Jay, come over my house now!" Bilal said with anger.
"What's up, Lal? You all right?"
"Fuck no I ain't all right. I need you over here now!" Bilal yelled into the phone.
"Okay, slim, I'm on my way," Jovan said, hanging up the phone.
Jovan then went into Mark's office and said, "Hey, Mark, I gotta make a run. Family emergency."
"Is everything all right Jovan?" Mark asked.
"I don't know yet."
"Look, go 'head and take the rest of the day off."
"Okay, thanks, Mark."
As Jovan drove out to Bilal's house, he couldn't stop wondering what was going on. Bilal had called him at work, and it sounded like he was crying and angry. What the fuck coulda happened?
As he pulled up, Bilal was out front. His eyes were red and swollen.
Jovan got out of his van, walked over to Bilal and asked him, "What's up, man? You a'ight?"
"Naw, Jovan. Come 'round back."
"What the fuck is going on, man?"

"Jay, they killed Los, man!" Bilal said, his eyes filling with tears.

"What?" Jovan asked him, not sure he'd heard him correctly.

"Man, they killed Los. They killed my man, Jay!" Bilal cried as the tears gushed outta his eyes.

"Who? Who killed Los?"

"Petey and Chicken Wing!" Bilal yelled.

"How you know that, Lal?"

Bilal laid the whole thing down to Jovan. Jovan had just met Carlos and this nigga had bought him an 850 BMW for a present. This nigga was a good dude, and he was Jovan's best friend's partner and comrade. The whole time Bilal was telling the story, he was breaking down how much he loved Carlos. Jovan could now see the pain that he had held back when Mal-Mal died. He had held onto that pain by loving Carlos.

Damn, shit done got fucked up, and there's only one way to get it back right, Jovan thought. Petey and Chicken Wing were some cruddy niggas, and they had to get what they deserved; but first, Jovan had to calm Bilal down so that he wouldn't make any dumb moves that could get them life in prison.

Jovan's loyalty to Bilal was concrete, so there was no way he was gonna let these niggas get away with this shit. They had pulled a fucked-up move, and Carlos died for some bullshit-ass two hundred thousand. They had just talked about getting outta this game the night before, but as he saw it, once you're in, there's no way out. Every time you try to make that step out, something always pull you right back in.

"Look, Bilal, this the move, but first you gotta calm down. Is Meeka in the house?" Jovan asked Bilal.

"Naw, she's at work."

"Good, then let's go in and have a drink and plan this shit out perfectly."

As Bilal tried to calm himself down, Jovan laid out his plan. "Look, Lal, you know that Madness party is tonight."

"Yeah, Jay."

"Don't you got tickets to that joint?"

"I got two tickets. Why?"

"I'ma need 'em. Most likely them niggas is gonna be there celebrating what they did. They got some free money, and you know they're gonna be flauntin'. How many guns you got, Lal?"

"I got three hammers, a .357 Desert Eagle, and two sixteen-shot Smith and Wesson nine millimeters with black talon bullets. Yeah, Jay, I got a silencer that fits both nines," Bilal said.

"A silencer? Where the fuck you get that?" Jovan asked Bilal.

"My connect sent that shit up to me the last time I copped from him."

"Okay, that's perfect. Give me those two nines and the silencer."

"What you gonna do, Jay?"

"What I do best: both those niggas will be dead within forty-eight hours or less."

"Hold up, Jay. If you're gonna go to that party, you gotta be right."

Bilal went upstairs and came back down with a jewelry box. "Here you go, man," Bilal said.

When Jovan opened up the box, the 18-karat Presidential Rolex and matching bracelet almost blinded him. Bilal's watch and bracelet had the biggest diamonds Jovan had ever seen.

"Man, Bilal, what you try'na do, get my arm chopped off tonight?" Jovan said, still staring at all the diamonds on the jewelry.

"Naw, Jay, that's yours now. It used to be Carlos's, but I know he'd rather you have it. That shit is worth almost three hundred thousand. You got an outfit for tonight, Jay?"

"Yeah, I got a black Versace suit I bought from California that I've never wore, and a black-and-gold Versace silk print shirt with Medusa heads all over it, and some black Versace slip-ons with the matching belt."

"Damn, nigga, you try'na kill 'em, ain't you."

"Bilal, I'ma keep my van over here tonight and push the 850 to the party."

"Okay. Jay, how you gonna put in the work?"

"I'll let you know everything after I do it. Just stay home and wait for my call."

"Cool."

On Jovan's way home, he thought about Bilal and Carlos. Damn, shit was going sweet. All they had to do was get that money and step off. Now it was Bilal and him, just like old times. Those niggas had violated his family, so in turn, they had violated him also.

When Jovan got to Grandma's house, he called Sonya.

Ring, Ring, Ring.

"Hello," Sonya said.

"What's up, baby?" Jovan said to Sonya.

"Jovan, I was just thinking of you."

"You mean to tell me that out of the whole day, you just started thinking about me?" Jovan said, smiling.

"No, actually I've been thinking about you all day."

"Me too. You been on my mind also. So what's up?"

"You, Mr. Jovan Price. You're what's up."

"Look, what are you doing tonight?" Jovan asked Sonya.

"Well, I promised my friend Germain that I would go to this hair show party with her downtown," she said.

"You mean the Madness Connection party?" Jovan asked her.

"Yeah, you heard about it?"

"I was thinking about going. You got tickets?"

"Well, Germain only has one ticket. She's trying to get the other one now."

"Guess what? You're in luck."

"Why you say that, Jovan?"

"I've got an extra ticket that you can have if you want it."

"Are you going to the party too?"

"Yeah, baby, I gotta come keep my eye on you, make sure you ain't getting too fresh with nobody," Jovan said jokingly.

"Like I told you before: you don't ever have to worry about that."

"I'm just joking wit'cha, boo."

"Jovan, you're the one who's probably going to be talking to all them bitches," Sonya said sarcastically.

"Naw, boo, you ain't got to worry about that, because I'm too focused on you."

"Well, that's good that you're going. Now I can keep my promise to Germain and see you at the same time," Sonya said, happy that Jovan would be at the party that night.

"How you getting there?"

"Germain is driving."

"Good, then I can take you home after the party."

"That'll be perfect, because Germain lives all the way out in Oxon Hill, and if she takes me home, it'll be out of her way."

"You can come on over now and get the ticket and meet my grandma at the same time, if you like."

"Where does she stay, Jovan?"

Jovan told her the address.

"First, I'ma call Germain and let her know about the ticket, and then I'll be over."

"Cool."

While Sonya was on her way over, he was still thinking about a master plan on how to lay his demonstration down. Jovan took out his suit, belt, and shoes and laid them out. He hadn't been to a party like this in a long time, so when he went, he was gonna do it right.

Sonya came over and got her ticket and met his grandmother. She didn't have a lot of time to stay, because she had to get back home and get herself together. Before she left, they kissed as if they had been together for years.

"I'll see you tonight, Jovan, and you better behave yourself."

"Like I told you—you ain't gotta worry 'bout that."

Sonya

Little did Jovan know I was all his. That night, I planned to look extremely good, so I got out my black Chanel dress, my Chanel shoes, my Cartier earrings, necklace, and bracelet with the matching watch. I let my long hair out so it could fall down my back. My dress was a perfect fit. I had never worn it before. It was strapless and exposed the crease of my back, and it felt so good and smooth, like another layer of skin on my body.

Germain was on her way to pick me up, but little did she know she wouldn't be bringing me back.

Jovan

It was ten o'clock and the party had just started. I was still at home contemplating my move. I showered and got myself together. I never went to parties when they first started; I always came in a little late to give that grand appearance, so I just lay back on my bed and thought about my plans.

After I killed these two niggas, I would take Sonya home, and who knew what would happen after that. I only hoped Sonya didn't follow me around, because I had to duck her for at least half the time we were at the party.

At eleven o'clock, I put on my clothes and took out the new Rolex and bracelet Bilal had given me. Damn, this watch was hittin'. I looked at my fine-ass image in the mirror and said to myself, "Jovan, you're a fly mu'fucka." I then grabbed about two thousand dollars out of my gym bag, all hundred-dollar bills, got in my 850 BMW, and headed to the party.

When I pulled up, I circled the block first to see if I saw Petey and Chicken Wing's cars. They wasn't out front, which was good. As I turned the corner onto Fourteenth Street, I saw Petey's Benz parked in the cut, and it was kinda dark, which was perfect. Then I looked down the street and saw Chicken Wing's Porsche parked at least a half block away. I parked my car three spaces from Petey's, got out, and went into the party.

As soon as I came through door, I heard D.C.'s number one party anthem, "Before I Let Go" by Frankie Beverly. The joint was packed with females, gangsters, and a few lames. As I made my way through the crowd, I could see bitches out the corner of my eye, tapping their girlfriends as I walked by, saying, "Girl, who is that fine-ass brother right there?"

I made my way upstairs to where everyone was chillin', and as I glanced through the party looking for Petey and Chicken Wing, I saw a few good men who were regarded as real niggas. In D.C., when real niggas acknowledge one another, we call it tilting our hat. The first MOBs I tilted my hat to were Don and AB. They were over by the VIP section, poppin' bottles with some bad bitches. Then I saw ED and Ty, the ones giving this party. Also I saw that paradise of MOBs: Block, Marlon, Pee-Wee and the number one super middleweight champion, Keith Holmes. Mark Johnson. who was the flyweight WBC Champ, was also in the house. Big Sweat and them Willington Park youngin's were there also. I also saw young Ish, J-Rock, Rat Man, Rudy, and Fat Troy; these young niggas were doin' it.

The dude Ish had a Rolex on his arm that looked so heavy it made him slow down when he walked. I respected these dudes ever since their man Li'l James got double life for a crime he didn't commit. It was rumored that they stopped hustling and ventured their money into the music industry so they could pay for his lawyer legitimately. I heard they were tryin' to get him Johnnie Cochran. Damn, that's real.

Then I saw Big Poo and Fats. They used to cop from me back in '91. As I walked through the party, all these dudes tilted their hats to me, and I returned the favor. Also, a lot of bad bitches I knew were coming up to me try'na get with a nigga. My Rolex was attracting bitches like a magnet. The first broad I saw was Peppa, and she was looking good as shit. I wanted to tell her to meet me outside after the party, but I had plans for something else, so we kicked it for a minute.

Then I saw Keda, and she also looked good. I hadn't seen or talked to her since I had been home. I let her know how much I appreciated what she did for me when I was locked up, and I told her if there was ever anything she needed, I'd help her out.

Then I saw Big Titty Tracey and her crew. Cha-cha and Nicki came over to talk to me, and Li'l Shana and her cousins, Nicki and Toya, were also there. I used to mess with Nicki back in the day, and she was looking good as shit, too. If I didn't have nothin' to do, I would have taken her straight to the hotel.

As soon as I finished talking to Nicki, my old piece, Barvette, walked up behind me.

"Hey, Jovan," Barvette said, hugging me around my waist.

"Hey, what's up, Barvette?" I said, turning around.

"I haven't seen you in years, boy. Where have you been?"

"I was away for a minute," I said to her.

"I can see nothing has changed."

"What do you mean?"

"You still fly, and you got a watch on that looks like it cost more than this building," she said.

"Yeah, you know me. Shit don't stop 'cause the nigga got knocked," I said, laughing.

"Jovan, you still the same."

As we were talking, I saw Petey and Chicken Wing with some bitches taking flicks, and it looked like they were already drunk. I locked my eyes in their direction, not looking directly at them, but I kept them in sight.

While I was peeping Petey and Chicken Wing, everybody rushed toward the stage where the hair show was. I didn't go down there, but I looked off the balcony. When I looked on stage, I saw the strangest shit ever at a party like this: there was Trina Boo and another girl modeling for a hair salon. I think it was Erotica. Trina Boo was behind this girl, motioning like she was fucking her doggy style with a dildo. The whole party was in an uproar. Niggas were trying to get on stage, and people were rushing up front to see what was happening. These broads were on stage acting out a lesbo scene. Throughout all the commotion, I still kept my eye on Petey and Chicken Wing.

After Trina Boo and her friend did their little lesbo trick, everything calmed down, and that's when I saw

Sonya and Germain downstairs by the bar. Sonya had on a black dress that look like another layer of skin, and she also had on some pretty diamond earrings and a necklace. I could see the shape of Sonya's ass through her dress, and her hair was falling straight down her back. Damn, she looked so good—a straight dime piece, and I mean a strong dime.

I went downstairs to greet her, but I still kept my victims in sight. As I crept up behind Sonya, I whispered in her ear, "Damn, you look gorgeous tonight."

She didn't even bother to turn around as she said, "I see you finally got away from all them bitches that were hawking you."

"What are you talking about, boo?" I asked her innocently.

"Jovan, I just left the ladies room, and every bitch that came in there was talking 'bout you."

"I can't help that, Sonya."

"I know, baby. You're just a smooth-ass nigga, and I can't get mad because other bitches want you. In fact, that shit kinda turns me on."

Sonya then turned around and looked at me and said, "My God, Jovan, you look very nice. Now I see why all these bitches try'na get with you."

"And you mean to tell me all the time you been here, ain't none of these niggas try to talk to you," I said to Sonya.

"Yeah, they have, Jovan, but I batted that shit down."

"What'd you tell 'em?"

"I told them that I was very involved with a man I hardly know."

We both laughed then Germain joined us. "Oh, hi, Jovan," Germain said.

"Hey, Germain."

"You know, we've only been here for a half hour and we've already heard a lot about you in the ladies room."

"Yeah, Sonya already told me," I said to Germain.

"Jovan, are you behaving yourself?" Germain asked me.

"Yes, indeed," I said, smiling at her.

"You better, 'cause if you make my friend mad, I'ma have to kick your butt."

"She know she doesn't gotta worry about that."

As I talked to Sonya, I could see that Trina Boo was on her way over. I didn't know Trina Boo personally, but I had heard a few rumors that would make a nigga want to get to know her fast, and I do mean real fast.

"Hey, cuz," Trina Boo said.

"Don't 'hey, cuz' me. I saw you on stage acting like you don't have no sense," Sonya said to her cousin Trina.

"Girl, that was just an act for the shop. Who is that with you?"

"Oh, excuse me. Jovan, this is my cousin Trina."

"Hi, Trina."

"Call me Trina Boo."

"No, Jovan, call her Trina. Her name is Trina."

"There you go acting like you somebody's mother."

As Sonya was talking to Trina, I saw that Petey and Chicken Wing were about to leave and they had that broad Pebbles wit' 'em. This was my chance to make my move.

"Hey, Sonya, can you excuse me for a moment? I gotta go talk to one of my clients in the lobby," I said.

"Sure, baby. I'll be right here waiting on you. Jovan, you sure take your work seriously. You at a party and you talking to clients."

"Gots to get that money, boo."

"That's right, baby. Go right ahead."

"Hey, you better behave yourself while I'm gone," I said.

"Boy, I told you once before—matter of fact, twice—that you definitely don't have to worry about that."

"Okay. I'll be back in about twenty minutes, maybe less."

As Petey and Chicken Wing were in the lobby still trying to talk Pebbles into leaving with them, I walked straight past them and out of the party. I looked around to make sure no one saw me as I went to my car and popped the hydraulic stash. I took out one of the 9 mm that Bilal gave me and screwed on the silencer. Then I got out of my car and went over to Petey's Benz. I took off my watch and bracelet, put them in my pocket, and crawled under Petey's car.

I waited for about ten minutes before I saw Petey and Chicken Wing walking toward their cars. Pebbles wasn't with 'em, which was good, 'cause if she was then I'd have to whack her too, and I wasn't try'na kill no bitch who ain't had a damn thing to do with this.

As they got closer, I could hear them talking.

"Damn, slim, I told you we shoulda got that nigga Bilal first. He the one wit' all the bank," Chicken Wing said.

"It's hard to get that bitch-ass nigga because he don't even be coming out," Petey said.

"Yeah, I searched the fuck out that party for him."

As I heard these niggas talking about killing and robbing my best friend, my only family, I knew I had to kill these niggas. I wasn't nervous or anxious; I just wanted this shit to be done right.

As Petey walked toward his car, Chicken Wing stepped off.

"I'll see you tomorrow. We can page that bitch nigga Bilal, tell 'im we got his money, and get him then," Petey said.

"Yeah, that's what's happening," Chicken Wing said.

Chicken Wing headed down the street to his car. Damn, that nigga Chicken Wing was getting away. Fuck it. I couldn't let the cat outta the bag. If I jumped out then, I'd have to kill Petey then chase Chicken Wing down the street, and that shit would be real sloppy and for sure somebody would see me. So, I stayed on Petey.

As Petey got close to the car, I positioned myself, and as soon as he put his key in the door, I rolled from under the car and placed my gun right up under his nut rack and said, "Nigga, if you still wanna make babies, then shut the fuck up!"

Petey was in shock. He couldn't move or scream, so he tried to negotiate. "Look, man, all I got is my Rolex and about fifteen hundred on me. You can have the shit."

"Naw, nigga, give it to your peoples for funeral arrangements," I said, and then I shot Petey in the nuts three times. *Pat-pat-pat.*

As Petey stumbled back in shock, holdin' his nuts, I got up and shot him three times in the chest. *Pat-pat-pat.* He then fell to the ground. I looked around for a second to see if anybody saw me, but no one was in sight. I then stood over him and delivered four shots to his head. *Pat-pat-pat-pat.*

I spit on him, and as he lay there dying, I said, "You deserved that, you bitch-ass nigga!" I wiped off the gun, took off the silencer, and put it in my pocket. I put my Rolex and bracelet back on, threw the gun down the sewer, and headed back to the party.

As I was walking up to the front entrance, I could hear the seductive melody of Teddy Pendergrass's voice penetrating through the speakers. On my way back in, I saw a good dude I knew by the name of Cat Eye Tony, on his way out.

"What's up, Jovan?" Cat Eye Tony said.

"What's up, Tony? Hey, the party over or what?" I said.

"Yeah, Jovan, you know when they play Teddy Pendergrass's 'Turn Off The Lights' that means it's time to roll."

"Yeah, I know. I'll holla at you, Tony."

"Okay. Good to see you, Jovan."

"Yeah, you too, Tony."

While maneuvering my way through the crowd of people who were leaving the party, I looked around and noticed that Sonya and Germain weren't standing in the same spot I had left them. After a few seconds I finally spotted them over by the picture booth, talking to a few of their female friends. I walked over and slightly eased my hand on Sonya's waist, pulling her away.

"What's up, boo? Did I take too long?" I asked her, nibbling on her ear.

"No, you said you'd be gone twenty minutes. That was only fifteen minutes," Sonya said.

"So, you clockin' me now?"

"How can I clock a man that's always on time?"

"Look, this joint 'bout over. You ready to go?"

"Yeah. Oh, Germain, Jovan is gonna take me home tonight," Sonya said.

"What?" Germain said, looking at her with an evil eye.

"Like I said, Jovan taking me home, so now you can get back to your husband early," Sonya said, giving Germain the same evil eye.

"Sonya, you nasty!" Germain said, laughing. "Shut up, girl. You so silly."

"Jovan, take it easy on her," Germain said, winking her eye at me.

"Bye, Germain."

"Bye then."

"Germain, you want us to walk you to your car?" I asked.

"Yeah, Jovan, thanks."

We walked Germain to her car and said our good-byes once again.

"You know something? Y'all two look cute together," Germain said, getting into her car.

"Bye, silly. Call me when you get in the house," Sonya said.

As I walked Sonya to my car, we saw a small crowd and the police up ahead.

"Look, Jovan, something happened."

"Well, boo, it ain't none of our business. C'mon, get in the car," I said, knowing that we had to get out of there fast now that the police had shown up.

"See, that's why I don't like going out. Niggas always out trippin'," she said.

"Yeah, I know. They always doing something stupid."

"Why can't they be more like you?" Sonya said.

"What do you mean?"

"I mean you got a job and you don't be around a lot of niggas. You just be chillin', and you still got the same things these niggas out here hustling got."

"I guess that's the life they chose," I told her, but in my head I was saying, *Baby, you just don't know. I'm the reason why everybody standin' there. I just gave ten shots to a nigga who deserved it.*

As we pulled off and made our way through traffic, I put in a CD that would fit the mood. Traffic began to flow and the music began to take over our emotions. I played Jon B & Tupac's song "Baby Are U Still Down." Out the corner of my eye I peeped Sonya staring at my watch as the street lights beamed down on its diamonds that reflected rays of rainbows. As my 850I BMW glided up Connecticut Avenue in the cool summer night like a space ship taking off, I placed my hand on Sonya's thigh and rubbed it softly as if I was rubbin' a lion's fur. I could see that just from me touching her like that, I put her at ease to a point where she placed her hand on top of mine and closed her eyes.

When I pulled up to Sonya's condo, she was sleeping lightly. "Hey, Sonya, we're here," I said to her, gently waking her.

She woke up in amazement and said, "Oh, I'm sorry, Jovan. I guess I got caught up in the music and fell asleep."

"So am I going to see you tomorrow or what?"

"Sure, Jovan," Sonya said.

"Would you like me to walk you to your door?" I asked, hoping that she would invite me in.

"Sure. That'll be nice."

I parked my car and walked Sonya to her door. Once we got to the door, Sonya turned around and planted such a wet, erotic kiss on my lips that I couldn't hold back. I held her soft body close and we kissed passionately for what seemed like an eternity. Then she placed her key in the door. As I turned around and began to walk away, Sonya stood in her doorway and watched me go down the hall. I turned around once more and looked at her staring at me.

"What's wrong, boo?" I asked her.

Sonya looked at me with those pretty eyes and said, "Jovan, please stay with me tonight."

That's all she had to say because as soon as we got in her apartment, Sonya grabbed my hand and directed me to her bedroom. All at once, I pressed my tongue deep into her mouth and slid off her dress with one stroke. As she took off my jacket and shirt, I admired her perfect body. Her titties were round, not too big and not too small, but perfect. She wasn't wearing any panties, and I saw that her pussy was neatly shaved.

I caressed her lips while she continued to unbutton my pants, and soon we were both completely naked.

As I placed her on the bed and kissed her more passionately, I began to run my fingers over her hard nipples and lightly sucked on them as if I was sucking on a fresh strawberry. I then ran my wet tongue all over her breasts, down to her navel, and then to her thighs. As her moans of ecstasy grew, I caressed her thighs and gently ran my tongue teasingly around the outside of her pussy. I could feel her body ripple and tense as I continued. I didn't move too fast or too slow; I patiently took my time exploring Sonya's sweet pussy.

As I kept going, I could feel her hands reaching behind my head, trying to get me to crush my face into her pussy, eager for me to lick more of her, but I wasn't going to make it that easy for her. Instead, I grabbed her hands and held them back and continued to tease her sweet, throbbing pussy, never penetrating her, only dabbing and rubbing it slightly.

She moaned as I felt her body shudder and all at once, I pressed my tongue deep into her pussy and she gave a soft cry.

"Oh my God, Jovan!"

I motioned my tongue in and out of her pussy as if it was my dick. Then I started licking on her clit as if it was an ice cream cone, up and down, side to side. While licking on her clit, I pressed one finger inside her wet pussy, and as her moans got louder, I placed two fingers deep into her pussy and positioned them in a motion as if telling someone to come here, until I felt a spongy spot of flesh. I continued to lick Sonya's clit until I found her G spot, and then her soft moans became a loud cry.

"Oh my God, Jovan. wWhat are you doing to me? Oh, Jovan, Jovan, Jovan!" Sonya screamed.

I could feel her body tremble and her legs shake as she closed her eyes tightly and let the waves of her orgasm rush through her body.

After Sonya had come repeatedly, I caressed her thighs for about ten seconds, letting her catch her breath. I lay on top of her in the missionary position and gently stuck my hard dick into her wet pussy. Sonya held me so tight that I could feel the rate of her heartbeat. As I stuck my dick deep into her pussy, Sonya pushed forward toward my dick, letting her clit rub up against my flesh as we joined in rhythm.

I ran my tongue around her nipples, kissed her neck, and enjoyed her moans as she whispered in my ear, "Oh, Jovan, baby, don't stop. Don't ever stop. This dick is so good, baby. Oh, Jovan, you don't know what you're doing to me!"

Again, I could feel her body tense and tremble as she came all over my dick, pussy juices flowing. Again I lay there for ten seconds letting her recoup, then I turned her around, massaged her back, and ran my tongue all over her body.

I grabbed hold of Sonya's ass, which was soft and pretty, and rubbed it for a few seconds. Then I pulled her up in a doggy-style position, spread her ass cheeks apart, positioned myself behind her, and slowly put my full-length, hard, throbbing dick into her wet pussy.

Sonya's pussy clung tightly onto my dick as I deeply penetrated her slowly with long, deep strokes and our rhythm came together at once. As I began to move in and out of her faster, her moaning got louder as her orgasm began to build.

"Oh, Jovan, you're fucking me so good, baby! Why are you doing this to me?"

My rhythm began to move faster and faster, and the more strokes I made, the wetter her pussy got. Sonya's pussy was so wet that her juices were dripping off my balls.

"Oh, yes, Jovan! Fuck me, boo! Fuck me, boo!"

As she cried out in pleasure, I began to pound harder into her. I pounded Sonya's pussy and caressed her ass at the same time with a ferocity that was sending her over the brink. Sonya's body tightened and her squeals of pleasure became sobs of ecstasy.

She looked over her shoulder into my eyes and moaned, "Jovan, I'm about to cum. Jovan, I'm cumming, boo! Oh, boo, I'm cumming! Oh, Jovan, I'm cumming!"

Sonya's pussy exploded on my dick as she sunk her head into her pillow trying to hide her tears of joy, pain, pleasure and lust, lovemaking and fucking, all wrapped up in one.

As she got herself together, I lay down beside her and placed her head on my chest, ran my fingers through her hair, and gently kissed her on her forehead and lips.

"Jovan," she said

"Yeah, boo?"

"Please don't leave me. I need you, boo."

"I ain't going anywhere," I said, stroking her breasts gently.

"You promise?"

"I promise."

With that, Sonya began to rub my dick and kiss my chest at the same time. She kissed all over my body while stroking my dick hard. Then she grabbed my dick and played with it before easing down and taking it into her mouth.

Her tongue moved around the head of my dick slowly as she stroked it up and down. Damn, that shit felt good. She then began sucking it slowly as the blood continued to swell my dick. Sonya was bobbing her head up and down, sending me to a place of ecstasy no woman had ever taken me before.

As I was about to cum, Sonya stopped sucking my dick and got on top and rode my dick, moving her hips back and forth, up and down, and harder and faster, until we both came and I exploded a load that was built up from the moment we met.

Sonya lay on top of me with my dick still in her pussy and her face buried in my chest. "Jovan, you don't know what you just did to me. Please don't hurt, me baby."

I made love to Sonya all night and all morning. After we took a shower together, I looked over at my pager and saw that Bilal was paging me. I called him back while Sonya was cooking breakfast.

Ring, Ring, Ring.

"Hello," Bilal said.

"Lal, what's up, nigga?"

"Man, why you ain't call me back last night? I got a little worried."

"Worried for what? Nigga, I'm like James Bond."

"Did everything go all right?" Bilal asked.

"Well, yeah and no, but I'll fill you in when I get there."

"You're okay, though, right?" Bilal asked.

"Most definitely, nigga. I told you I'm like Double-O Seven."

"Yeah, okay."

"What time you coming over?" Bilal asked.

"Soon as I eat my breakfast."

"Where you at anyway, nigga?"

"I'm over a friend's house."

"Who?"

"Her name is Sonya."

"You talking about that female you met in the courthouse?"

"Yeah."

"Damn, slim, you work fast, don't you?"

"I wouldn't call it that. I'd just say it was something destined to happen."

CHAPTER 20

"The Tightest"

After Jovan got off the phone with Bilal, he ate the veggie omelet Sonya had cooked and drank some freshly made orange juice. Sonya just sat there looking at him.

"What's wrong?" Jovan asked her, enjoying his breakfast.

"Nothing," she said, smiling.

"Then why you looking at me like that?"

"You just don't know, Jovan."

"Know what?"

"You don't have a clue what you're doin' to me."

"Yes, I do, and I feel the same way about you," Jovan said.

"I hope so."

"Look, I've got some business to take care of this morning. Then I'm going to the gym. What are you going to do today?" Jovan asked.

"Germain and me were gonna go to Chevy Chase Pavilion and do a little shopping."

"So am I gonna see you later on?"

"Jovan, you can see me whenever you want."

"I'ma call you after the gym. Maybe we can repeat last night," Jovan said, grinning.

"I like that idea," Sonya said, also grinning. They laughed, kissed, and said their good-byes.

"Oh, Jovan, I forgot to tell you that's a nice watch you have."

"Yeah, I had to confiscate it from a client who couldn't pay his bill," Jovan lied.

On Jovan's way over to Bilal's house he was putting his plan together on how he was going to deal with Chicken Wing. Only thing he knew about Chicken Wing was that he loved hood rat bitches. He didn't know where he lived at or nothing. He didn't even know if this nigga had a baby momma or not. Only thing Jovan knew was that he hung around Trinidad and drove a black Porsche. Damn, he had to think of something quick. Even though Petey was dead, Chicken Wing still may have had something planned for Bilal.

Before Jovan got on the highway to Bilal's, he stopped in Georgetown and went to Up Against The Wall. He saw this nice blue-and-white DKNY spandex gym suit with a matching baseball cap and thought it would be perfect for Sonya. Even though mostly hood rats wore this, he bought it anyway. Jovan also bought a pair of thick DKNY shades. He went down to the sex store beside Houston's Restaurant and brought a few things and then got back on the highway and headed to Bilal's house.

When Jovan reached Bilal's, the only cars he saw sitting out on the lawn were his MPV van and Meeka's Lexus coupe.

Bilal greeted Jovan at the door.

"Hey, Lal, what happened to all your cars?" Jovan asked him, looking around.

"I went out to Eagle Motors this morning and sold all that shit back to 'em."

"What'd they give you for them?"

"Four hundred fifty thousand all together."

"Damn, Lal, they got over on you," Jovan said, amazed that he had settled for such a low price.

"Not really, Jay. Only by like about fifty to seventy-five thousand."

"Well, anyway I'm glad you got rid of all that shit."

"Me too, Jay. I'm serious about this Atlanta thing."

Jovan went into his van, got out the Hugo Boss sweat suit and New Balance 996 tennis shoes he had bought the other day, and then they went downstairs to talk. Jovan told him about how he had hid under Petey's car and how he heard them talking about robbing and killing him. He talked about how he had shot Petey in his nuts first, and the way he was looking at him when he did it.

"Damn, Jay, you shot him in the nuts?" Bilal said.

"I had to make him know not to ever fuck with my family."

"Yeah, slim, from what you telling me, you straight punished that nigga."

"Yeah, and guess what, Lal? The whole time I was doing this shit, my broad was in the party thinking I'm in the lobby talking to a client."

"Damn, Jay, you smooth as shit!"

"I told you, Lal, I'm like James Bond!"

"Yeah, and outta all the killers in the city, can't none of 'em fuck with you. Now, I've heard of niggas doin' similar shit, but none of it was as smooth as yours, and what makes your work tighter is nobody never knew you did it, and besides that fact, you're a fuckin' lawyer."

"Not yet, Bilal," Jovan said, reminding him once again that he was not a lawyer yet.

"Yeah, but soon though, Jay. Anyway, this is what's up: while you lay the demonstration down on Chicken Wing, I'ma send this money down to Mexico. We got six million now, and I'ma cop with three and hold the other three back. I want you to take the other three with you and put it up over Grandma Price house."

"Why?"

"'Cause I'm 'bout to sell the house."

"Good idea."

"After I get these bricks, it may take me about three weeks to get rid of 'em. Jay, we can make eight point five million on this, and I sell the house for a cool three and a half, plus the three you holdin', that's fifteen million altogether."

"Man, Lal, I got a suggestion."

"What's up, Jay?"

"Look, we already got six plus the house. Why don't we just sell the house and keep the six? That's ten million, and we can step off with that. Fuck the extra five mil. You know the feds try'na get at you, and ain't no sense to keep hustling, slim. We can get the money and step off, go somewhere and do this shit legally, man," Jovan said to Bilal.

"I already got all my clientele waiting for me to get down. Shit, Jay, I already got at least three million as soon as I get the shit. These niggas out here hungry. Niggas ain't got nothing, and the ones who do can't beat my prices, so everybody coming straight to me. Two to three weeks tops, Jay, and we're gone. Remember, I'm the hustler. I know what the fuck I'm doing. I've been doing this shit since '91, and look how far it got us."

"Okay, Lal, whatever you say. It sounds good. Three weeks for an extra five mil. I can't argue with you on that. When you say you copping again?"

"I got these two suitcases full of money. I'm taking 'em to my carriers today. My shit should be here first thing in the morning."

"I need to take a shower, Lal."

"You ain't take no shower over that girl's house?"

"Yeah, but I really wasn't washing up. I was laying down the pipe."

"You a trip, Jay. Use the shower upstairs. It got a Jacuzzi in it too."

"Naw, I don't need all that, but I can use a razor."

"Just look in the cabinet. There's some brand new razors in there."

After Jovan took his shower, he shaved off his goatee and mustache, put on his clothes, and headed for Trinidad. Before he left, he paged Sonya, and she called right back. Jovan thought, *Damn, I musta really put it on her, but little did she know she put it on me also.* Sonya was the baddest and sexiest female he'd ever had, and to be honest, she had the best pussy ever.

"Hello."

"Baby, what's up, sweetheart?"

"You," Sonya said.

"Is that right?"

"Yes, sir, Mr. Price."

"Hey, look, what time you gonna go up Wisconsin Avenue to Chevy Chase Pavillion?"

"What time is it now?"

"Almost twelve thirty."

"We should be finished by two o'clock. You wanna meet me somewhere?"

"If you want you can tell Germain to drop you off at the gym. I'll be finished working out by then."

"Which gym are you going to be at?"

"Finley's boxing gym on Tenth Street."

"Oh, I know were that's at. My li'l brother Tony used to box for Mr. Finley."

"Okay, boo. I'll see you then."

"Oh, Jovan."

"What's up, baby?"

"Don't be letting anybody mess your handsome face up."

"Boo, you must not be hip to my work. I'm like Mike Tyson when it comes down to that," Jovan said, laughing.

It was one fifteen when Jovan got around Trinidad. He pulled his van around the corner at the top of Sixteenth Street and looked around for a second to scope out the scenery. After he saw that there were no spectators around, mainly because it was still early in the day, he jumped in the back seat of the van, pulled out the binoculars he previously had from when he killed Fat Mike, and focused them perfectly.

As Jovan looked down Sixteenth Street, he spotted Chicken Wing's car. He looked over to the left and saw two guys standing in front of their stash house. Chicken Wing was nowhere in sight. A gold four-door Acura Legend pulled up and the driver rolled down the window to talk to the two guys out front. One guy yelled toward the house, and Chicken Wing came out front.

The dudes in the Acura got out. They looked familiar, and as Jovan beamed in closer he could see that it was Big Poo and Fats. They were talking to Chicken Wing. Poo reached in his car, pulled out a bag, and gave it to Chicken Wing. It was obvious this was a drug transaction taking place.

After Poo and Fats left, Chicken Wing stayed out front and sat with the other two guys. Jovan assumed that Chicken Wing had gotten everything Petey left behind and was selling the remaining bricks before he put his lick down on Bilal.

As they sat out front, Jovan was changing his clothes in the back of the van. He put on the DKNY spandex suit he had bought from Up Against the Wall, and he put on the ass pads and fake tittie bra he had bought from the sex store. Jovan then put on the ponytail wig he got from the costume shop in Georgetown, and the matching DKNY baseball cap, pulling the ponytail through the hole in the back of the cap. He looked in the mirror at his disguise and wasn't satisfied, so he put on Meeka's bright red lipstick that he had taken from the cabinet when he took a shower at Bilal's. Jovan then put on the big shades that covered most of his face and looked in the mirror again. This time he was satisfied with what he saw.

It was 1:45, and for the next ten minutes, Jovan was going be a certified hood rat. He popped his stash spot and retrieved the 9 mm and screwed the silencer on it. He placed it in Meeka's Coach bag that he had also taken from Bilal's house.

Jovan got out of his van and walked around Bladens- burg Road, came through the cut on Sixteenth Street, and walked by Chicken Wing and his crew. Jovan knew Chicken Wing was on hood rats hard as hell, and this butt pad made his ass look like Mary J. Blige's. Although he felt humiliated wearing this costume, he knew it would serve its purpose, so he did what was necessary.

As he walked past Chicken Wing, he started switching and Chicken Wing came off the porch and fell right into his trap.

"Damn, she phat as shit. Girl, come here!" Chicken Wing yelled.

As Jovan walked faster up the street, Chicken Wing began to follow. Jovan put his hand into his bag and held onto the gun like glue. As Chicken Wing got closer, Jovan looked around and saw three little girls playing jump rope. This was his chance, and he couldn't blow it. He needed to get this nigga. As the little girls were playing, Jovan started walking faster to get them out of reach.

Chicken Wing started a light jog, saying, "Hey, hold up for a minute. Let me holla at you."

Jovan slowed down, and when he heard Chicken Wing's footsteps getting closer, he waited for a second until Chicken Wing was about two feet away. Jovan didn't panic. He was going to give it to a nigga who truly deserved it. When Jovan felt Chicken Wing's breath damn near on the back of his neck, he turned around and shot Chicken Wing four times in the solar plexus. *Pat-pat-pat-pat.* That way Chicken Wing would instantly lose his breath and wouldn't be able to holla for help.

As Chicken Wing clutched his stomach on the way down to the pavement, Jovan shot him once in the forehead and quickly put his gun back in the bag. He didn't run from the scene. He just began to walk away fast.

As Jovan was walking away, he could hear the little girls laughing. "Ooh! You see that? He tried to touch that girl's butt and she turned around and punched him in his stomach. That's what he get!"

As Chicken Wing was curled up on the sidewalk dead, those little girls thought he was punched in the stomach for touching Jovan's ass. This came out better than Jovan had planned. He headed back to his van, and no one saw him get in. As he drove off, he could see Chicken Wing's crew walking toward him, laughing, not knowing he was through, finished, done like a hot turkey on Thanksgiving.

It was just turning two o'clock, and Jovan pulled up on Ninth Street, took off his costume, wiped the lipstick off of his lips, wiped down the gun, placed everything in Meeka's big Coach bag, and placed the bag in the dumpster.

Jovan walked in the gym through the back way on the Ninth Street side and came out front on the Tenth Street side. Sonya and Germain were just pulling up when he came out on Tenth Street, and when Sonya got outta the car, instantly Jovan was aroused and pleased at what he saw.

She had on a pair of tight Moschino jeans and a T-shirt with some open-toed sandals. She had her long hair in a ponytail. Sonya looked good even in regular gear. Her beauty was natural. She didn't need makeup or nothing. She was a natural queen, ready to claim her spot.

"Hi, Jovan," Germain said.

"Hi, Germain," Jovan said.

"How you doing?"

"I'm fine."

"That's good. How'd you like the party last night?" Germain asked.

"It was cool."

"What about the after party?" She started laughing.

"What after party?" Jovan asked, even though he knew she was insinuating about the explosive sex that Sonya and Jovan had.

"The one on Connecticut Avenue," she said, still laughing.

"Bye, Germain. You talk too much. Open the trunk so I can get my bags," Sonya said as she tried to hide her embarrassment.

Sonya got her bags, and Germain and she said their good-byes.

"Bye, Jovan."

"See you later, Germain. Sonya, let me get them bags for you." Getting her bags out of Germain's truck, he joked, "Damn, girl, you got a lot of shit."

"Wait 'til you see what I got."

As they walked to Jovan's van, Sonya started looking at him funny.

"Jovan, you look different, boo," she said.

"What you mean? I don't appeal to you no more?"

"No, silly, it's just something different about you. You're still fine, but I'm sure you know that already."

"Naw, I only know what you tell me. Now, what's different about me?"

"You look younger."

"Younger?"

"Yeah."

"Oh, I know what you're talking about."

"What?"

"My goatee is gone."

"Yeah, that's it. What you do, shave it off?"

"Naw, I went to a different barber shop this morning and they fucked my shit up, so I told him to shave it off. Don't worry. It'll grow back in two days."

"I didn't say anything was wrong with it. You're still handsome, but—" Then she laughed.

"But what?"

"You look so young."

"Okay, so now you calling me a youngin'?"

"No, baby, you still look nice. I'm just playin'. You ain't mad at me, are you?"

"Naw, I ain't mad."

"'Cause if you were then I got something to cheer you up, but we gotta go to my house to get it," she said with a sly grin on her face.

"Well, in that case, I'm mad as hell," Jovan said, laughing.

"I bet you are, Jovan."

Sonya kissed him once they got in the van. "I missed you all day."

"Me too, but before we go over to your house, I gotta go down the street to my grandma's first."

"Okay, baby."

Jovan's grandma only lived a few blocks down the street from the gym. He still had the three million in the suitcases Bilal had told him to put up. When they got to his grandma's house, he pulled out the suitcases and began to take them in the house.

"What's up, Jovan? You packing up and moving out?"

"Naw, Sonya, this is just some old things I had in storage while I was in school," Jovan said, lying.

Jovan went upstairs and put the suitcases in his room. When he came back downstairs, Sonya and Grandma were kicking it like old friends. Grandma liked Sonya, which was cool, because Grandma usually didn't bond with just anybody. Jovan kissed Grandma, told her he'd be back later, and they left.

On the way to Sonya's, they stopped at a 7-Eleven and Sonya went inside and got a few things. When they got to Sonya's condo, Jovan cooked dinner, which was baked fish and baked potatoes and a tossed salad. They ate, cuddled, and watched TV, but after a while, they went right back to what they were doing the night before.

This time Jovan was less aggressive and more gentle as they made love in the living room first, then the kitchen, the bathroom, and finally they found ourselves on the bedroom floor, dripping from sweat and lovemaking.

Jovan held Sonya against his chest as she gave him little kisses and rubbed her hands over his chest.

"Jovan, you're a king. You know that?" Sonya said.

"If I'm a king, then what that make you?" Jovan asked.

"I don't know if I want you to say it," Sonya said as she playfully pulled the hairs on his chest.

"I rather not say it. I'll just show you."

"You already have, baby. You already have. You treated me like a queen from day one."

"Vice versa," he said.

Sonya then got up, and Jovan loved watching her walk around in the nude with her ass jiggling and titties bouncing. She went into the living room and came back

with her shopping bags. She gave Jovan one and said,
"Here."

"What's this?"

"It's yours. Open it."

Jovan reached in the bag and pulled out a black-and-silver Giovanni Versace sports jacket. First thing he did was look at the tag, which was $2,750.

"Sonya, this is nice, but where you get the money to buy this?" Jovan asked her.

"Jovan, stop playin' with me."

"Okay, then how you know I don't have this jacket already?"

"That jacket was just brought in today. They didn't even have it on the rack, and Arthur, the faggot that works in there, said that it wasn't going to be on sale until two weeks from now. You were at the gym all day. It would have been impossible for you to go all the way up Wisconsin Avenue and meet me back at the gym by two o'clock. Shit, Jovan, I damn near had to pitch a bitch for him to sell it to me."

"Well, boo, thank you very much. I like it. Come here and give me a kiss," Jovan said, pulling Sonya into his arms.

Sonya got back on the floor with Jovan and they kissed and made love all night long.

CHAPTER 21

"Against All Odds"

Bilal sent his carriers down to Mexico by plane, and he was to get a call from them as soon as they landed. At 8:30 p.m., Bilal's connect called and told him that no one had exited the plane with the briefcases. Bilal then called the airport to see if there was a delay in the flight. He was told there was no delay, but another flight was to land at 2:00 a.m. Bilal called his connect back and told them that another flight was to land at 2:00 a.m. and that his carriers, which were Meeka's and Carlos's female cousins, probably missed the flight. The connect said that he would call when they arrived.

Bilal was at home wondering what the hell had happened to the carriers, but he didn't panic even though he was going through a lot. Carlos had been killed, Meeka was pregnant, and his pager was blowing up from niggas who was try'na spend money. Bilal had to keep calling niggas, telling them to hold fast because that shit would be ready soon.

At twelve o'clock, Jovan called Bilal from Sonya's.

Ring, Ring, Ring.

"Hello," Bilal said.

"Damn, Lal, you picking shit up on the first ring."

"Oh, hey, what's up, Jay?"

"I'm just trippin' right now," Bilal said.

"What's up?" Jovan asked.

"You know my people ain't get there yet," Bilal said, worried as shit.

"What time was they supposed to be there?"

"Around eight thirty," he said.

"Well, they mighta had a delay. You call the airport?"

"Yeah, I called. There wasn't any delay, but another flight is due to land around two a.m."

"Cool, then they're probably on that joint."

"Jay, where you at?"

"Over Sonya's."

"You over there again?"

"Yeah."

"Damn, nigga, that pussy must be good. Don't let me find out you fallin' in love, nigga," Bilal said, laughing.

"Go 'head wit' that shit, Lal."

"Jay, did you handle that?" Bilal said, referring to Chicken Wing.

"Most definitely. Like a pro."

"Yeah."

"My smoothest one so far. I'll give it to you raw when I see you."

"Okay, slim. You coming by in the morning?"

"Naw, tomorrow's Monday. You know I gotta work in the morning, man."

"Oh, yeah. I forgot you a big-show lawyer," Bilal said, once again jokingly.

"Not yet, Lal, but soon," Jovan said.

"I see you later, Jay."

"Okay, Lal," Jovan said as he was about to hang up the phone.

"Oh, Jay."

"What's up, Lal?"

"I love you, nigga"

"I love you too, Lal."

It felt good talking to his best friend. Even though he had been through a lot lately, he sounded better, like everything was going as planned. Jovan would be glad when Bilal got that shit and dumped it off fast so they could get the fuck away from there and do their thing legally. He could finish school in Atlanta, start his own law firm, and have a few other businesses on the side.

While Sonya was still asleep, Jovan tried on his new jacket. This joint was tight as fuck. Jovan was going to wear it the next day with his black Versace slacks and white Versace mock neck shirt.

Jovan knew Cindy wanted a nigga to slam meat up in her, 'cause every time he came in, she was always looking at him, complimenting him and shit. Jovan wasn't gonna go at her, though. Shit, Sonya was enough, and right now she was all a nigga needed.

As Jovan went to get a glass of juice outta Sonya's refrigerator, he didn't hear her creep up on him.

"So you couldn't wait to try it on, huh?" Sonya said, smiling.

Jovan turned around fast, butt-ass naked with his jacket on, and said, "So how does it look on me, boo?"

She laughed and said, "It would look better if you had on a pair of pants to go with it."

"Yeah, you're right, but right now since you're up, let me do something that'll make you smile."

"What's that?"

Jovan took off his jacket, blindfolded Sonya, fed her some fruit, then smothered her body with chocolate and licked it all off, not missing a spot. He could tell Sonya loved every bit of his lovemaking, because no matter how he gave it to her, she accepted it with multiple orgasms.

Jovan woke up the next morning around 8:00 a.m. Shit, he had to go to work, and his pager was blowing up, but he was in too much of a rush to look at it. Sonya was taking the day off, so she cooked breakfast while he showered.

After Jovan got out of the shower and looked at his pager, he saw it was Bilal hitting him up with *911*. Jovan immediately called back.

Ring, Ring, Ring.

"Hello," Bilal said.

"Lal, it's me," Jovan said.

"Yeah, Jay. Look, you gotta get over here fast."

"What's up, Lal? You sound worried."

"I can't talk on the phone. Shit's looking fucked up."

"You a'ight?"

"Physically, yeah, but mentally I'm fucked up, Jay."

"Look, I'm on my way, but first I gotta call the office."

Jovan called the office and lied to Mark.

Ring, Ring, Ring.

"Good morning. Law office of Rohon and Robinson," Cindy said.

"Cindy, this Jovan. Is Mark in yet?"

"Yes, Jovan, he just came in."

"Mark, Jovan on line one," Cindy said to Mark.

"Jovan, what's up, buddy?" Mark said.

"Hey, Mark, I'ma be a little late today."

"Okay, Jovan, what time will you be in? You know we have a new case."

"Yeah, I know. I'm going to be working on that while I'm out anyway."

"What are you going to do?" Mark asked Jovan.

"Well, you know the case we got where the guy was supposed to be selling drugs within a thousand feet of a school?"

"Yeah, Jovan, that's the new one."

"Well, I don't think he was within that distance, so I'm going to go out and measure it and take a few pictures."

"That's good, Jovan. Take your time."

"Okay, Mark. I'll see you later."

"All right, buddy."

Jovan kissed Sonya and told her he was in a rush and that he wasn't gonna be able to stay and eat breakfast. She kissed him and told him how proud she was of him for taking such pride in his job. Little did she know Jovan's duty right now wasn't to the law firm; it was to and for his loyalty to his truest friend, Bilal, his nigga for life.

As Jovan drove to Bilal's house faster than normal speed, he got there around nine o'clock. As soon as Jovan came through the door, he knew something terrible had happened.

"C'mon downstairs, Jay," Bilal said, heading downstairs. Bilal's eyes were bloodshot red, and Jovan could tell he didn't get any sleep.

"What's up, Lal?"

"Jay, shit done got twisted. I should have listened to you from the jump," Bilal said, pacing.

"What happened?"

"Well, last night, you know my carriers missed the first flight, or at least that's what we thought."

"Man, Lal, don't tell me them bitches rolled out with the money."

"Naw, Jay, just listen, man. I stayed up all night, and at two a.m. the second plane landed, and my connect tells me ain't nobody get off the plane but some old people."

"What?" Jovan said, still not understanding.

"So what I did was called around looking for my carriers, and nobody gave me any information, so I stayed up pacing the fucking floor all night, wondering what the fuck happened. I even called Customs to see if them bitches had gotten locked up. Then I get a call around seven thirty this morning from the precinct.

"Come to find out these bitches never made it to the airport. That bitch, mu'fuckin' Detective Tony Bridges, was following me when I gave them bitches the suitcases," Bilal said.

"Man, Bilal, I told you that mu'fucka wasn't playing."

"I know, Jay. That white cracker had it out for me ever since I took Orleans Place over."

"Did the bitches tell?"

"Naw, not yet, but who knows what they'll do?"

"Lal, we gotta go."

"I know, Jay, but now ain't the time."

"The fuck you mean now ain't the time? Man, in the next twenty-four hours them people's gonna be swarming the streets looking for your ass. Nigga, fuck that. Pack your shit and let's go!" Jovan told Bilal.

"Jay, I gotta—I mean *we* gotta do something fast."

"What? We already got three million, and I know you still got something stashed in the cut for hard times. Let's go, Lal. I know how these people play."

"Yeah, I got like three hundred thousand over Meeka aunt's house, but that's around Orleans Place."

"So fuck it. We'll send for it when we get to Atlanta."

"Jay, I can't leave now. Meeka's pregnant, and I still gotta get that money, and—" Bilal started, but Jovan cut him off.

"And what? And what, Lal?"

Lal looked Jovan straight in the eyes with all the sincerity he had ever seen and said, "Jay, you gotta kill Detective Bridges."

"What!" Jovan said, shocked by Bilal's request.

"Look, Jay, I ain't never ask you for nothing. I've never asked you to kill nobody for me. You killed them other niggas outta your love for me. Jay, I'm asking you outta love and loyalty. If you want me to do it with you, I'll do it, but you already know I ain't no killer, Jay. This mu'fucka stole our dream from us, and if we don't take care of him now, then he'll haunt us forever."

"Lal, you trippin'. That's a fucking police officer. Do you know the feds will be on your ass for that?"

"Jay, I know we can get away with this. I know we can, man."

When Jovan looked at Lal, he had tears in his eyes and he was looking at the tattoo on his arm which read: *In loving memory of Mal-Mal, my truest love.* At that moment, a sense of guilt came over Jovan.

After all these years, Jovan still felt responsible for Mal-Mal's death. Bilal showed his loyalty to Jovan at the tender age of fifteen, and Jovan had failed him when he let his little brother die. He had always wanted to do something in return; he had always wanted to fix that void in their relationship, because he knew that deep down in Bilal's heart, he held him responsible for Mal-Mal's death. Bilal just loved Jovan too much to show it.

Bilal and Jovan had never talked about what happened that night when Mal-Mal died, but Jovan knew Ms. Cookie went to visit Bilal before she died, and whatever was said on that visit, Jovan would never know. He owed this nigga. He stood on principles of loyalty and honor, and plus, he loved this nigga. He was his only friend. They were like brothers. They made a vow at a young age that would never be broken.

"Okay, Lal, listen good. I'll make a deal with you."

"What, Jay?"

"After I handle this business, we're getting the fuck outta here. Fuck that waitin' around to see what happens shit. We're taking the three million plus the two hundred thousand I got, and we're going to Atlanta, you and me. We'll leave Meeka up here to sell the house and get the three hundred thousand from over her aunt's. Let the house go for three million to get an easy buy. Altogether that's six and a half million plus assets. We sell my BMW, and that's about fifty thousand, plus the jewelry that's about two hundred, and I know you got some jewelry too."

"Yeah, Jay, I got about half a mil in jewelry."

"Okay, altogether that's seven point two million. We take that shit to Atlanta, legalize all of it, and live comfortable and peaceful for the rest of our lives. Lal, that's a one-shot deal, and if you ain't try'na do that, then I'm gone," Jovan told Bilal seriously.

"But, Jay, the feds don't even know who you are. Why you try'na leave?"

"That's good they don't know who I am, and I ain't try'na stick around so they can find out either. So, you in or what?"

"Nigga, you're my best friend and I love you. Jay, you my only family, and I got no choice but to be in," Bilal said.

"Okay, and when we get to Atlanta, ain't no hustling," Jovan said to him.

"It's a deal, Jay."

"Okay, now I gotta put this shit together."

"How you gonna do it, Jay?"

"I dunno yet. Where's that Desert Eagle?" Jovan asked Bilal.

"It's upstairs in the room."

"Go get it."

Bilal went upstairs to get Jovan the gun, and when he came down, Jovan was still in a daze, wondering why the fuck he had just commited himself to do this crime. Damn, Bilal was trippin' like shit, but Jovan laid the deal on the table, and Bilal had agreed with his plans. If everything went as planned, then they wouldn't have nothing to worry about, and plus, Bilal was right; if they left now, Detective Bridges would track them down. He had to be dealt with.

Bilal came downstairs with the biggest gun Jovan had ever seen, a silver .357 Desert Eagle—one shot, one kill.

"Jay, this here is my house gun. I keep it at home for protection."

"How many bullets does it hold?"

"Ten."

"This big-ass gun only holds ten bullets?" Jovan asked, amazed.

"Yeah, Jay, but that's the most powerful gun out there. One shot will send a mu'fucka straight to la-la land."

"Okay, Lal, you got any money on you?"

"Nigga, my name is money. How much you need?" Bilal said.

"About five thousand in big bills."

"You got that, Jay."

Bilal went upstairs to get the money, and as Jovan was downstairs still contemplating his next move, he heard Bilal and Meeka arguing about something. Jovan knew Meeka wasn't trippin' about the money Bilal was giving him. If so, then Bilal didn't have his people in check.

"Here you go, Jay. That's six thousand in case you need extra."

"A'ight thanks. Look, Bilal, I'ma lay these demonstrations down proper. Tomorrow morning get all your things together, and when I call you, be ready to leave."

"Okay," Bilal said. "Oh, Jay."

"Yeah, what's up, Lal?"

"What's up with that girl you've been spending all your time with?"

"Man, Lal, for real I'm diggin' the shit outta her, but right now I got a more serious situation to deal with, and if I gotta leave her behind, then she's staying behind."

"Damn, slim, I wish I could leave Meeka behind, but she's pregnant."

"Bilal, that's your decision. If you think it'd be better for her to stay, then don't bring her."

"I'll think about it, Jay."

"Yeah, well, by tomorrow morning I hope you come up with an answer. Look, I'm gone. I'll talk to you later."

It was 10:00 a.m. when Jovan left Bilal. He drove back to the city so fast that he got there in half an hour. Jovan went straight to Sunny's Surplus and purchased a blue police department T-shirt and hat. He also bought two Metropolitan Police Department stickers and two envelope folders.

Jovan drove down Benning Road to the automobile shop that sold old taxicabs and unmarked police cars with the big spotlight on the side. The dealer was an old man who didn't care if you had ID or not. He just wanted to see cash.

Jovan bought a late model 1986 Caprice Classic, white with black interior, and shiny hubcaps for $4,000. He parked his van on the side street next to Club Chateau and took out all of the things he had bought from the supply store. He put on the T-shirt and hat, took out an ink pen, and wrote *Bilal Davis* on both folders. Jovan then placed a Metropolitan Police Department sticker in the back window and one in front, on the left side by the spotlight.

Jovan was about to drive around to Orleans Place, but before he did, he rode through Eighteenth and D's drug market to test his disguise. When Jovan rolled through the strip, niggas immediately scattered like roaches, and he was satisfied with his disguise. He rolled through Orleans Place looking for any signs of Detective Bridges, because he knew for sure he was out there looking for Bilal.

Jovan spotted an unmarked police car sitting in the alley. He rode past and entered the alley from the other side so that their cars would be opposite each other and that both driver's sides would meet.

As Jovan drove up, he could see that everything was working out perfectly. Detective Tony Bridges was sitting in his car, looking at something in his lap, sipping on some coffee.

Jovan pulled his hat down and pulled up alongside Detective Bridges' car and said, "Hi, how are you? I'm Detective J. Newman from the seventh district."

"Well, Newman, what brings you into my territory?" Detective Bridges said.

"Well, I'm investigating a case of some big drug dealer who's controlling drugs in certain southeast neighborhoods."

"What's his name?"

Jovan held up the two folders with Bilal's name on them. "Bilal Davis. Don't know much about him, though."

"Well, Newman, I think you just hit the jackpot. I'm here looking for the asshole. I just popped two of his carriers this morning," Detective Bridges said.

"Are they talking?"

"Well, yeah, they're cooperating, but I think I need a little time with 'em."

"How long you been out here, Detective . . . Bridges, is it?"

"Tony Bridges. Well, I just came out here about ten minutes ago," he said.

"Yeah, me too. I've been cruisin' up and down these streets. I haven't even stopped to get a bite to eat yet."

"Well, Newman, the best thing I can do for you is a Snickers bar," Detective Bridges said.

"Well, hell yeah. That beats nothin' at all."

As Detective Bridges went into his glove compartment to get the candy bar, Jovan pulled the .357 Desert Eagle from under his leg. This was the only time he was paranoid and nervous. With butterflies creeping in his stomach, he was in a state of oblivion.

Detective Bridges was bringing the Snickers bar up, and as soon as he turned back in Jovan's direction, exposing his face into the barrel of the gun, Jovan shot him one time right between the eyes. *Boom!* The impact of the bullet was so powerful Jovan could practically see brain matter scattered all over the inside of the car.

Jovan then wiped off the gun and threw it in Detective Bridges' car. He pulled off slowly and headed back down Benning Road at a normal speed.

Once Jovan got back to his van, he parked the car, took off the temporary tags, and set the title and registration on fire, because even though it was in a bogus name, he still didn't want to take any chances. He took off the T-shirt and hat and threw everything in the garbage. He then parked the car right behind the dealership so that if the police were ever looking for a white Caprice, they wouldn't bother to look at this one, because the dealership had about twenty white Caprice Classics.

Jovan walked across the street to his van and drove back to work.

"Hello, Cindy," Jovan said, walking into the office.

"Hi, Jovan. How are you?" Cindy asked.

"Fine, thanks. Cindy, is Mark still in his office?"

"Yeah."

Jovan left Cindy's desk and walked into Mark's office, where he was sitting at his desk, going over some paperwork.

"Hey, Jovan," Mark said, looking up from his work.

"Hey, Mark, how you doing?"

"Well, everything's going okay, but I still gotta get this kid's motion straight. Did you measure the distance?"

"Yeah, and from where they're saying he was standing, he was definitely within a thousand feet. It was more like seven hundred feet, to be honest."

"Shit, Jovan, we gotta find some kinda technicality for this kid, because if not, he's a goner."

"Don't worry 'bout that, Mark. Just give me a little time in the library."

"Okay, Jovan. Do your thing."

Jovan went into the library, but he could hardly work because the thought of what he had just done and the anticipation of going to Atlanta was putting him in a state of confusion. He sat back for a moment and got his thoughts together. He then realized that what he had just done was for the better and that from now on his life would be at peace.

Jovan got all the motions ready for Mark. It was a rush job, but it was complete. Mark read over Jovan's motions and asked him to change a few things, so he went back and put his all into them and delivered the best motions he had ever put together, just like the motion that helped set him free when he was in Lewisburg. Mark liked the motions so much that he made copies and placed them on the desk of all the associate attorneys.

Before Jovan left work, he called Sonya at home. He missed her badly and he wanted to ask her to leave with him, but he couldn't.

Ring, Ring, Ring.

"Hello," Sonya said.

"What's up, baby?" Jovan said.

"You, Jovan. I miss you so much."

"Sonya, I've only been out of your sight for a few hours."

"I missed you the moment you walked out that door this morning, and I've been thinking about you all day," Sonya said seriously.

"Me too. You've been on my mind so much I couldn't even work."

"Jovan, we gotta do something about this."

"Ain't too much we can. Or do you got any suggestions?" Jovan asked.

"Yeah, come stay with me tonight," Sonya said, hoping Jovan would agree to spend another night with her.

"I was planning on doing that anyway."

"I bet you were. What time you coming?"

"I'll be there right after work."

As soon as Jovan got off from work, he went straight to Sonya's condo. When he came in, Sonya was butt-ass naked with a pair of red pumps on. His kinda girl, she wanted it morning, noon, and night, and he gave it to her.

While Sonya and Jovan were lying together cuddled up after a long session of lovemaking, they began to talk.

"Hey, my king," Sonya said.

"Yeah, my queen," Jovan answered.

"Have you ever felt something but was scared to address it because of what the outcome may be?"

Jovan wanted to say yes in relation to what he did earlier, but instead he said, "No, boo, if there's something I feel that needs to be addressed, then I'ma shoot my shot."

"Well, Jovan, in that case, I don't know what the outcome of what I'm about to say is gonna be, but I'm prepared."

"Is it something that I need to know?" Jovan asked, curious about what Sonya was about to tell him.

"Maybe, maybe not. Depends on how you take it."

"Well, go 'head and shoot your shot."

"Jovan C. Price, I think I'm falling in love with you," Sonya said, smiling.

"Well, Sonya C. Duncan, I feel the exact same way about you," Jovan said, taking her into his arms.

They hugged tight and kissed as Jovan wiped tears from Sonya's eyes. He knew that he was filling in that missing spot in her life, and he accepted it. They made love again and fell asleep in each other's arms.

***

The next morning, Jovan called Bilal's house, and when he didn't get an answer, he thought he must be out getting shit together so they could leave. The more Jovan looked at Sonya, the worse he felt, because she had told him she was in love with him, but she didn't even know that he was leaving and she would never see him again. As bad as he wanted to tell her he was leaving, he couldn't, because he was in love with her also.

Jovan tried to call Bilal's house again, and still there was no answer. "Where the fuck is Bilal at?" Jovan wondered.

Jovan waited a few more minutes then decided to call Mark and tell him he would be leaving his job and going back to school.

Ring, Ring, Ring.

"Good morning. Law offices of Rohon and Robinson," Cindy said.

"Cindy, get me Mark." Jovan said.

"Oh, hello, Jovan," Cindy said.

"I'm sorry. How you doing, Cindy?" Jovan said, apologizing for his rudeness.

"I'm fine, thank you. Hold on."

Mark didn't pick up the phone; instead, he put Jovan on the intercom.

"Hey, Jovan," Mark said.

"Hey, Mark."

"I got some good news, Jovan."

"What's that?"

"I've got an old client who just got locked up this morning, and he's got plenty of money to give us."

"Who's that?"

"Remember Bilal Davis?"

A sharp pain hit Jovan in his heart. "What? Who?" He did not want to believe Mark had just said Bilal was arrested.

"Bilal Davis, the guy we just got out, he's back in trouble again, and guess what the fool did, Jovan," Mark said.

"What?" Jovan said.

"Do you remember the cop who walked up on us in court that day?"

Jovan damned near dropped the phone. This shit couldn't be real. Instantly, Jovan started to get dizzy, and after a few seconds, he finally pulled himself together, though he was still trembling with fear for what he was about to hear.

"Well, yesterday that cop was killed on one of Bilal's drug strips, and the gun that was used was left on the scene."

Jovan was saying to himself, *I wiped the gun off,* but he said to Mark, "Were there fingerprints on the gun?"

"No, Jovan, no prints, but there was something worse than that."

"What?"

"The gun is registered in his fiancée's name."

Fuck! Why the fuck didn't Bilal tell him that shit? Bilal did say that it was his house gun, but hell, he still didn't tell him it was registered in Meeka's name. Maybe that was what he and Meeka were arguing about. Fuck! Shit was all fucked up now for real.

"Mark, when did they get him?" Jovan asked.

"This morning. They locked him and his fiancée up. This is some major money for us, Jovan. You coming by the office?"

"Yeah. I'll be there in a few."

After Jovan hung up with Mark, he kissed Sonya and got in the shower while she went downstairs to cook breakfast. In the shower, he started getting his thoughts together. Damn, Bilal's shit was all fucked up. Jovan knew he had to leave now for sure. He knew Bilal wasn't saying a word, but Meeka knew Bilal gave him that gun, and he know how scared females could get. They wasn't used to this shit. Plus, she was pregnant, so he knew she was gonna tell.

Jovan had $3.5 million, his van, the 850 BMW, and two hundred thousand worth in jewelry. What he was gonna do was leave Mark a retainer fee, tell him that it was from Bilal's family, pack his shit, and head to Atlanta or maybe California. Wherever he went, it had to be far the fuck away from D.C.

Jovan got out of the shower, ate a little something, and told Sonya he had to leave for work. When he got to the door, he grabbed Sonya and held her tight. Jovan gave her the most passionate kiss ever. He put his heart and soul in it, because this was the last time he was ever gonna touch her.

She looked at him and said, "Damn, Jovan!"

"What, boo?"

"You just kissed me like this is the last time we're ever gonna kiss."

"Naw, boo, I ain't going nowhere. I'll be back later on to finish it up. Bye."

As Jovan walked down the hall, he was crushed that he was lying to Sonya, 'cause if there was anybody he wanted to be with, it was her. He knew he wouldn't find anyone else like her.

CHAPTER 22

"The Unforgiven"

Jovan went straight to Mark's office when he got in, because he wanted Mark to fill him in on everything before he packed his shit. Mark told Jovan everything about their old client, Bilal Davis. He said that he wouldn't be able to see him until about three days from now, after all the processing.

"Okay, Mark, before I get too deep into this case, I first gotta go take care of something at home," Jovan said.

"Okay, Jovan, but hurry back. I'ma need your special services on this one."

"You got it, Mark," Jovan said, leaving Mark's office.

As Jovan was leaving the building, cars pulled up from everywhere. Uniformed and plainclothes officers, even the FBI, had their guns in Jovan's face.

"Don't fuckin' move. You're under arrest!" someone yelled at him with a gun in his face.

"What?"

"Put your hands on your head!" another one yelled.

Now, as Jovan was putting his hands on his head, the Channel 5 News van pulled up. At that time, Mark came out of the building and said, "What the hell is going on?"

Mark knew some of the agents who were arresting Jovan, and one of them said, "Mark, it's a long story. Come on down to Homicide and I'll fill you in."

"Homicide?"

"Yeah, Mark, it's a real messy situation," the agent said to Mark.

As Jovan was being handcuffed and hustled past the TV reporter, he held his head down, trying to cover his face from the camera. He heard the reporter say, "Jovan Price is being arrested for the murder of D.C. Police Narcotics Detective Anthony T. Bridges."

Jovan was taken downtown to the Homicide Division and interrogated. They knew he was in the legal field, so they did everything according to the law. Once Jovan was arrested, he was read his Miranda rights, and while attempting to interrogate him again, they asked him if he wanted to exercise his rights.

Jovan replied, "Yes, I wish to exercise my Fifth Amendment right to remain silent. I also would like to request an attorney from the law offices in which I'm employed," Jovan said.

At that moment, Michelle Robinson walked in and said, "Excuse me, gentlemen. It is obvious that my client wishes not to speak with you. I ask that you leave so I can converse with him in private."

The feds were mad as fuck, but they couldn't do anything. Everything was according to the law.

"Jovan, what the hell is going on?" Michelle asked him once the feds had left the room.

"I don't know, Michelle. That's what I'm trying to figure out," Jovan told Michelle.

"They said they got an indictment on you in two hours, and you know with all the publicity in this case, it's gonna be hard for me to get those grand jury transcripts."

"Yeah, I know, but work your way around and try and get them as fast as you can."

Jovan really didn't need the grand jury transcripts. He already knew that it would say that Meeka snitched. She probably told the police that Bilal gave him the gun and that she argued with Bilal not to give it to him. She would have said that Bilal was at home with her when the murder took place, and that left only one suspect: Jovan.

Jovan's main thing now was that outta all the murders he had committed, he didn't set up an alibi for this one. Fuck, his tightest job ever turned into his sloppiest work overnight.

"Look, Jovan, I'm gonna take the case. Mark can't be your attorney because you're his employee, and he also can't take your co-defendant, because it would be a conflict of interest issue," Michelle said.

"So it's you and me, Michelle?"

"Yeah, and we're gonna ride this thing out until the wheels fall off, Jovan. Well, there isn't too much we can do right now but go ahead and let 'em process you. When you get over to the D.C. jail, we can get everything together. Is there anyone you want me to call?"

"Yeah, listen."

Jovan told Michelle to come closer so he could whisper in her ear. She understood everything he said very clearly, and she nodded her head and left.

Sonya

While I was still at work, Germain came running downstairs as if a bomb was about to go off in the building, screaming, "Sonya, Sonya!"

"What, Germain? What's going on?" I asked her.

"Oh my God, Sonya. Look!" she said, pointing to the television.

"Look at what, Germain? You're scaring me," I said, full of fear that something terrible had happened.

Germain then grabbed my hand and led me to the television. When I looked at the television, I saw Jovan's face. Instantly my whole body went numb as I listened to the news reporters. As I collapsed on the floor, Germain and another coworker had to pick me up and shake me back to reality.

"Oh, my God. Please tell me I'm having a nightmare! This can't be true. Not Jovan. It can't be. Nooo!" I cried out loud as I covered my face with my hands and slid off the wall onto the floor. "No, not the man I'm in love with. This shit ain't supposed to happen to me!" I said as I continued to cry my heart out.

I cried so hard that the pupils in my eyes began to swell. Nothing in the world could explain what I was feeling at that moment, and I mean nothing! I was in such a daze that Germain had to wave her hand across my face as if to wake me from a hypnotic spell.

I took off work and went straight home to wait for Jovan to call and tell me what to do—for him to tell me that this wasn't him, that someone was trying to frame him, that it was some type of lawyer scheme. I wanted him to tell me anything, but just not tell me that it was him. Hell, no. Not Jovan, not my boo. I wouldn't believe it if it wasn't on camera, because that was not his style.

While at home, I cried so much that I cried myself to sleep without eating or drinking anything. I fell asleep in my living room with Jovan's T-shirt on, smelling his scent. I was missing my man, wondering when was he gonna call and tell me to come visit him. Whatever Jovan wanted me to do, I'd do it. If he needed money for a lawyer, I had that. Every visiting day, I'd be there looking fly, representing for my man. If he needed me to run errands, then I'd take all my leave from my job to be his aide. I'd do anything for Jovan. Anything.

Jovan

I was fingerprinted and processed at central cell booking then transported to the D.C. jail, also know as the Lion's Den. I was given an orange jumper, some blue karate shoes (that's what they call 'em) and a bedroll. I was sent straight to the hole and placed on special handling lockdown, mainly because of the publicity in my case. As I was being transported, handcuffed and shackled, through the hallway and escorted by a white-shirt lieutenant, I could hear dudes talking as I went by.

"Slim, ain't that the lawyer dude that was on TV today?" one inmate said.

"Yeah, that's him. They say he put in that work on that policeman," another inmate said. Normally, other dudes would take that as a compliment, but I was ashamed. I never wanted my work to be known.

As I was led to my cell and locked in, I could see everybody standing in their cells looking at me. Some were whispering to each other; others were asking the corrections officer what time they would be able to come out for their one hour of recreation. They could use that time to take a shower or use the phone, play basketball, or just go around and talk to other inmates through the bars.

As I was making my bed, I heard someone call my name. At first I thought it was Bilal, but the voice was different.

"Jovan. Hey, Jovan," the voice said.

"Yeah, who dat?"

"Chaz."

"Who?"

"Li'l Chaz from the Valley!" he said as he screamed through the bars.

"Yeah, nigga. What's up, youngin'?" I said, remember-ing him.

"Ain't shit, slim. I saw you come through the door."

"Then why you ain't say nothin'?"

"I was gonna let you get your shit together first. Look, I'm on detail, and I come out in about ten minutes. I'ma come down and holla at you, 'cause I ain't try'na scream through these bars. You know how the walls got ears around here," Chaz said.

"Yeah, I'm hip," I said, knowing that niggas were eavesdropping.

Chaz was from Valley Green Southeast. When I was doing shit on Whaler Place back in the day, shorty was my number one youngin'. He used to pump coke, and plus, he wasn't no dummy. I had always liked this youngin', but the thing was his ass stayed locked up.

After hearing Chaz tell me he was on detail, I was somewhat glad, because even though this was a lockdown block, they still had at least two detail workers who cleaned up, and in return, they got to come out of their cells for a few extra hours and walk the tier or use the phone. I figured when he came out I'd get him to make a call for me.

When Chaz came out for recreation, he came straight down to my cell and started sliding me shit through the bars. He gave me a bag of soap, toothpaste, lotion, peanut butter and crackers, and some cigarettes so I could buy food off of other niggas' trays, and a big-ass knife with ridges on the side. In D.C. jail, it was a must that one kept a knife on him, or at least somewhere close by.

I put the knife up in a good spot, and shorty and me kicked it for the next hour.

"Yeah, Jay, I saw that shit on TV earlier," Chaz said.

"Yeah, you know that's some bullshit," I said, looking him in the eye.

"Whatever it is, I know you can handle it."

"Hey, Chaz, you see them bring my man Bilal in here?"

"Naw, but I heard they got him in the intake block."

"The intake block?"

"Yeah, you know Bilal got that power in here. These mu'fuckas do whatever he says."

"How long you think they gonna keep me on special handling?"

"Most likely until the publicity dies down. Look, Jovan, I've only got like twenty minutes left. You want me to call somebody for you?" Chaz asked.

"Yeah, hold up." I wrote Sonya's number down and gave it to Chaz. "Tell her I said to call my grandmother and comfort her, and to come see me tomorrow on visits."

"Okay, slim, is that all?"

"Oh, tell her I said I love her."

"A'ight, slim."

"Oh, Chaz," I said before he left to make the call to Sonya.

"What's up, Jovan?"

"Why you in here on lockdown?" I asked him curiously.

"'Cause I had to put that knife in one of them bitch niggas upstairs who wasn't hip to my work."

Sonya

At 10:00 p.m. I received a collect call from the D.C. jail. The operator said, "You have a collect call from Jovan. Press five if you accept."

"Hello, baby. Please tell me that wasn't you," I said anxiously.

"Hold up. This ain't Jovan," a man said.

"Then who the hell is this?" I said.

"I'm a friend of Jovan's. He asked me to deliver you this message."

"Okay, I'm sorry," I said.

"I understand. He wants you to call his grandmother and comfort her. Also, he wants you to come visit him tomorrow, and he told me to tell you he loves you," Chaz said.

At that moment, tears gushed outta my eyes like a waterfall. "Tell him that I'll be there and that I love him also."

"I sure will."

"Thank you, and hey, I'm sorry for cursing at you," I said, embarrassed.

"It's okay. Like I said, I understand," Chaz said.

The call I had been waiting for all night had finally come through, and it wasn't even Jovan. Even though it wasn't him, the message that he sent still rang in my ears like church bells.

Jovan

The next morning, I was told to get ready for a visit. Visiting hours didn't start until 1:00 p.m. and it was only 9:30 a.m. I thought it must have been Michelle coming to talk about the case. Well, whoever it was, I was ready, because I had to get a message to Bilal to get me outta this hole.

The lieutenant cuffed and walked me to the visiting room, and when I came through the door, they led me to the same conference room I'd interviewed Bilal in. It was Michelle and Andy, Mark's investigator.

"Hey, Jovan, how they treating you?" Michelle asked me.

"Like shit. They got me locked down because of all the publicity."

"Don't worry 'bout that. I'll call the jail and pull a few strings for you," Andy said.

"Okay, Andy. Thanks."

"Now, Jovan, this is it. The prosecutor says she got some concrete evidence on you, but she's not gonna disclose that information to me. She and I don't get along that well, so I'ma have Mark try and pull it outta her no later than within the next couple of weeks so we'll have it," Michelle said.

"Good."

"Also, I called the number you gave me. Everything is okay on that end."

"What 'bout the lab reports on the gun?"

"I have that. There are no fingerprints, and only one shot was fired. The gun is registered to a Ms. Tameka Gonzales," Michelle said.

"That's all it says?" I asked Michelle.

"Yes."

"What about the grand jury transcripts?"

"We're still working on it. Have you seen your co-defendant, Bilal Davis, yet?"

"Naw, they got him in the intake block."

"Don't worry. You'll get to see him soon. Maybe in a week or so."

"Yeah, try to work that out."

"Ain't too much we can do right now but wait for this evidence the prosecutor has and the grand jury transcripts," Michelle said.

"Okay, Michelle. Oh, how's Mark handling this?" I asked, afraid to hear her answer.

"He's pissed because of how he used to brag on you, and now he's got a few dickheads clowning him about you."

"Tell him I'm sorry, but this is something that didn't happen. It's some type of mistake."

"I'm sure he knows that. Oh, Jovan, Cindy ain't taking it to well either," Andy said.

"What do you mean, Andy?"

"She's been crying, asking about you all day," Andy said, laughing. "Hey, tell me something, Jovan. Did you tap that ass?"

"Naw, Andy, I don't confuse work with pleasure."

CHAPTER 23

"6 Months Later"

Sonya came to visit Jovan every visiting day, but this day was the most intense visit they had. Jovan's case was still at a standstill, and his trial was not going to start for two weeks. The prosecutor was still holding back on evidence, and Michelle couldn't get her hands on those transcripts. Jovan was prepared, because no one could place him at the scene, not even Meeka. The only thing she knew was that Bilal gave him the gun, and he could argue that, because she wasn't downstairs when Bilal gave it to him.

Jovan had only seen Bilal once, and that was in the infirmary. He said everything was cool on his end and that they should get a severance on their case. Jovan had already done that, because there wasn't no sense in both of them going on the same trial. They each had a better chance going in there alone.

Jovan talked to the lieutenant, who said that the publicity on his case was down and that he'd let him out into population the next day. When Jovan talked to Sonya on the phone, he asked her not to come to his trial and to stay home and wait for his calls. She wasn't try'na hear it, but Jovan being the man, he had to put his foot down.

At twelve o'clock, the lieutenant came to Jovan's cell. At first Jovan thought he was coming to tell him to pack up so he could go to population, but instead he told him to get ready for a visit. Now, Jovan had already seen Michelle and Andy yesterday, and Sonya's visits didn't start until 1:00 p.m., so who the hell could it be? He knew it wasn't the Homicide Division, 'cause they already knew he wasn't talking.

Jovan got ready for the visit and was escorted to the visiting room. When he came through he saw Mark, Michelle, and Andy. This was the first time Jovan had seen Mark since he was arrested.

When Jovan entered the room, everyone was quiet. Mark did the talking.

"Look, Jovan, I had to sell my soul to get you this," he said. There was a big yellow envelope on the table, and as Jovan reached for it, Mark grabbed his hand and said, "Don't look at it in here. Take it back to your cell, and when you finish, make sure this envelope and its contents self-destruct."

They got up to leave, and Jovan asked, "That's it?"

"Yeah, Jovan, trial starts in two weeks, so get ready to rumble."

Jovan was so eager and curious to open the envelope. He pressed for the guards to take him back to his block.

"Hey, C.O., my visit over wit'. I'm ready to go back!"

"Okay, here I come. Hold up. You're on special handling. You gotta wait for a white shirt," the C.O. said.

Lazy bitch, Jovan thought as he began to get mad. A lieutenant was walking past, so he said, "Excuse me, Lieutenant, my visit is over with. Can you take me back to my block?"

"C'mon. You're Price, right?"

"Yeah."

"Well, you know you're going to population today," the lieutenant said.

"Oh, yeah," Jovan said, glad to be getting out of solitary confinement.

"Have your shit packed by three o'clock."

"Okay."

As soon as Jovan was placed back in his cell, he opened the envelope. There were only two pages. The first one read:

> *On May 12, 1994 Defendant Jovan C. Price was indicted in Washington, D.C. Superior Court for the following murders in the 1st degree:*
>
> *Count 1: Michael A. Jones, aka Fat Mike*
>
> *Count 2: Peter C. Milligan, aka Petey*
>
> *Count 3: Corey L. Washington, aka Chicken Wing*
>
> *Count 4: Anthony T. Bridges, Detective MPPD 6th District*
>
> *Additional Summary: It is also known that Defendant Jovan C. Price committed several other murders dating back at least to 1985.*

As Jovan read off his indictment, his heart started beating so fast that he thought he was gonna have a heart attack. He hurriedly moved to the next page. It read:

> *It is May 21, 1994 and this is the interrogation and debriefing of Bilal Ali Davis. Mr. Davis informed that he was the head of a multi-million dollar drug operation and that Mr. Jovan C. Price was his hit man. Mr. Davis said that most of the weapons used in the murders committed by Mr. Price were discarded, and that Mr. Price was an extremely careful professional. Mr. Davis gave extreme detail of most crimes Mr. Price committed, but acknowledged that he was not present at*

*any dating from 1992 on up. He informed us
that Mr. Price committed a murder in 1985
in his presence, and that he, Mr. Davis, was
arrested and did time in Cedar Knoll and Oak
Hill Youth Division for that crime.*

At that very moment, Jovan didn't think there was any definition in the dictionary that could describe his pain. He dropped to his knees, the same knees he dropped to when Bilal got Juvenile life for a crime he had committed; the same knees he dropped to when Mal-Mal and Ms. Cookie died. Jovan couldn't stop the tears from coming down his face, because he realized that Bilal had tricked him. He now knew that Bilal still held him responsible for his little brother's death.

Jovan got up off the floor, tore up the envelope and papers, and washed his face. When he looked in the mirror, he saw a reflection, a true resemblance of his father. Then those jewels that were handed down to him as an innocent child came back: *trust no one, master your condition,* and *keep the suckers within the bounds of moderation.* Those precious jewels were given to Jovan at a tender age, preparing him for the future. He always knew that he'd have to live by them, but when it came down to Bilal Ali Davis, they didn't apply when they should have.

It was now one o'clock and Sonya was like clockwork when it came down to Jovan's visits. She'd be the first one in line outside. She told himm that she came at least an hour early just so she could get in first and get her full visit.

"You got a visit, Price!" the lieutenant called out to him. "Cuff up," he said.

When Jovan got into the visiting room, Sonya was looking good as shit. She always came fly, representing her nigga to the fullest, and she had the deepest glow ever. Jovan knew this woman loved him, and he knew he loved her, but it would break her heart to know that he was a cold-blooded killer, that he killed outta loyalty and love, and that his best friend whom he killed for was now doing a Houdini trick.

"What's up, boo?" Jovan said, picking up the phone to speak, while at the same time looking at Sonya and wishing that they were able to touch each other instead of speaking on these damn phones.

"I love you, Jovan," Sonya said, picking up her phone also.

"I love you too."

"Good. Now that we got that outta the way, Jovan, I wanna ask you a question."

"What, boo?"

"Why don't you want me to come to your trial?" she asked, still not understanding why he would not want her there by his side.

"I have my reasons and that's it. I don't wanna talk about that," Jovan said, not wanting to reveal the reason why he didn't want her at his trial. "My trial starts in two weeks, and every day after trial, I'll call to inform you of what's going on. I promise."

"Okay, Jovan, but I miss you. I miss you so much," Sonya said, not wanting to spend the little time they had together arguing.

"I miss you too, Sonya."

They talked for a while, and then all of a sudden, Sonya got up out of her seat.

"Jovan, I love you very much, probably more than you'll ever know."

"I love you too, baby, now sit down," Jovan said to her, wondering why she was standing up all of a sudden.

"No, Jovan, I have something to ask you," she said, still standing.

"What is it, and why can't you ask me sitting down?" Jovan said.

"Because, Jovan, what I have to ask you is very important."

"Okay, boo, go 'head. Ask your question."

"First, I want you to look at me in my eyes and know that what I'm saying is true and from the bottom of my heart."

As they talked through the glass, Sonya got down on one knee in the visiting hall in front of everybody.

"Jovan Conrad Price, will you marry me?" Sonya asked.

Jovan thought, *What the fuck is she trippin' off of? I'm facing life and she's proposing to me.* He had never seen or heard of this shit before.

"Sonya, get up off the floor. Everybody's looking at you. You're embarrassing yourself," Jovan told her.

"So what? I love you, and I want to be your wife. I'm not getting up until you give me an answer," Sonya said, refusing to get up off her knee.

"Look, Sonya, there's a lot of shit about me that you don't know," Jovan told her.

"So what, Jovan? I don't care about that. There's a history with me also, but I love you so much that I'm willing to bury it for you."

"I don't think yours is worse than mine."

"Trust me, Jovan, if it ain't, it's running neck and neck."

"Sonya, if I marry you, there are certain things you must do."

"Whatever it is, Jovan, I'll do it. Whatever it takes, I'll do it baby. I know you've got skeletons in the closet. Who doesn't? I've got some too, baby. Whatever you try'na do, I'ma follow that pattern. You're the king, baby," Sonya said, meaning every word of what she was saying, because she loved Jovan more than life itself.

Sonya's eyes got watery as she stayed there on one knee. "Baby, can I get an answer?"

"You sure you're ready for that?" Jovan asked her, still unsure of his answer.

"Yes, baby."

"You know if I marry you, you gotta be down to the end?"

"Like I said, Jovan, I'll do anything, even if it involved anything like Bonnie and Clyde and when I say that, nigga, I mean it."

"Sonya, you gotta be down with the move."

"Baby, you lead, I'll follow, and if you fall down, I'm picking you up and carrying you the rest of the way, even if it breaks my back. Now, what's the move, and can I get an answer?"

"Yes, boo, yes, I'll marry you," Jovan finally said to her.

Tears started gushing outta Sonya's eyes. "Baby, you are my life, and I vow with my life that I'll be by your side through any storm."

"Okay, boo, I love you too. Now will you please get up off the floor?"

After their visit was over, Jovan was escorted back to his cell. It was two o'clock, and since he had packed his shit earlier for population, he did about fifteen hundred push-ups, a thousand crunches, and a few bend-and-reaches. He was thinking about how he was gonna get out of this shitty situation.

Jovan was hoping they would put him in the same block as Bilal, and then he could really figure it out. Jovan wanted to look him in his eyes, because the fact that he did this to him made him feel like he was half dead—not his man, his best friend, his only family. Jovan had killed at will for this nigga. He had protected him and fed and clothed this nigga when his dopefiend-ass mother wouldn't. How the fuck could he empty his brain and sell his soul like that? What Bilal did to Jovan was unforgiving. He had committed the greatest sin.

The lieutenant came down to the cell and said, "Price, you got your stuff ready?"

"Yeah, I'm ready. Where I'm going?"

"You're going to NE three, cell sixty-three."

As soon as Jovan got to the block, the first people he saw were Li'l Rat Man from Glass Manor and Li'l Hog from down Southwest. They were running the block. These niggas had all types of tennis shoes, commissary knives, street food, weed, and liquor. They said they had a cellular phone, but the police took it when they got shook down last week. Damn, Jovan would have loved to use that cell joint right about now.

It was almost 2:15, and the C.O. came and started calling for Jumah, the Muslim prayer service.

"Jovan," Li'l Rat said.

"What's up, Rat?" Jovan said while lying on his bunk.

"Look, if you try'na see your man Bilal, you better get on that Jumah list."

Jovan went over and signed the Jumah list and asked Li'l Rat, "When are they gonna take us up there?"

"They be back in 'bout five minutes. What size shoe you wear?" he asked.

"I wear a nine."

"Hog, get Jovan a pair of them Jordans out my room when you come up."

"Thanks, youngin'," Jovan said.

"Ain't shit, slim. I got a lot of that shit, and plus, you a real nigga. You used to look out for me when I was a young nigga," Li'l Rat said.

Jovan went downstairs to his cell and got the knife that Li'l Chaz had given him. This was a big-ass knife, and it had ridges on the side like a hacksaw.

The C.O. came back into the block and said, "Everybody who signed the Jumah list, let's go, front and center!"

"Jovan, you got a joint?" Rat asked.

"Yeah, I'm a'ight, Rat."

"Stand on this side so he won't pat you down," Rat said, pointing to the opposite wall from where Jovan was standing.

Jovan stood on the side of the Sally-Port and watched the C.O. pat down all the dudes in front; then he crept back in like he had already been searched. On the way to Jumah, Jovan let everybody walk ahead of him so he would be in the hallway damn near by himself.

As Jovan turned the corner to where the Jumah services were held, he heard the most beautiful chanting sound ever. There wasn't a crack in the voice, and it sounded milky and smooth. As he got closer, he heard it louder, "Allahu-Akbar. Allahu-Akbar." When Jovan peeped through the door, he saw where the sound came from. Young Rico, aka Ali Katabb, was standing in the middle of the floor with his hands behind his ears, singing this beautiful song. Rico was back from Allenwood Penitentiary on his appeal. Later, Jovan came to find out that this song wasn't really a song. It was a call to prayer for Muslims.

As Jovan entered the room, he looked around for Bilal, and when he looked to his left, he saw him in the corner making Salat, the Muslim Prayer. Jovan always knew Bilal was a Muslim, but he had never seen him do the prayer. Bilal's father, Saleem, was Muslim, and if Saleem knew that his son was a cold ho, he'd probably kill him himself.

At Jumah, everybody came because this was where co-defendants met up to discuss their case. This was where niggas passed shit off, or it was just something else to do other than be in the block. Only a few dudes in there were true Muslims. Most of these niggas were faking it, just trying to be accepted, and were punks for real—like Bilal, for instance.

Jovan went to the back of the room and found a seat. When Bilal finished his Salat, he looked up and saw Jovan in the back of the room. Bilal's eyes were like Pop Rocks, like he had just seen a ghost or something. He put his shoes on and headed toward Jovan with a fake-ass smile. He had on his D.C. jail jumper, a black kufi, a platinum chain with the word *Allah* in Arabic writing, a pair of Cartier glasses, and some brown suede butta Timberland boots.

When Bilal came over, Jovan greeted him. "Damn, nigga, even in jail you lookin' slick."

"Yeah, you know me, Jay. Shit don't stop 'cause the nigga got knocked," Bilal said.

"That's right, slim."

"So, what is your lawyer saying, Jay?" Bilal asked.

"Oh, they bullshittin'. They're saying that the prosecutor got some damaging evidence on me," Jovan said.

"Did they give it to you?"

"Give me what?"

"The evidence."

"Oh, naw, they ain't try'na disclose that info to me."

"So what else they say?"

"They said somebody gave the feds some type of info on me or something."

At that moment, Bilal tightened up. "Who they say it was, Jay?"

"I don't know, Lal. They won't tell me."

"You sure they ain't gonna tell you, Jay?"

"Naw, they ain't gonna tell me. So who you think it is, Lal?" Jovan asked him, already knowing the answer.

"I dunno, Jay, but hey, don't even worry about that. We're gonna beat this shit. Did they give you another indictment or anything?"

"Naw, the only indictment I got said accessory or conspiracy to commit murder. Why you ask?"

"'Cause I heard that they be try'na fuck with niggas and give 'em another indictment right before their trial."

"Oh, naw, they can't indict me on anything 'cause you the only nigga I've ever done something with, Lal, and that was in '85. Everything else I've done by myself with no witnesses. You're the only one I've told about my work, Lal, and I know your loyalty with me, so hell naw, they can't indict me on nothing."

"Yeah, Jay, you're right."

As Lal sat there and lied to his face and tried to compose himself, Jovan smiled and said, "Lal, you know I love you, right?"

"Yeah, Jay, I love you too."

Jumah was now over, and everybody was leaving. Bilal and Jovan stayed behind so that they could walk the hall and get a little extra time in.

"What block you in, Jay?" Bilal asked.

"NE three. Where you at, Lal?" Jovan said.

"NW three."

"Oh, we're going the same way then."

As they walked into the hallway, Jovan could see that it was only Bilal and him. As Bilal kept talking, Jovan knelt down as if he was tying his shoe and let Bilal walk in front of him. Jovan then reached into his jumpsuit and grabbed hold of his knife as if his palm was dipped in Crazy Glue. He held onto its handle with the tightest grip ever.

Now, Bilal was cut the fuck up, two hundred pounds, big as a brick house, and he also was the boxing champion down Oak Hill, so if Jovan made any mistakes, he would capitalize on that and kill him with his own knife. No matter how many blows Jovan gave him, his first blow had to be his best, most vicious and vital blow.

Bilal was positioned about one foot in front of Jovan on his left side, and since Jovan was right-handed, that was perfect. He wasn't nervous or scared; he was just cautious because he knew that this was a once in a lifetime golden opportunity.

Jovan sent his first blow with the hardest hook shot he ever took, and the knife went straight through Bilal's jugular vein. As Bilal held his neck, trying to stop the blood that was squirting out like a water fountain, Jovan's second blow went straight through his heart. Jovan pushed the knife with such force that when he pulled it out, strings of flesh were hanging off.

Bilal fell to the floor with blood gushing out of his neck and heart, and when he hit the floor face first, Jovan already knew he was dead—but he wasn't finished with him. He had to teach him a lesson. Jovan had to let him know that he lived and would be willing to die by the code of loyalty. He held his knife high in the air with both hands and drove it right in the middle of his back.

He then wiped the handle of the knife off and left it in his back, and before he turned around, he spit on him and said, "Now you know how it feels to be stabbed in the back, mu'fucka!"

As Jovan walked back to his block, no one was in sight. He held back the tears, the pain, and the hurt and held tight to the jewel his pops had given him: *Trust no one.*

CHAPTER 24

"The Cruelest Lie"

Sonya

Trial started for my fiancé, and I'd been up all night anticipating this day. Now that it was finally here, I eagerly wanted it to go away. Jovan had asked me not to come to his trial. He said he had his reasons. Like I told you before, I was from Trinidad NE, and there wasn't too much you could get past me. Obviously, Jovan was hiding something from me, and I wanted to know what it was. Was it that he had another woman, maybe a wife and child? Was it that something may come out in trial that would hurt me or make me ashamed of him? I didn't know what it was, but Jovan needed to know that no matter what, I still loved him to death and wanted to be with him for the rest of my life.

CHAPTER 25

"Get Ready to Rumble"

Jovan

My trial started, and I couldn't sleep all night long. I was back in the lockdown special handling block 'cause when the lieutenant came to my block and told me that my co-defendant had been killed in the hallway, I immediately told him that I wanted to go back to lockdown. I told him that if anybody wanted to do something to Bilal for whatever reason, then they might try to do something to me.

He understood and escorted me back to special handling. While in lockdown, I still exercised every day. I did push-ups, crunches, sit-ups, and jumping jacks, and I also got my trial strategy together. I subpoenaed everyone I felt necessary that would aid in my defense. I knew that the government's star witness was Bilal and his earlier grand jury testimony, but with him not there to testify to that, if they tried to use it, all I had to say was the he lied about everything he said I did, he was really the perpetrator, and he wanted to destroy me because I wouldn't take his case on the murder of Detective Bridges.

As I prepared to go into the courtroom, I was wearing a suit that my attorney, Michelle, brought me. Sonya had dropped it by the office for me the day before. It was a black silk Armani suit, white shirt, and tie to match. She also bought me a pair of Armani glasses that would give me that distinguished, innocent look. I was brought in by the marshall and sat at the table opposite the prosecutor.

At my table was my attorney, Michelle Robinson, and Andy, sitting there with their briefs, reading notes. Mark was in the audience seated right behind us, because if there was any suggestion he had, he'd be able to reach over and say it. The courtroom was packed with all types of lawyers, paralegals, and secretaries. The trial was cut off from the public at my attorney's request, and only a few important people were allowed in. I told Sonya and Grandma not to come and that I'd fill them in daily about the trial.

As I sat down, I acknowledged Mark first, and he winked and gave me a thumbs up.

"Good morning, Jovan," Michelle said.

"Good morning, Michelle."

"Hey, Jovan," Andy said.

"How you doing, Andy?"

"Are you ready to rumble?" he asked.

"Yeah, let's get this mess over with."

"Okay, buddy, put on your hard hat."

"I had it on a long time ago, Andy."

The bailiff stood and said, "All rise. This is the court-room of Judge Patricia A. Queen."

After Judge Queen came into the room and was seated, she motioned for everyone else to be seated. "Thank you. You all may be seated. Prosecutor Debra White, do you wish to proceed in this case?"

"Yes, I do, Your Honor. First I would like to present to the court and the jury that Mr. Jovan C. Price is the sole perpetrator in the murders of Michael A. Jones aka Fat Mike, Peter C. Milligan aka Petey, Corey L. Washington aka Chicken Wing, and Anthony T. Bridges, a detective for the Metropolitan Police Department," the prosecutor stated.

"Okay, Miss White, is that all?" the judge asked.

"Yes, Your Honor," the prosecutor said.

"Okay, now would the defense like to say something?" the judge asked Michelle.

Michelle stood and said, "Yes, Your Honor. I would like to present to the court that my client is innocent of all charges, and that if there is any physical evidence linking my client to any of these crimes, I ask that it be known to the court now."

"I would like to ask that the government produce its evidence that is requested by the defense," the judge requested.

"I call into evidence the grand jury testimony of Bilal Ali Davis," the prosecutor said.

The judge asked, "Is Mr. Davis here today?"

"In fact, no, Your Honor, Mr. Davis was subsequently killed two weeks ago while incarcerated at the D.C. jail," the prosecutor answered.

"So you're saying you're ready to proceed in this trial with only the transcripts of a grand jury proceedings?" the judge said.

"Well, yes and no, Your Honor. I have certain witnesses that will corroborate Mr. Davis's testimony transcripts," the prosecutor said.

"Okay, you may hand that discovery over to the defense," the judge said.

When the prosecutor handed over the discovery, I read all the testimony Bilal had given. He told these people our life story, but as I read more, I could see that the only physical evidence that Bilal gave was the 1985 murder, and I wasn't even charged with that one. Also he said that he gave me the .357, which was registered in Meeka's name, but that was argumentative. That didn't prove I killed Detective Bridges. It only proved he gave me the gun that was later used in a homicide, and I could twist that.

Also in discovery was the witness sheet. The only witness the government had other then Bilal was Tameeka Gonzales. The prosecutor was lying, saying she had other witnesses.

All day long the prosecutor and my attorney presented their opening statements. Michelle was on point with everything she told the jury: that there was no physical evidence that would link me to Bilal, no photos of us together, no phone taps, no fingerprints, nothing but the fact that I was hired as a paralegal on his previous case. I was proud of the way Michelle handled things that day.

Sonya

I went into the courtroom and grabbed a seat all the way in the back, outta Jovan's sight. It wasn't that hard for me to get in. I told the guard at the door that I was a paralegal working on this case, and he let me in. When Jovan came out he looked nice. He didn't look like he was on trial for murder; he looked like the attorney representing a client for murder. I could see that the Armani suit and tie I picked out looked very nice on him, and he looked conservative with those glasses on.

As the prosecutor was saying all these terrible things about my fiancé, I knew they weren't true. Jovan couldn't have done all those things. He didn't have time to, because most of the crimes they said he committed were on dates and times when he was with me. I knew for sure it wasn't true.

Jovan

As soon as I got back to the D.C. jail, Chaz came down to my cell.

"How it go today, Jovan?" he asked me.

"It went okay, Chaz."

"That's good to hear. By the way, you need anything while I'm out?" Chaz asked.

"Naw, the C.O. supposed to let me out for my rec in about ten minutes."

"A'ight, I'ma holla at you later."

"Okay, Chaz."

When the C.O. let me out, I went straight to the telephone and called my fiancée.

Ring, Ring, Ring.

"Hello," Sonya said.

"You have a collect call from Big Daddy. If you wish to accept, press five," the operator said.

Sonya pressed five and said, "Yeah, I got your Big Daddy."

"What's up, boo?" I said to her.

"Nothin'. I'm just sitting here missing you," she said.

"Yeah, me too."

"So how'd it go today, baby?" Sonya asked.

"Oh, everything went smooth. I'll be home to you in no time."

"I wish you'd hurry up, 'cause my pussy is throbbing for your dick."

"How do you think I feel?"

"I don't know, Jovan, but if it's anything like me, then I know you're in misery."

"You miss a nigga like that?"

"Hell yeah, boo!"

"So how was your day at work?"

"Baby, I took off for two weeks. I'm thinking about not ever going back."

"You can't just quit like that, Sonya. You gotta have something to fall back on."

"I know, baby, but I'm just so frustrated."

"Pull yourself together, boo. Everything's gonna be fine. You're my queen, remember?"

"Yeah, and you're my king."

Sonya

Jovan called me at 6:00 p.m. and we talked for a while. It was good to hear my baby's voice. I wanted to tell him how good he looked that day in the suit I bought him, but I couldn't, 'cause he didn't know I was there.

Jovan had told me not to worry and to pull myself together. How could I not worry when he'd been charged with four murders, three of 'em I was not supposed to know anything about? Why was he hiding them from me when I knew he was innocent? He was with me when those crimes were committed—well, not all of 'em, but the first three he was with me.

Damn, Jovan told me there were things I didn't know about him. Well, there was something Jovan didn't know about me, but regardless of that, I still loved him no matter what.

Jovan

It was the fifth day of my trial, and everything that the prosecutor presented had been batted down by my attorney. Michelle had been doing a tremendous job. On the fifth day the government said they had a witness to corroborate Bilal's grand jury testimony, and my attorney said they had witnesses that could prove I was somewhere else during the time of those crimes. The judge informed them that she would hear the defense first, and then the government could call their witness.

Judge: Okay, Ms. Robinson, would you like to call your first witness?

Michelle: Yes, Your Honor, but first may I have a brief moment with my colleagues?

Judge: Go right ahead.

Michelle: Okay, Your Honor, I'm ready to call my first witness in the defense case.

Judge: Call your witness.

Michelle: I'd like to call to the stand Ms. Kathy Morris.

Bailiff: Ms. Morris, do you swear to tell the truth, the whole truth, and nothing but the truth so help you God?

Kathy: Yes, I do.

Michelle: Ms. Morris, can you please state your full name and occupation?

Kathy: My name is Kathy Marie Morris, and I'm employed as a waitress at Phillips Restaurant.

Michelle: Ms. Morris, were you working on the day of May 8, 1994?

Kathy: Yes, I was.

Michelle: And what were your hours?

Kathy: From 11:00 a.m. to 7:00 p.m.

Michelle: Ms. Morris, at any time between the hours of 12:30 p.m. and 3:00 p.m., did you see my client, Mr. Jovan C. Price, enter the restaurant?

Kathy: Yes, I did.

Michelle: And what time did you notice this person?

Kathy: A young lady and he came in around 12:30 p.m. I was assigned as their waitress, and I seated them out on the patio.

Michelle: How long did the couple stay at the restaurant?

Kathy: They stayed a while, and it was obvious that they were in a heavy conversation, because they stayed longer than the normal customer would stay.

Michelle: Do you know what time they left?

Kathy: Yes. It was exactly 3:00 p.m.

Michelle: Ms. Morris, at any time did you see the defendant here get up and leave the restaurant?

Kathy: No, not at all.

Michelle: Thank you, Ms. Morris. That'll be all.

Judge: Ms. White, do you want to cross-examine the witness?

Prosecutor: Yes, Your Honor, if I may.

Judge: Go ahead.

Prosecutor: Ms. Morris, do you know the defendant?

Kathy: No, I do not.

Prosecutor: Well, can you tell me how, out of all the customers you see and after months, how could you be exact with the time and identity of this person?

Kathy: First of all, I was their waitress, and Mr. Price was kind when they came in. He asked to be seated while I was still telling them the menu. Also, he's a very handsome man, and I was attracted to him. It's hard to forget a face when you're attracted to them.

Prosecutor: Thank you. That's all, Ms. Morris. You may step down.

Michelle: Your Honor, I would like to ask that the government strike the murder of Michael A. Jones off the defendant's indictment. The government hasn't met its burden of proof, and it is clear that the defendant wasn't at the scene of the crime.

Judge: If the government doesn't have anything concrete to meet its burden, I'll have no other choice but to strike the charge according to the law.

Prosecutor: Well, Your Honor, my star witness is deceased, and no, I don't have any other witness to meet the burden, but as the trial continues, I'm sure I can find something.

Judge: Well, Ms. White, we're in the middle of trial now and you haven't found anything yet, so I'm not going to waste any time on this. I'm going to strike this charge, and if you find some concrete evidence in the near future, you can always bring the case back before this court.

Prosecutor: Thank you, Your Honor.

Judge: Now, Ms. Robinson, do you have any other witnesses to call?

Michelle: Yes, I do, Your Honor. I would like to call a witness to clarify that on the weekend of May 16th, my client was in Orlando, Florida, in Disney World with his girlfriend and child. There is no way possible he could have murdered Peter C. Milligan and Corey L. Washington.

Judge: Okay, Ms. Robinson, you may call your witness, but first let me tell you something. I'm not going to keep striking these charges all day. This is a trial, and in the middle of trial, anything can develop.

Michelle: Okay, Your Honor, I understand completely. I would like to call my second witness for today, Keda Jones.

Bailiff: Ms. Jones, do you swear to tell the truth, the whole truth, and nothing but the truth so help you God?

Keda: I do.

Michelle: Ms. Jones, please state to the court your full name and occupation.

Keda: My name is Makeda Ivory Jones, and I'm an employee at Erotica Hair Gallery.

Michelle: What is it that you do at the Erotica Hair Gallery?

Keda: I'm a hairstylist as well as a manager.

Michelle: Ms. Jones, can you tell the court how you know the defendant, Jovan Price?

Keda: Yes. He's the father of one of my sons.

Michelle: Ms. Jones, were you with your son's father during the weekend of May 16th?

Keda: Yes, I was. In fact, my son and me were with his father on my son's birthday, which was May 16th.

Michelle: And where did you go for your son's birthday?

Keda: Jovan took us to Disney World in Orlando, Florida.

Michelle: And how long did you stay?

Keda:We stayed for two days, Friday and Saturday, and we left Sunday morning.

Michelle: Your Honor, I'd like to exhibit Ms. Jones's testimony in showing that my client wasn't even in the city of Washington, D.C. during the time of these crimes.

Judge: It is accepted, but first let's see if the government wants to cross examine.

Prosecutor: Well, yes, I do, Your Honor, and I'd appreciate it if the defense lets me do so before entering any kind of showing to the court.

Michelle: You can do whatever you like, Ms. White. I'm just being a lawyer.

Prosecutor: I'm sure you are.

Judge: Okay, knock it off! We won't be having any catfights in my courtroom.

Michelle: Sorry, Your Honor.

Prosecutor: Sorry, Your Honor. Ms. Jones, how long have you known Mr. Price?

Keda: Eight years.

Prosecutor: And how old is your son?

Keda: Seven.

Prosecutor: Would you say Mr. Price is a good father?

Keda: Yes, I would.

Prosecutor: Ms. Jones, do you love Mr. Price?

Michelle: Objection, Your Honor. The prosecutor is badgering the witness.

Judge: Overruled. She can answer the question.

Keda: Well, yes, I love him for the fact that he's an excellent father and he does for his child.

Prosecutor: So, would you lie for the man you love?

Michelle: Objection, Your Honor. Prosecution is leading the witness.

Judge: Overruled. She can answer that.

Keda: No, I wouldn't lie. I wouldn't lie for no one.

Prosecutor: Ms. Jones, other than your testimony, do you have any proof that Mr. Price was with your son and you on the weekend of May 16th?

Keda: Well, yes, I do. I have the stubs from the flight, and I also have a few pictures.

Prosecutor: Well, Ms. Jones, I can see that the stubs are valid, but Mr. Price isn't in any of these photos.

Keda: He was the one taking them.

Prosecutor: I see. Thank you. You may step down.

Michelle: Your Honor, I'd like to ask at this time that her testimony be accepted.

Judge: Well, I'm not going to accept it just yet. If the government can't prove Mr. Price's whereabouts, then I'll consider it.

Prosecutor: Your Honor, I'll need a little more time.

Judge: Look, Ms. White, I'm not going to be giving you all this time, but what I will do is adjourn the trial over the weekend, and you can pick back up on Monday.

Jovan

When I got back to the jail, I came out for recreation and went straight to the phone to call Keda. She was my gangsta, and she had come through like a soldier for me.

When I first got arrested and Michelle came into the interrogation room, I whispered in her ear to call Keda and give her the alibi. Keda wasn't even in Florida over the weekend. Her sister Carla took her sons to Disney World, and before they left, Carla took a few pictures of them.

Damn, Keda was a soldier. She had lied for me and said I was the father of one of her sons. Even though I looked out for her son, I never thought she'd say I was his father. Keda did shit right, and for that I was going to bless her with something real nice when I got out.

I dialed Keda's number.

Ring, Ring, Ring.

"Hello," Keda said.

"You have a collect call from Jovan. If you wish to accept, dial five now," the operator said.

Keda pressed five and said, "Hello, Jovan."

"Hi, Keda," I said.

"Yeah, what up, boy? How'd I do?" she asked.

"You did good. Thanks, baby. I'll never forget that."

"That white lady was a bitch," Keda said.

"Yeah, I know. Now, look, don't talk too much on this phone."

"Okay."

"This what I'ma do. I really, really appreciate what you did, and for that you will forever have my loyalty. You're more real than some of these bitch-ass niggas out here."

"Jay, I fucked wit' you. I know we ain't together, but the shit you did for me and my sons, I'll never forget, and for that, if I can do anything for you, I will."

"Okay, shorty, thanks again. Look, Keda, I'ma call my grandma. I want you to go over there. She's gonna give you a gym bag."

"What's in it?"

"It's a present for you."

"Okay, Jay."

As soon as I got off the phone with Keda, I called Grandma and told her to go upstairs and grab the gym bag, not the suitcases, and give it to Keda when she came by.

"Okay, baby, when is she coming?" Grandma asked.

"She should be ringing your doorbell anytime now."

After I got off the phone with Grandma, I called Sonya.

"Hey, baby, what's up?" I said to Sonya.

"Nothing," she said. For some reason, Sonya sounded upset.

"What's wrong Sonya?"

"Ain't nothing wrong with me," Sonya said.

"Damn, you sound like you mad with me 'bout something."

"Why? Am I supposed to be mad at you about something?"

"Naw. Look, I see you got a bad attitude, so I'll call you some other time."

"Oh, so now you don't wanna talk to me no more. What, you gonna call one of your other bitches?"

"Man, what you talking 'bout, Sonya?"

"Nothing, Jovan. Nothing,"

Sonya

When I was in court today, everything was going good, until I saw that bitch get up on the stand and lie for Jovan. I didn't care about her lying, but the fact that Jovan had a son and didn't tell me fucked my head up. Now from her testimony I knew Jovan committed those murders. He wasn't in Florida; he was at that party, and that night was the night we first made love. That was the night my soul took flight. If anybody remembered anything about that night, it would be me.

Also, the next day Jovan was at the gym, or at least that was what he told me. He was probably somewhere laid up with that bitch Keda. But anyway, one thing I did know was he wasn't in no damn Florida. He was at my house fucking my brains out.

I didn't care if Jovan was a killer or not. I knew he had things in the closet, but so did I. That's not what I was mad about. I was mad because I was his fiancée and I told him I was down for whatever, and he still ain't tell me he had a child.

Jovan

It was Saturday and visits were starting in twenty minutes. I doubted Sonya was coming, even though she hadn't missed a visit yet. She was probably still mad I hadn't called her since we last talked. Shit, she was trippin' for nothing. I told her that it was a lot she'd have to deal with by being with me. If she was frustrated by the whole thing and couldn't hold fast, then she could go ahead with her life. I needed a soldier, a gangsta who could weather the storm, who wouldn't get mad at me 'cause I wasn't home yet. This kinda shit took time.

The C.O. came to my cell and said, "Price, you got a visit."

"Okay, thanks, C.O."

After I got myself together, the lieutenant escorted me to the visiting room. Sonya was sitting there, looking mad as hell, with her arms crossed. What the fuck was she trippin' off of?

As I entered the booth, Sonya still didn't smile. I sat down and looked at her for a second. She still ain't said nothin'. She was probably still mad I ain't called her.

"What the fuck is wrong with you? Why you looking so mean?" I asked her, picking up the phone to talk.

"'Cause, Jovan," she said.

"'Cause what?"

"Look, I told your ass I love you a million times! You act like you can't hear me. I got on my knees in this fucking visiting room, cried my heart out to you and embarrassed myself. I asked you to marry me, and you still ain't recognize. I done told you I was down regardless of anything, and you still ain't realize, nigga, that I love you and will die for you," she said, crying.

At that moment, I was shocked by what she was saying, but nothing was making any sense.

"Okay, Sonya, what are you getting at? And please make it plain so I'll understand."

"Jovan, I was in the courtroom Friday."

Instantly I knew what she was mad at. "Sonya, I thought I told you not to come to court."

"Yeah, I know, but I couldn't hold that back. Listen, Jovan, I'm not mad at the shit you did. I know you're a good person, and whatever happened, happened for a reason. You gotta do what you gotta do, and the fact that you do it so well is even better.

"I understand you don't want me to know, and I won't ask. That's not the problem. I'm down with you on that part all the way to the bloody end, and will do whatever to protect you, and I mean whatever, but what fucks me up is that you got a fuckin' kid!" she said, getting upset again.

"Hold up, boo. See, that's why I ain't want you to come to court, 'cause I knew you would take it like this," I said.

"Well, Jovan, how else am I supposed to take it? You're about to be my husband."

"Look, Sonya, that's not my son. It was part of the move. Look at you. You feel stupid, don't you?" I said to her. Now I was getting upset.

"Baby, I'm sorry, but I thought—" Sonya said, but I cut her off before she could finish her sentence.

"Yeah, I know what you thought, but now you know everything, so where do we go from here Sonya?"

"Jovan, baby, I'm still here. I ain't going nowhere. We're still gonna get married, have babies and all that, but now that I know about you, it's time you know about me. We'll both have something over each other's heads, and forever we shall remain loyal to each other."

Sonya told me some shit that I would never believe even if I saw it. She told me how she killed her father for cheating on her mother, and that her little brother took the beef. She told me all about her past, and about the day we met in the courthouse. She was going to see her probation officer that day. Sonya had done time in federal prison for being a drug carrier for that bitch-ass Ray.

She told me so much shit that I knew for sure that I had the perfect one, the perfect soldier, a straight-up real bitch, down for the ride to the bloody end, just like Bonnie and Clyde. So, I put her down with the move, the political move, and she graciously obliged.

Sonya

My visit with Jovan went well. We put everything on the floor. Now there was nothing for us to hide, no more lies. I knew that one day I'd have to stop living a lie, but I couldn't let the world know. Only my man, my love, my soon-to-be husband, who was also living a lie, and no one else, would ever know.

Jovan

It was Monday, and after my visit with Sonya, I felt unbeatable. I already had three bodies out the way; now I had to get this last one over with and then I was a free man. Some way I had to discredit Meeka's testimony. If I could do that, then I was free. Michelle was doing a good job, but for real, I was just tight like that, so any lawyer who would have taken my case woulda walked straight through it.

When I entered the courtroom, I looked in the back for Sonya. She wasn't there. I told her she could come now since we had talked about everything.

"All rise!" the bailiff said.

When I stood up for the judge, I was still looking for Sonya, but I don't see her. This was the last stage of my trial, and I needed her support.

Prosecutor: Your Honor, you gave me an extension of time last week to meet my burden. I feel that it's a shame for me to concede with the defense in accepting Ms. Jones's testimony and ask to strike the other two charges, but I do not have any other witness to corroborate the grand jury testimony of Bilal Davis.

Judge: So, Ms. White, you're telling me to strike those charges?

Prosecutor: Well, no. Actually, Your Honor, I'd like to ask that they stay until the end of the trial.

Judge: Ms. White, I'll hold these charges, but if you can't get me a credible witness, then I'll have to strike them.

Michelle: Excuse me, Your Honor, I'd like to file for a mistrial on the basis that the government has no physical or material evidence that can convict my client.

*In all actuality, Your Honor, this is a waste of time and
a defamationof Mr. Price's character.*

*Judge: I agree with you in part, Ms. Robinson. If the
government cannot provide anything else, I may just
consider your motion, but until then let's proceed.*

*Prosecutor: Your Honor, I'd like to call my witness to
the stand who will show that Mr. Price was the perpetrator in the murder of D.C. Detective Anthony Bridges.
I'd like to call Tameeka Gonzales to the stand.*

Damn, Meeka was gonna fuck the whole thing up. She
was a hot snitch-ass bitch, just like her man. She walked
to the stand all fat and pregnant.

*Prosecutor: Ms. Gonzales, will you please state your
whole name and occupation?*

*Meeka: My name is Tameeka Marie Gonzales, and I
work for Geico Insurance.*

*Prosecutor: Ms. Gonzales, do you know the defendant,
Mr. Jovan C. Price?*

Meeka: Yes, I do.

Prosecutor: And how do you know him?

Meeka: Through my fiancé, Bilal Davis.

*Prosecutor: Ms. Gonzales, did Mr. Price enter your
home on May 19, 1994?*

Meeka: Yes.

Michelle: Objection, Your Honor!

Judge: Overruled.

Prosecutor: Can you tell me what he was doing there?

Meeka: He was talking to Bilal about something.

*Prosecutor: Do you know what they were talking
about?*

Meeka: No.

*Prosecutor: At any time did you see Mr. Davis go back
and forth upstairs?*

Meeka: Yes, I did.
Prosecutor: Did you see Mr. Davis give Mr. Price a gun?
Meeka: No, I did not.

At the moment, I was shocked that Meeka didn't tell. Damn, Meeka was a soldier. She was keepin' that shit on the street. It was Bilal the whole time who snitched. Meeka was willing to do some time for her nigga, and he was the one who snitched. Damn, that's fucked up. I shoulda known Meeka was down. She came from a family of hustlers, and they taught her well. Damn, I respected that shit to the fullest degree.

Prosecutor: Excuse me. I'd like for you to repeat that answer.
Meeka: No, I did not see Bilal Davis give Jovan Price any gun. Matter of fact, I didn't see Bilal Davis give Jovan Price anything.
Prosecutor: No further questions.
Judge: Okay, now would the defense like to cross-examine?
Michelle: Most definitely, Your Honor. Now, Ms. Gonzales, did you purchase a .357 Desert Eagle from a gun shop on Marlboro Pike?
Meeka: Yes, I did.
Michelle: And where was that gun kept?
Meeka: Upstairs in my bedroom.
Michelle: Now, at any time did that gun ever leave your home?
Meeka: Yes, it did.
Michelle: When was that?
Meeka: Right after Jovan Price left the house. Bilal was mad that Detective Bridges had arrested his carriers with his money. This was the second time Mr.

Bridges had done that, and Bilal was mad at that. He said he was gonna kill Detective Bridges.

I tried to stop him, but he knocked me down and took the gun and left. Before he left, he told me that if I called the police, he would also kill my family and me.

Michelle: Thank you, Ms. Gonzales. You've done a wonderful job.

Your Honor, surely this is grounds for a mistrial. Not only that, but a judgment of acquittal would be the proper channel according to the law.

Judge: Now, Ms. White, if you can't come up with something else, I have no other choice but to rule in favor of the defense, but, Ms. Robinson, there isn't enough material to put in for a judgment of acquittal. We still have the grand jury testimony of Bilal Davis, and according to the law, a grand jury's testimony can still be used, even if the person is not present. It's more like a last will.

Michelle: I understand, Your Honor. A mistrial would be fine, and if we have to come in here again with the boxing gloves on, then we will.

Damn, fuck a mistrial! I needed that judgment of acquittal. If I got a mistrial, that meant I had to stay in jail until another trial, and that may take about a year. Who knows? I might not even beat the next trial.

Prosecutor: Your Honor, before you rule, I have another witness, a surprise witness.

Who the fuck could that be? A surprise witness. Now they puttin' shit in the game.

I leaned over and said, "Hey, Michelle, what the fuck is going on?"

"I don't know, Jovan. This is all new to me. Hold up. I'ma try and do something."

Michelle: Your Honor, we've already heard everything about the case. Another witness wouldn't help the government. I ask that you don't let the government proceed, and that you go ahead and rule for a mistrial.

Judge: Now, Ms. Robinson, you heard the government. They don't just have a witness, but a surprise witness. Now, Ms. White, if this witness doesn't help your case, not only will I rule, but you're putting me in a spot that I may have to rule in favor of judgment of acquittal.

Prosecutor: Okay, Your Honor, but I believe this witness will do very well. Matter of fact, I think this witness can bring back those charges that were stricken. I'd like to call to the stand Sonya Chanel Duncan.

What the fuck! Man, I knew Sonya wasn't going out like that. I was fucked up. I told this bitch everything, and this bitch done flipped the script on me. Naw, not Sonya. I loved this woman. Damn, it seemed like everything I loved turned into hate.

Prosecutor: Ms. Duncan, please state your full name and occupation.

Sonya: My name is Kia Lynett Daniels, and I'm currently unemployed.

Prosecutor: Hold up! Your name is what?

Sonya: My name is—

Prosecutor: Yeah, I heard that, but this isn't what we talked about.

Sonya: You asked me my name, and I told you.

Prosecutor: You're supposed to tell the court how Jovan Price committed these murders.

Michelle: Objection, Your Honor! Apparently the government's witness is a surprise to the government.

Prosecutor: Your Honor, I'd like to strike this witness.

Michelle: Before you strike the witness, Your Honor, may I have permission to cross-examine? Maybe there's something the court needs to know.

Judge: Somebody do something in here. I'm totally confused.

Michelle: Ms. Daniels, who are you?

Sonya: My name is Kia Daniels. I had my name changed in 1993 when I was released from Danbury Federal Prison for women.

Michelle: And why were you in prison, Ms. Daniels?

Sonya: I was convicted in 1989 for being a drug carrier.

Judge: Ms. White, you just called a convicted felon as your Defense and you didn't even know it?

Prosecutor: Apparently not, Your Honor. I don't know what the hell is going on.

Judge: Ms. White, I won't tolerate that language in this court. Furthermore, your case is weak. It doesn't even hold enough merit for a mistrial. The fiancée of Bilal Davis just proved to us that his testimony was a lie, and now this witness here just proved to us that the government will try anything to convict someone, even if he is innocent. I have no choice but to rule in favor of a judgment of acquittal. The defendant, Jovan C. Price, is cleared of all charges brought against him, and it is further ordered that he be released from this prison immediately. Court is adjourned!

Michelle: Thank you, Your Honor.

Jovan: Thank you, Your Honor. You've handled this case fair and just.

Judge: Now, Mr. Price, I think in the near future that you should be careful about the people you meet.

Jovan: I sure will, Your Honor.

Everyone in the courtroom was clapping, and Sonya got off the stand and left. I wondered where she was going and what the fuck she was doing up there in the first place.

Sonya

This time when I entered the courtroom, I sat way, way in the back so no one could see me. I saw that Jovan kept looking back for me, but I had on a disguise. I was dressed as an old woman. I wanted to help my man, show him that I was down.

The purpose for my disguise was for Meeka. If Meeka had fucked my man around, I was gonna follow her out of the courtroom and put a knife right in her neck. When I saw that she didn't snitch, I knew my baby was coming home. I knew I would hear the judge say that she may rule for a mistrial and not the acquittal. Shit, if Jovan got a mistrial, that wasn't nothing. That only meant he had to stay in jail and wait for another trial, and that may take at least another year. Fuck that. I needed my man home now! This was my fiancé. I couldn't let him go out like that.

When they called for a recess, I went into the ladies room and took off my disguise and found the prosecutor in the hallway. I told her I hated Jovan for what he did, and that he had a child on me and I knew everything he did. She instantly told me to testify. I knew if I got up there and told them my real name and how I went to jail, it would fuck the whole trial up and cripple the prosecution so much that the judge would flip the fuck out and rule for an acquittal.

I had to do it. I had to do something to free my man. I couldn't be a witness for his defense. They wouldn't have believed me because I was his fiancée and they knew I would lie for him, so instead I turned it around and still lied. The best lie ever.

Jovan

On my way outta the courthouse, I was still looking for Sonya, and she wasn't nowhere in sight. Fuck it. She mighta left, rolled out. I was still fucked up as to why she got on the stand. Was it to help me or ruin me? As Michelle, Mark, and I walked out of the D.C. Superior Court, Michelle gave me a hug and told me I owed her some money. I told her to put it on my tab.

"So, Jovan, what are you going to do now?" Mark asked me.

"I don't know yet. Maybe I'll go back to school, Maybe I'll just chill," I told him.

"Well, whatever you do, you know you gotta be smooth about it."

"Yeah, I know."

"Hey, Jovan, let me tell you something so you'll know lawyer strategy and stay two steps ahead," Mark said.

"What's up, Mark?"

"I always knew that Bilal and you were friends. I just didn't say nothing."

"Get the fuck outta here! How you know that?" I asked him, amazed that he knew of our friendship.

"You gotta finish law school to learn that, Jovan. Look, you need a ride?"

"Naw, I think I'ma go catch a cab, walk around a little, get some peace of mind and fresh air."

"Okay, buddy. I'll see you around. Take care, and finish school, man."

"Okay, Mark."

As Mark left and got in his car, I took off my tie and glasses and started walking down the street. Damn, I'd done killed six mu'fuckas—well, seven—who truly deserved it, and I got away with it. Damn, I lived a lie—a good lie, my best lie ever.

As I got to the curb to hold my thumb out for a taxi, a black limousine pulled up. The light was green, but the limo stopped. As the window rolled down, I still wasn't paying attention, until I heard a voice.

"Looking for somebody?"

Sonya was smiling the brightest smile I'd ever seen. I immediately jumped in the limo, and we started kissing as the limo pulled off. She told me what she did for me, and I knew I had the perfect one.

"Baby, we lived a lie," Sonya said to me.

"I know, Sonya. A good lie."

"Naw, boo, a bad lie."

"Yeah, baby, a vicious lie."

I put my finger on Sonya's lips to tell her to keep quiet, and I said to her, "It was a cruel lie, Sonya, but yet it was told in silence!"

CHAPTER 26

Two Years Later

After they left the courthouse, Jovan and Sonya went past Grandma's and got the suitcases with the three million, sold the 850 BMW, but kept the jewelry. Then they went to Sonya's and got all of her things, sold her car, packed up, and headed to Atlanta.

Now they were Mr. and Mrs. Jovan and Kia Price, the proud parents of an eighteen-month-old boy named Jovan Jr. They had a seven-bedroom house worth seven hundred thousand, and three cars: a burgundy Range Rover 4.6SE, a green 500SL Mercedes-Benz, and the new black 600S V12 Mercedes-Benz coupe.

Jovan went back to school for two years. He passed the bar exam in Atlanta, and now he was the youngest person ever to have his own law firm.

Kia was doing modeling and had a string of hair salons all over Atlanta.

THE END

Dear Readers,

As you can see, I tried my hardest not to expose too much game. Although this book may give you a harsh sense of reality, it is my duty to let you know that this book is not a true story.

J. Rock